IRISH AUTUMN

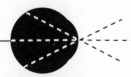

This Large Print Book carries the
Seal of Approval of N.A.V.H.

IRISH AUTUMN

Margaret Evans Porter

Thorndike Press • Thorndike, Maine

Library of Congress Cataloging in Publication Data:

Porter, Margaret Evans.
   Irish autumn / Margaret Evans Porter.
     p. cm.
   ISBN 1-56054-086-9 (alk. paper : lg. print)
   1. Large type books. I. Title.
[PS3566.O653I7   1990]   90-21574
813'.54—dc20   CIP

Thorndike Press Large Print edition published in 1991
by arrangement with Walker and Company.

Cover design by Carol Pringle.

The tree indicium is a trademark of Thorndike Press.

This book is printed on acid-free, high opacity paper.

IRISH AUTUMN

1

A lady from the south country
with a finish of fairy ivory.
— Muireadach O'Dalaigh

The dining room at Dromana House was not large, but on a morning when the skies outside were pewter grey and the damp chill of early autumn seemed to seep through even the substantial brick walls, it was a cosy place to be. Certainly the party of five gathered around the breakfast table thought so. A trio of boys, ranging in age from seven to fourteen, chattered among themselves in between bites, dominating the conversation.

Berengaria Ivory, the lady presiding over the meal, was the younger of the two present, a slim creature whose oval face wore a thoughtful expression. Her soft, dark hair, an indeterminate shade between brown and black, was pulled back to reveal the graceful contours of her white brow and high cheekbones. Her nose was rather pointed and the grey-blue eyes a trifle large for classic beauty, but these could hardly be counted faults.

At least, that was the opinion of Miss Judith Laverty, her aunt, who was seated at the foot of the table wondering, as she often did, how Garia could be so lovely without possessing anything like a conventional sort of prettiness.

Judith Laverty took advantage of an unaccustomed lull to interject a question. "Have you heard the news, Garia? The servants are saying the Earl of Lindal arrived at the Castle last night."

The young lady nodded, but her murmur of affirmation was lost in the sudden babel of youthful voices. Garia reached for the platter making the rounds and speared a piece of bacon with the silver serving fork. As she placed it on Bennet's plate, she commented, "His lordship was bound to return to County Waterford sometime."

Jeremy, who was sitting on her left, leaned forwards. "It is my duty to call upon his lordship now that Papa is gone, isn't it, Garia? I am the man of the family, after all."

She strove to conceal the mix of emotions she felt on hearing her stepbrother's first attempt to assume the role of her late father. However endearing, it was dismaying proof that Jeremy was no longer a child. "If he has only just arrived at the Castle, he might prefer that you wait a day or two," she said gently. "It will not do to behave as freely with this

Lord Lindal as we did with his grandfather. Remember, the new Earl has been away for a decade at least and is not used to our ways. Oh, Bennet, can you not manage that meat by yourself?" she asked, conscious of the struggle taking place on her other side.

The youngest boy raised his blue eyes and piped cheerfully, "Too tough!"

"I'm sorry, dear, but it can't be helped. Let me cut the rest for you."

"Shan't I be able to go to the Castle library any longer?" asked Egan. He was the middle child, in age as well as stature. "Mr. Montrose says I may work there whenever I please, just as Lord Lindal let me do."

Judith took it upon herself to answer him, saying, "Mr. Montrose has only been running the estate during his cousin's absence, Egan, and there may be changes now that the new Lord Lindal has come to Ireland. I'm sure you can write your poems and make your sketches here at Dromana House."

With an encouraging smile, Garia Ivory interjected, "At least until we find how well disposed our neighbour is towards your assaults upon his bookroom. For now, perhaps you had better spend less time with your writing and drawing and take more exercise. Jeremy, why don't you invite Egan to go shooting with you this morning?"

"Take me too, Jeremy!" cried young Bennet. "Oh, Garia, do say I may go! Egan's only three years older than me — why should I not go shooting too?"

"Because you weren't asked," his elder said loftily.

"Oh, dear," Judith Laverty murmured ruefully.

But the mistress of the household lost none of her customary poise in the face of a potential dispute. "Bennet, I know you'd prefer to go with your brothers, but I desperately need your help this morning." She gazed fondly at the deceptively cherubic face and its crown of copper curls. "I will be exceedingly busy and thus unable to exercise Brutus. Do you think you could possibly . . ." She let her voice trail off meaningfully and cast a speaking glance at the oldest boy.

Jeremy, responding to her appeal, broke in swiftly. "But Garia, you don't really want *Bennet* to ride Brutus, do you? He's too young. Let me do it for you. Or Egan."

"No, no — she said she wants me!" Bennet objected, nearly overcome with self-importance. "Thank you, Garia — I'll be ever so careful!"

"I hope you will be. Now finish off that bit of bacon, and then you may go round to the stables. Erris will be waiting for you."

Bennet quickly finished his breakfast. As he dashed out of the room, Judith Laverty asked if he was capable of handling the horse.

"Oh, he'll come to no harm," Garia replied. "Brutus is as safe an animal as you'll find in all Ireland, and Erris has been my groom since I was Bennet's age. That child is so restless these days, and I'd rather he be led tamely around on Brutus than have him dashing about with a gun."

"Little nodcock," Jeremy muttered through a mouthful of dry toast. "Egan wasn't so bothersome at that age."

This backhanded compliment went unacknowledged by Egan, who continued to stare abstractedly at the foggy world outside the dining-room window.

"For shame, Jeremy," said Garia in gentle reproof. "You should know better than to speak in such a soft voice when you address your brother."

"But I wasn't talking to him, I was talking about him," the youth protested.

"That's even more inexcusable, and not at all what I expect from the man of the house," Garia said pointedly.

Egan turned towards his sister. "Just because I don't reply doesn't mean I haven't heard, Garia."

After the two boys left the dining room —

11

in their usual noisy fashion — a slight frown marred the serenity of Garia's face. Judith, well acquainted with her niece's concerns, said comfortingly, "You manage those children better than anyone could, my dear." It was true, as she had learned during her year of residence at Dromana House. Garia, at twenty-six, was eminently capable of looking after herself, her stepbrothers, and the estate she had inherited upon her father's demise.

"It isn't the boys worrying me," Garia sighed, shaking her head. "I was just remembering that I am supposed to meet with my bailiff at noon, and I know he's going to scold me and I probably deserve it. How I dread hearing his report on the harvest! This morning's interview with Mrs. Aglish and the empress of our kitchen was quite enough to depress my spirits." The housekeeper and cook were longtime antagonists, each taking the credit for any household economies and blaming the other for extravagance. Garia kept the peace as best she could, but invariably emerged from battle more alarmed than ever about her precarious finances.

"But the larder and the stillroom are overflowing," she went on, "despite all the moaning I heard earlier today. And I know I have you to thank, Aunt, for the way our poultry and geese have prospered. The shooting season has begun, so with luck the boys can keep plenty of wildfowl on the table. If I can continue to maintain a surplus of foods, then I can hope to offer relief to the poorer of my tenants if it is a bitter winter." She squared her shoulders and rose from the table, shaking the crumbs from her brown skirt.

This reminded Miss Laverty of something she had intended to ask earlier. "Garia, my dear, when do you intend to leave off mourning Sir Andrew? It has been a year now — high time you had some new gowns, whether or not you think you can afford them."

Garia glanced down at the stuff of her skirt, which was indeed showing wear. "I might see my way to purchasing some new dress lengths," she conceded, "if we make them up ourselves."

"We'll do no such thing! My father the General wouldn't be best pleased if I let his granddaughter go about looking like a country dowd. And as for your sister Rosamund — "

"Fashionable Lady Kelsey, the ornament of Dublin society," Garia murmured, her eyes bright with humour. "Oh, very well, if you threaten to publish the news of my lamentable appearance, I have no choice but to go to the dressmaker in Cloncavan village sometime this week."

"You'll visit the dressmaker in Carrick, and

you'll do it tomorrow! We shall both go and take your brothers to that inn they like so, the one that serves the meat pies."

"What a termagant you are," Garia said, laughing. "And I'm no match for the daughter of a general! To be perfectly candid, I have not yet set aside my mourning for fear Mr. Ruan would be emboldened to offer for me. And I'm not at all prepared to give him an answer."

"You should have had it ready a year ago," her aunt declared.

"I suppose so." Garia's tone was noncommittal, but she sighed.

"A rich lawyer — it's more than you deserve, after refusing nearly every gentleman in the district. Your father should have married you off years ago — before you settled so comfortably into spinsterhood. I blame myself for presenting so cheerful and comfortable a picture of the single life," Miss Laverty said with mock severity. "It might have been a better example to you if I'd complained more about how annoying it is to be at the beck and call of one's relations."

But Garia only laughed as she kissed her aunt and went into the hall, leaving her to puzzle over Garia's reluctance to marry the persistent Mr. Ruan. It was true that in Jeremy, Egan, and Bennet the lawyer from Waterford had three rivals for Garia's affections, very formidable ones. Now that the foolish girl had entered her twenty-sixth year she often declared she should give up any thought of marriage. What need had she of a husband? The answer to that was plain to Judith, who knew how worn down she was from shouldering the heavy burdens fate had forced upon her. Dromana had been left outright to Garia, and it was more of a trial than a windfall, although the property was finally clear of the debt that had encumbered it for so long.

As delightful as Garia's stepbrothers might be, they were a great drain upon her income. For a year Judith had seen her favourite niece pinch pennies and squeeze rents from her reluctant tenants, all for the sake of three children who were not even her blood kin. But it was pointless to raise that argument with Garia, who hated to be reminded that the boys' surname was Howard, not Ivory.

Judith's expression became fierce as she let herself dwell upon the painful subject of the second Lady Ivory. The false-hearted Josepha had possessed a provocative beauty, no fortune whatsoever, and three young sons — each one doubtless sired by a different father, Judith fumed, though all bore the name of that shameless creature's first husband. But Josepha was in India now, too far away to make more trouble. The reappearance of one ghost from poor Garia's past was more than enough, Judith told herself.

And only then did she recall that her niece had given no hint of how she felt about the return of the heir to Cloncavan Castle.

Mr. Brian Doyle, senior tenant at Dromana, had served as bailiff for as long as Garia could remember. As soon as he crossed the threshold of the library, he began to question Miss Ivory's recent acquisition of ten acres along the northern boundary of her estate, and his thick, bushy brows, which resembled fat black caterpillars, wriggled furiously.

The lecture she received was not unexpected, and for some minutes Garia listened patiently to a scathing denunciation of her new purchase, which he referred to as a mere bog. And when at last she interrupted his tirade, it was to say calmly, "Yes, I know you were opposed, but you must agree that the price was a fair one."

"Faith, Miss — the old man was anxious to sell at any price. The land was of no use to him, any more than 'twill be to you. Your great lawyer from Wateyford-town did a decent job of bargaining, but though he may be a fine man for writing out a deed or a will, he's a city dweller and knows naught of land value. Meanin' no disrespect to him or yourself, but you'd have done better to heed me. You've not capital enough to be flinging it after bad land," he persisted.

Garia folded her hands in her lap and said staunchly, "Mr. Ruan says I've made a good investment."

"It's an investment only if there's a return, and all you'll grow on that bog is furze and wildfowl and rabbits."

"Well, since we're on that subject, didn't you and my brother Jeremy come back with four brace of birds apiece last week?" she asked with a show of spirit.

He was quick to correct her. "Four and a *half*. Sure, and 'twas the prettiest day's shooting I've had since I don't remember when. If 'tis your wish to load your table, no doubt you will, young Jeremy being that grand a shot. But it's a wasteland, it is, and will never be more," he said with a despondent air.

Privately she suspected he could be right, as much as she might wish it otherwise. When Charles Ruan had first suggested that she enlarge her holdings, she had been reluctant. But in the end he had persuaded her with his talk of drains and ditches. She had realised, too late, that although improvements of that kind would turn the bog into arable land, they would also entail further expenditures.

"How many of the Midsummer rents are

still outstanding?" she asked the bailiff.

"Too many, that's all," was his gloomy reply. "But I hear Robbie O'Patrick sold half his sow's litter and two geese, and I'd not be surprised if he sold more than a few bottles of his potheen, besides. If he's so full in the pockets, I'll have his back rent out of him before sundown, Miss Garia, or my name's not Brian Doyle."

He gave her his brief and discouraging report on wool and flax production, and although Garia listened with every appearance of interest, part of her mind continued to mull over the vexing problem of unpaid rents. Mr. Doyle was too eager to begin badgering the delinquent O'Patrick to remain with her much longer. After he left, she spent half an hour reviewing her household accounts. It was just possible, she determined, to purchase a new gown or two, and perhaps a pelisse, and still be able to buy a new hunter for Jeremy. And as she had done for the past thirteen months, she longed for her father, who had been so knowledgeable about horseflesh. A deal was always made to the advantage of the trader, never that of the buyer, and as a female she was far more likely to be taken in over the price, or to end up with an unsound animal.

She closed her account book, prey to a strong wish that the new Earl of Lindal had remained on the Continent, or in England, or wherever he considered himself to be most at home. For if he had not returned, Jeremy could have continued to borrow hunters from the Castle stables. The late Earl, a generous old man with a warm regard for the mistress of Dromana House, had always been happy to mount her brothers.

She went in search of her aunt, who was seated in the drawing room, her greying head bent over her embroidery hoop. Garia obligingly offered to straighten Judith's workbasket, and as she did so, the two ladies discussed current fashions and debated which colours were best suited to a lady with dark hair and a milky complexion.

But at the first opportunity, the older woman asked, "Aren't you the least bit curious about Lord Lindal, Garia? This morning you said scarcely a word about him."

"What is there to say? Surely you cannot be thinking of that sorry business years ago?" Garia replied with a dismissive shrug. She saw that this reply had disappointed her aunt, and a spark of understanding flashed in the smoky depths of her eyes. "You *are* thinking of it!"

"How can I help it? The marriage so near — the settlements agreed upon and the betrothal contract signed."

A shadow passed across Garia's face, but an instant later she was smiling. "Yes, I was most shamefully jilted! And Viscount Melbury, as Lord Lindal was in those days, added insult to injury by running off with a chambermaid from the Castle! But since he and I never met, not even once, I have since comforted myself with the thought that his actions were not meant as a reflexion upon me. He was merely wild and bad and dissolute. And if he had married me, I daresay we'd have been perfectly miserable together."

"You are a strange girl, Berengaria. Don't you feel the least flutter at the thought of meeting him?"

"A tiny one, perhaps. But recollect that it was ten years ago, and busier years for him than for me. His grandfather often spoke of the foreign parts he visited, and of his many adventures. If I were a young man who had travelled so widely, I should find it quite easy to forget a sixteen-year-old girl I'd never set eyes on and had agreed to marry merely to oblige my grandpapa and his best friend. No, Aunt, I'm more a-flutter thinking that our boys will continue to buzz round Cloncavan Castle as they did when the late Earl was alive."

"Poor lads, they miss him. And he had such a fondness for them."

"But his heir may not be best pleased to discover three boys running tame on his property, riding his horses and fishing his waters. I hope my warning this morning will be sufficient, but I think I had best speak to Thomas Montrose. A hint from him will carry more weight with my brothers."

Miss Laverty, smiled. "If Lord Lindal is anything like his cousin and his grandfather, he won't care a fig what they do."

"But his disposition remains to be seen," Garia pointed out. "Did you know you are nearly out of blue silk thread?"

"I must remember to purchase some tomorrow in Carrick."

"And I must buy more drawing paper for Egan when we're in town," said Garia, whose stepbrothers were never very far from her thoughts. "He has begun to illustrate his poems, and very well at that. And of course we must indulge Bennet somehow, or there'll be a grand fuss."

Judith smiled. "You may be sure something will catch his eye in the shops!"

Garia looked up from the skein she was untangling and said ruefully, "What he really wishes for is a dog of his own. But when I told him he might have a spaniel pup, he said the gundogs belong to Jeremy and that he would prefer a different breed. He turned up his nose at a harrier, for which I was thankful — a hound would be too rambunctious and

21

noisy to keep in the house."

"What about the old rat terrier in the barn?" her aunt suggested.

Garia did not even dignify this with a reply.

"A sheepdog, perhaps?"

"My shepherd would be up in arms if I let Bennet make a pet of one."

"Well, there are dogs enough in Ireland, my love, and Bennet will find his one day."

"Oh, what did I ever do to deserve such a boy?" Garia cried in despair. "Boys, I should say, and all three of them so different! Jeremy excels at whatever he does—shooting, hunting, his studies. Egan doesn't excel at anything save for his art and his writing—he is perfectly content to dwell forever in that dream world of his. His deafness only increases his tendency to withdraw. And Bennet—"

"Bennet is too young to care for much but mischief and aping his brothers. That is perfectly natural at his age."

"But he'll grow up so quickly, just as the others are doing! I don't know how I will manage it, but I am determined that they shall have everything in the world — good schools, a university, some kind of employment. Jeremy might make a fine lawyer. And Egan wants to be an artist, so he'll require a patron one day, and I have so few connexions myself."

Judith Laverty looked up from her needlework and found that increasingly familiar pucker of worry between Garia's dark brows. She said severely, "My love, your forehead will be permanently indented by the time you're thirty if you don't stop frowning. I know you'd give your stepbrothers the world if you could, but it's beyond your power. Tell me, did you have everything you wished for when you were a child?"

Garia gave the question due consideration before answering. "To be sure, Papa was inclined to spoil me, especially after Mama died, and most particularly when Rosamund married and went to live in Dublin. He tried to give me my heart's desire, and it was not his fault that ultimately he failed. But I was very silly at sixteen, and prone to foolish, girlish dreams — the sort that are made only to be shattered."

Startled, Judith asked, "Whatever do you mean?"

"Why, that the first serious disappointment I ever suffered was when Torin Montrose, then Viscount Melbury, now Earl of Lindal, jilted me sight unseen and ran away with a chambermaid!" Garia laughed suddenly and softly, and the crease in her brow vanished, making her look a great deal younger than her twenty-six years.

2

Bring thee through mist and foam to thy desire,
Again to Irish land.
— Colman

For centuries Cloncavan Castle, seat of the
Earls of Lindal, had loomed impressively
above the surrounding countryside and appeared to be as permanent a part of the landscape as the Comeragh Mountains to the west.
But it had been altered by successive generations of the Montrose family, and the only
remnant of the original medieval fortress was
a small tower at the rear of the house.

At the very moment Berengaria Ivory was
making light of her disappointment at his
hands, the Earl of Lindal could be found there,
seated at a small, uncomfortable desk. He was
sorting a sheaf of papers, holding each one
up to a branch of candles to read it before
adding it to one of a number of growing piles.

Thomas Montrose, his lordship's cousin and
agent, walked over to the single window cut
into the thick stone wall and looked out at
the river flowing through the finely wooded

demesne. Then he shifted his gaze to Lord Lindal. "Well, Torin?"

Torin Montrose placed the final sheet of paper upon the stack and leaned back in his chair. "Admirable, Thomas. Most admirable!" And when he smiled at his cousin, the faint lines of dissipation writ upon his swarthy countenance were less noticeable. "My few objections have already been made, so I'll not repeat them, except to say that in some cases your lenience with the tenants is to be wondered at."

"You must remember this is Ireland, not England, Torin. Many landlords in this country have been harsh and as a consequence are routinely troubled by uprisings."

The Earl pushed his chair away from the desk, freeing his cramped limbs. "You recommend that I preserve the status quo? I half expected you to suggest that I inaugurate sweeping improvements at Cloncavan. Am I not to be encouraged to create a model estate?"

Thomas Montrose was quick to catch the gleam of humour in the green eyes. "Nay," he said, "for Uncle Matthew and I went as far as we dared with enclosures and draining bogs a few years ago. To interfere any further would be futile. In any case, your philanthropy would be wasted here — 'twould be like pouring money into a ferret's hole."

"And I've no turn for it, unlike the rising breed of gentlemen farmers in England. I was only jesting." Torin closed the account book and climbed to his feet. He was a tall man, whose black head topped his cousin's brown one by several inches. "Shall we ride my ancestral acres this morning? It's damp, but not drizzling yet. Today I mean to please myself, tomorrow I shall call upon the spiritual leaders of our village on my way to Carrick."

His cousin nodded, adding as an afterthought, "You'll scarce recognise the Rectory. Mrs. Ashgrove has made it almost comfortable now, not at all as it was when you read Latin under my father."

As the two gentlemen traversed the lawn separating the vast stony pile from the stable block, they reminisced about their shared youth. The cousins had been inseparable as very young boys, before being sent away to school. Torin, Viscount Melbury, had attended Eton and later Oxford, from whence he had duly been sent down; Thomas had been educated at home by his father, former Rector of the parish. But the late Earl, his great-uncle, had dispatched him to Trinity College in Dublin, where he had distinguished himself, but afterward he chose to be his great-uncle's estate-agent and remain near his boyhood home.

The stable block, like so much of the Castle,

had been enlarged by the individual known within the Montrose family as the "Improving Earl." As Torin entered the vast horse barn and inhaled the familiar scent of hay and horse, he knew beyond all doubt he was home. At this early hour many of the stalls were empty, their inhabitants either grazing or being exercised, but a goodly selection of mounts still remained. He chose a nervy, black-tailed chestnut for himself and admired the roan that was his cousin's favourite hack. The gentlemen declined assistance from the liveried groom Torin had brought with him from London, and saddled the horses themselves.

They laughed and joked to the accompaniment of baying hounds, for it was feeding time in the kennels. "Sounds like they're crying for a good run," Torin said as he mounted. "Who's the Master these days?"

"Sir John Neale. I've heard he's got the earth-stopper out this week, in preparation for our next meet."

Torin led the way out of the stableyard, and Thomas followed. "It's as if time has stood still here," his lordship observed. "Even old Toby is the same as she ever was, for last night she called me her naughty, black-haired lad."

"Aye, she still spends her days in the housekeeper's room, humming to herself and knitting caps and shawls for Father Rourke's charity children. But you should be warned that Mrs. Tobin's nose has been put out of joint by your decision to install that toplofty Cobbe as butler."

"Dear coz, you know as well as I that Grandfather always said he'd retire Blaney after thirty years' service. Only he never quite got round to it, did he? Poor old fellow, he must have been wondering these dozen years why he hadn't been relieved of his duties! He's a rare one, old Blaney — when I told him I'd brought my own butler, he shook my hand and called me a promising youth, for all my prankish ways." Torin shook with laughter.

"Well, it isn't only the arrival of Cobbe that your housekeeper resents. Was it really necessary to bring a groom and a steward and a valet to Cloncavan? Not to mention the French chef and the English cook! This isn't the end of the earth, you know, and I don't blame old Toby for taking umbrage."

"That's gratitude for you," said Torin, wrinkling his aristocratic nose. "Toby may think she's ageless, but the fact remains she was head housemaid when I was born, and I'm two-and-thirty now. But do you think she would consent to being pensioned like old Blaney? No chance of it."

"So you imported that army of servants

without a single thought for your own comfort?"

"Naturally," said the Earl, whose wicked smile belied his answer. "But we've talked enough of household and estate business for one day. What say you to a contest — will you race me to the ancient oak on the hilltop?"

"It fell during a windstorm three years ago," Thomas retorted. But there was no one to hear, for the Earl of Lindal had already left him behind.

The following morning, Thomas Montrose could hardly keep from yawning over his breakfast. It was his noble cousin's habit to seek his bed at an advanced hour, and Thomas, unaccustomed to late nights, was feeling rather the worse for the experience.

Although business matters had been resolved the previous day, several questions of a more personal nature were rolling around his sleepy head. Foremost among his concerns was the fate of that chambermaid with whom Torin had absconded a decade before. Watching Torin pry the backbone out of a trout with great precision, then consume the fish with evident relish, Thomas could only suppose he had enjoyed Betty O'Brian with similar enthusiasm and had cast her away just as carelessly as he had the bones.

But it was doubtful that Lord Melbury had been the first to sample the charms of that saucy lass: the tales about her had been legion among the servant class. And gentle Father Rourke had been preaching sermons with thinly veiled references to her fall from grace long before Torin had decamped with her. Versions of those sermons were still trotted out every once in a while when the priest thought a parish girl to be on her way down the same path as the former chambermaid.

Torin, conscious of the silence at the other end of the table, eyed his cousin curiously. "Cobbe set that platter of fish before you quite five minutes ago — it'll soon be stone cold. I'd forgotten how excellent our river fare can be, and the only thing that could possibly eclipse it is the game you and I shall bring in these next few weeks. A fine time of year to come into the country — the shooting begun and the hunting just round the corner."

"It's hunting season nearly the year through in Ireland," Thomas reminded him. "Tell me, do you really mean to immerse yourself in country pursuits? Won't they seem awfully tame for one of your adventuring spirit?"

"After my encounter with the *banditti* a few years back, and those Bedouins outside Damascus, I've lost my inclination for adventures."

"World-weary, Torin? I'll not be believing that for an instant! By the way, what was the outcome of your encounter with the *banditti?*"

"Well, my friend Halsey and I joined forces with them until we were able to effect an escape of sorts, so I suppose we had the best of that one."

"You make it sound so dull and matter of fact. I would love to hear of the details of your adventures."

"I wearied of a nomad's dull existence long ago. Paris, Spa, Vienna, Athens, Damascus — one and the same, ultimately. My experience of travel has led me to conclude that it loses its appeal in time."

Thomas shook his head. "Easy for you to say, who's had your fill. I've never set foot off this dearly green, sadly soggy island and would welcome the chance to see something of the world."

"Then I must send you to London to carry out a commission for me one of these days. Only then I might lose you forever, and how would I manage my affairs?"

The other man grinned. "If London's at all like Dublin, I'd find my way back to the country soon enough!"

"Well, I haven't visited the Irish capital in years, but there is ample opportunity to lose yourself in the Metropolis. Just think of Betty

O'Brian — the city swallowed her up."

Thomas choked. When he recovered his composure, he asked, "What do you mean?"

"Spare me your shocked airs. You've been dying to know all about her — only your great delicacy prevented your asking outright. If you must know, one day Betty went out, ostensibly to go shopping, and never returned. Two weeks later I discovered her in what is popularly, if inaccurately, termed a nunnery — as prime an article of pleasure as you'd wish to find, and too popular by half! The last news I had of her was some time ago, but she was already an abbess herself. My word, Thomas, don't look so dismayed! All the girl wanted was passage to England, in return for which I received — well, I'm sure your imagination can supply you with what was my recompense. A most enjoyable interlude, and probably more remarkable to everyone here at Cloncavan than it ever was to me."

"Because it was so commonplace?" Thomas wondered if Torin had forgotten the other circumstance that had made his sudden flight from the Castle so remarkable. "Or because it paled in comparison with the adventures that came after?"

"Still hoping for travellers' tales, Tom? You'd be better entertained by a fellow I met everywhere abroad during the past two years

— in Spain and Portugal, Greece and Turkey. George Gordon was as capable of romanticising his adventures as I am not. He's just published them as *Childe Harold's Pilgrimage*."

"Can you be speaking of Lord Byron, the poet?"

"Does his reputation extend to these shores? I had no notion you read poetry, coz."

"I don't." But Thomas knew someone who did, and had recently visited the premier bookseller's shop in Waterford at the request of young Egan Howard. He had been agog to read Lord Byron verses and had saved up his pocket money to purchase the coveted volume. But Thomas hadn't been able to spend a penny of Egan's small hoard; he had paid for the book himself and made a gift of it. He commissioned one of Egan's drawings in exchange, saying that because he dealt in coin every day of his life, he would prefer something of real value. Remembering the child's pleasure, Thomas smiled to himself.

"Yes," he said, "I have heard of your Lord Byron. Someone of my very near acquaintance is especially fond of verse." Perhaps, he thought, it was time to inform his cousin of the Howards' *carte blanche* to roam the lands of Cloncavan and fish the river.

But the discussion of literature had reminded the Earl of a pressing matter, and he was even now discussing his plans to have the book collection at the Castle appraised. "Building up a fine library was one of my grandfather's greatest joys, but it must be catalogued to be of any worth."

"I suppose so, but I know nothing about estimating the value of old books."

"No, but it will be your responsibility to contact someone in Dublin who can perform an appraisal. Trinity College has a library of considerable renown, and I'm sure you keep up your friendships from your university days. You might start there."

"I'll write today," Thomas assured him. "Do you still intend to go to Carrick?"

Torin nodded. "After I've called upon the parson and the priest. Will you join me?"

Mr. Montrose threw up his hands in mock surprise. "What, and neglect my duties here? I'd be cast off without a reference, much less a shilling, did I fail to convince you of my industry!"

"Ah, but you forget that I've seen those impressive reports!" Yet Torin's smile was swiftly replaced by a frown. "I do wish you would consider my offer of land and a house, Thomas, in those spare moments when you aren't settling accounts and enriching my coffers through your excellent management. I can't think why the Earls of Lindal don't possess a Dower House."

"There hasn't been a Dowager Countess for more than a hundred years, Torin — not since your great-great-grandmother's time. Dromana House and its lands were sold outright to Sir Andrew Ivory's father a century ago. It was formerly the Dower House."

"Sir Andrew Ivory — he was Grandfather's friend. I remember him well. I daresay I ought to call at Dromana too, while I'm making my tour of the neighbourhood."

"You'll not find the gentleman there — he died a year ago." And still not a word of that business with Garia Ivory had passed Torin's lips, Thomas thought.

"A pity. He was a good man." Rising from his chair, Torin said, "I suppose there are new families here, and I will have to ingratiate myself with the old ones. And catch up on a decade's worth of gossip!" He said musingly, "Strange how my estates in England have never interested me as much as the Castle. London is a dead bore these days, and I'm glad I decided to close up Lindal House and visit Ireland. I might even remain fixed here till spring. Being lord of the manor in this part of the world is tantamount to being a king, and I anticipate an enjoyable reign. But do not worry, my dear Thomas — I shall strive for an enlightened monarchy!"

★ ★ ★

After making his calls Torin went into the village of Carrick-on-Suir. He stopped at the single bookshop and purchased a newspaper with which to while away the evening hours, then went to the inn and hired the small front parlour for himself, to the bemusement of the proprietor and the other customers.

From the window he commanded a view of the entire street. He watched a pair of ladies and two little boys enter the dressmaker's establishment directly across the street. Almost immediately one of the children darted out and made for the bookseller's next door. A moment later Torin's eye was caught by a flash of red-gold curls, and he looked up to see that the other child had also emerged from the modiste's shop. This lad was less decisive than his sibling, and for some time he simply stood there in the road unbuttoning and rebuttoning his jacket. Then he spotted something that must have exerted a powerful attraction, for suddenly he, too, hurried away and out of Torin's view.

"Well done, my lad!" he murmured in approval as the coppery head vanished around the corner. And he lifted his glass of what he judged to be an excellent French wine — probably smuggled — in a toast to the enterprising boy.

A short time later the two ladies left the shop,

clearly seeking their runaways. The older lady immediately entered the bookseller's.

The younger woman stood slim and straight in the middle of the street, wearing a black pelisse, a black bonnet, and gloves. A widow, Torin decided, and he suddenly wished he could shake that curly-headed rascal for plaguing his poor young mother so.

Torin left the inn wondering if he could offer his assistance, but by the time he'd settled his bill she was no longer standing there. He returned to the innyard where he had left his curricle. Of the groom there was no trace, but the boy with the copper curls stood on the mounting block, talking to the horses and stroking their noses.

"This is a bang-up carriage!" he cried, looking up. "I never thought to see Trinket and Tory pulling such a fine rig as yours, sir!"

Torin smiled. "This is a racing curricle, designed by the finest carriage builder in Long Acre — that's a street in London. You seem to be well acquainted with my horses. Who might you be?"

"I'm Bennet Howard. And you're the Earl of Lindal, I know that. I thought you'd be older — like the other Earl. I mean, you *are* old, but you don't have white hair like he did."

"Thank you for that crumb of civility, Master Howard!" Torin eyed the child's crumpled trousers, the shirt stained with juice from a meat pie, and the wild, dishevelled locks.

"Bennet!" Torin and his new acquaintance both turned to see an angry youth approach. "Climb down from there at once! I'm sorry, sir," he told Torin apologetically, "but my brother *will* disappear. I should have known it had something to do with an animal. He's as mad for horses as Egan is for books." He made a disgusted face and took hold of his brother's coat. "Come along, little looby, and leave his lordship alone. You and Egan ought to know better than to frighten everyone by running off."

It seemed to Torin that this was an exaggeration, for neither of the ladies had seemed particularly fearful. But the statement had the proper effect: Bennet hopped down from his perch.

"I didn't mean to worry them, Jeremy, truly I didn't!" he said as his brother led him away. "But I had to leave that shop — it was so very stuffy and it smelled dreadfully of dead flowers!"

The encounter forced Torin to rewrite his little drama of the bereaved young mother as he drove back to the Castle. The lady in mourning was entirely too youthful to be the mother of a lad in his middle teens. She must be the boys' sister, and he did not envy her the care of three such lads.

A few days later an Assembly was held at the village hall. Although at first Torin resisted, he finally gave in to his cousin's urging and agreed to attend. When he made his entrance, a silence betokening mass astonishment fell upon the company. Suddenly he was besieged by a host of gentlemen and their ladies, who either greeted him with unwarranted familiarity or begged Mr. Montrose to introduce them to his lordship. In a very short time Lord Lindal had made or renewed his acquaintance with the locals.

After being made welcome, Torin was left to amuse himself as he pleased. Although he accepted a glass of punch, a single sip was sufficient to change his mind about being thirsty. He retired to the sidelines and watched as several tireless couples danced reels and jigs at the end of the room, occasionally joined by one or more of their elders. He made a game of matching the younger people with their progenitors. There were three handsome brunettes who strongly favoured Lady Neale, and Mr. Horace de Lacy's hawklike nose could be traced in the visages of two of his sons. The delicate, blonde little person whom he had originally supposed to be the parson's daughter, Miss Ashgrove, seemed to be the

Manahans' child. Miss Ashgrove, most unexpectedly, turned out to be the big-boned, jolly creature dancing with a de Lacy scion. Torin was pleasantly surprised by the number of single ladies and gentlemen present — perhaps more than a dozen, if he included himself and his cousin in the reckoning.

Thomas had become lost in the crowd, but eventually Torin spied him standing in a hallway, in deep conversation with a dark-haired lady in blue. She was the young woman Torin had seen in Carrick earlier in the week. Was she a neighbour, too?

Mr. Montrose greeted him with a smile, saying, "Torin, dear fellow, is there any need for me to introduce you to the most admired lady in the parish, Miss Ivory? You must have met long ago — " He broke off, uncertain of whether or not he had overstepped himself.

"No, Mr. Montrose," Miss Ivory said quietly, "as strange as it seems, his lordship and I have never met." She looked at Torin, waiting for him to reply.

3

You have found me again at last
after many travels, a test of skill.
— Mael Isu O'Brolchain

Although Garia met Lord Lindal's scrutiny
with apparent unconcern, her fingers tightened involuntarily around the wineglass she
held. She had known the meeting was inev-
itable and preferred to be over the hurdle,
but she desperately wished she had been
warned of his attendance at the Assembly. He
was exceedingly handsome, this gentleman
with coal black hair, olive complexion, and
intense green eyes. But she could hardly believe he was that heartless petticoat chaser,
the monster who had signed his name to a
marriage contract one day and run off with
a chambermaid the next.

The Earl echoed her thoughts, saying wryly,
"I must say, this is altogether unexpected. And
are you the very lady to whom I was engaged,
so briefly and so long ago? Just how long ago
was it?" he asked, wrinkling his brow.

"Ten years," Garia replied promptly.

"Not as long as that, surely! If you will forgive my saying so, you are the merest child!"

She had to smile at that. "I'm no child now, my lord, though I certainly was then."

The Earl turned to his cousin and declared, "You are a villain, Thomas, for not informing me that I would sustain a shock this evening. I am most displeased and must banish you forthwith. Miss Ivory and I are entitled to some privacy, given our unfortunate history. Don't you agree, ma'am?"

Garia immediately turned imploring eyes upon her friend Mr. Montrose, but to no avail. With an apologetic smile and a shrug, he abandoned her.

Torin led her to a battered sofa in the narrow passage and said, "Here is a secluded spot where we may sit and talk." He moved some of the cloaks and hats aside to make room, and they sat down. "I was sorry to hear of your father's death," he told her. "So you are his daughter — I can scarcely credit it."

"You are not precisely what I imagined, either, my lord," she said candidly. "Although I daresay you are different now from what you may have been ten years ago."

"Quite distinguishable from my former self, I assure you," said Torin. "How extraordinary that we meet as strangers, considering that your father and my grandfather were such fast friends. But as we are now very near neighbours and will constantly be running across one another, I hope you'll attach no awkwardness to this or any future encounter."

"Oh, no," Garia murmured.

"I'm grateful for your forbearance, Miss Ivory, for I know you have every right to fling your wine in my face and call for your carriage. Tell me, was it your brothers I met in Carrick two days ago? I saw you there, from a distance, but naturally I had no idea you were the Miss Ivory I had jilted. I'm afraid that if I had known, I'd have fled the country in a panic!"

"You met Jeremy, the oldest of my brothers, and Bennet, the youngest — and the naughtiest, as you must have surmised," she said, smiling.

"Haven't they a different surname than yours?"

"They are the sons of my stepmother by her first husband. But though they may be Howards by name, they are as dear to me as any blood relation!" she said staunchly.

"And was the lady I saw with you Lady Ivory? I hope you will introduce me — I must offer her my condolences."

After the briefest hesitation, she replied, "You saw my Aunt Judith — Miss Laverty. Lady Ivory is not at Dromana House. She lives abroad."

The Earl said nothing and Berengaria sensed his awareness of having hit upon an unpleasant subject.

She said softly, "But you, too, have sustained a loss, my lord. The neighbourhood was deeply distressed by the Earl's death, and none so much as my brothers and myself. You are very like him, you know."

"Am I? You are kind to say so, for I regard that as a compliment of the highest order. I regret that our paths seldom crossed after I left Ireland. The last time we met was in London five years ago, just before I went to Russia."

"Yes, I know," Garia said. "He appreciated the books you bought for him there. And my younger brothers were fascinated by the Russian alphabet. They thought it was some special code. The Earl often read your letters aloud to us, with the descriptions of the many foreign places you visited. Although he took great care to delete the more shocking of your exploits." Her eyes brightened with amusement.

With a smile Torin told her, "If Grandfather and I were anything alike, he must have been delighted with your company, Miss Ivory."

Garia was unaccustomed to this sort of quizzing, and she ducked her head. "Oh, he and I always remained on the best of terms, even after — but I mustn't speak of that episode, for I'm sure he never did."

"Anything you know to my grandsire's discredit must be disclosed!" Torin declared. "Then I can apologise for the family."

With heightened colour she said, "He made me an offer of marriage once, that is all."

"All? The old rogue — why, he must have been thrice your age! And to think that you might have been my step-grandmama — that would be a joke indeed!"

"It would have been a most unequal match, and not only because of the difference in age," she said gravely. "He only meant it as a favour to me — a means of providing me with an escape from someone — from something unpleasant in my life. He said as much at the time. But he also said there was no cause for awkwardness between us, just as you did a moment ago, and that's what reminded me of him so particularly."

Privately Torin wondered if perhaps his grandfather had been trying to make amends for his heir's rejection of the same match. He said musingly, "An alliance between our families was the wish of his heart."

"It was once," she agreed, "but in later years I often heard him say you did me a favour by running away!"

Torin had to agree with that assessment, and for a moment he hated himself, or rather, the young man he had been a decade ago. He judged it time to change the subject, so he asked, "Is that lady across the room your aunt?"

Garia seized this opportunity to make her escape. "She will wonder where I have got to — if your lordship will excuse me, I had best go to her."

"I will, albeit reluctantly," he replied, also rising. "Will you honour me with a dance later?"

She shook her head. "I'm afraid I must refuse, though I thank you. I am only just this week out of mourning for my father and cannot yet accustom myself to the thought of dancing."

"Some other time, perhaps?"

She nodded, doubting very much that he would remember.

On the way home later that evening, Judith Laverty expressed her surprise at his lordship's attendance at a small country Assembly, when he must be used to grander fêtes. "For anyone can see that he is accustomed to moving in the first circles of society. Although we were not introduced, I own I was pleasantly surprised by his manner, considering all I've heard about him. And none of it good, I might add."

"It is hardly fair to judge him by what he was a decade ago," Garia declared, echoing his very words. She was startled to find herself championing the very man who was responsible for breaking her heart. And although she had been prepared to detest him on sight, he was too handsome and too conciliatory, with a cosmopolitan air and a hint of world-weariness that was not unattractive. It was flattering, too, his having singled her out, though of course she would not have admitted it for the world.

She ran her hand idly over the shabby upholstery. When new, the dark, rich velvet had been the perfect complement to her stepmother's sapphire eyes. But she was determined not to dwell on that now and asked her aunt if any interesting gossip had made the rounds during the evening.

"No," Judith said, sighing. "Although there is much speculation about where Miss Frances Ashgrove's fancy lies this week. I daresay you know the answer to that better than anyone, the two of you are so close."

"From all I observed, she seems to have embarked upon a flirtation with Ralph de Lacy. The Neale girls *will* be despondent — they regard him as their personal property."

"Their papa asked me if you mean to hunt with the Cloncavan pack this year. Do you?"

"Oh, yes, provided my household duties permit it." Garia heaved a small sigh. "It will be strange, hunting without Papa, but Jeremy says he's quite old enough to look after me.

And now that I'm out of mourning there can be no objection, can there?"

"I don't think so, dear, for Sir John told me he hoped to see you at the next meet."

Garia gave a soft laugh. "Then my hunting must be considered unexceptionable, for he and Lady Neale are very high sticklers indeed."

She lapsed into silence, and once again reviewed her curious encounter with Lord Lindal. How long would he remain at Cloncavan Castle, she wondered, and after considering the matter she decided that if he departed on the morrow she would be more relieved than otherwise.

Torin was disinclined to retire immediately upon his return to the Castle, so he persuaded his cousin to share a bottle of port before going up to bed. Comfortably seated before the cavernous fireplace that dominated the library, they exchanged opinions on the evening's entertainment. Thomas Montrose was greatly amused by his lordship's sharp and accurate perceptions of the neighbours. "But tell me," he said at last, "what do you think of Garia Ivory? You should be flogged for stealing her from me as you did!"

Torin replied that he had been amazed to discover Sir Andrew Ivory's daughter was a woman grown and still residing at Dromana House. He did not add that if he had thought of her at all during the intervening years, it had been as a sixteen-year-old schoolroom miss. "She appears to be a quiet, sensible creature," he concluded. "I can't help but wonder why she is still unwed."

"She hasn't lacked for suitors, you may be sure."

"I understand that at one time my grandfather was among their number." Something in Thomas's wistful smile made him exclaim, "Not you, too?"

His cousin nodded. "I proposed twice."

"And she refused you? Surely she knows what an estimable fellow you are! Shall I tell her?"

"I have very little in the way of fortune," Thomas replied.

"That shouldn't weigh with a woman of Miss Ivory's quality."

Thomas smiled faintly. "It didn't, of course. I'm afraid I chose my time ill in both instances. When I first offered, she had just endured a season in Dublin and was in no mood to entertain a proposal from any man. I made my last offer shortly after Lady Ivory left Dromana, and nothing would have induced Garia to leave her father and the boys then. But she may be more favourably disposed towards wedlock now."

"Indeed? And have you renewed your suit?"

Mr. Montrose sipped his wine thoughtfully.

"Oh, my *tendre* for Garia is long past, though I shall always consider her the most admirable woman of my acquaintance. It's Charles Ruan who is generally regarded as the lucky fellow."

"Charles Ruan? Now there's a familiar name." Torin stared at the dancing flames for a moment, then said, "I have it — that ragged boy who used to stand at the Castle gates and demand that we let him join in our play."

"The very same. He lives in Waterford now, practicising law and growing richer every day from it, they say."

Torin settled back in his chair and said consideringly, "From what I remember, the family hadn't a shilling to spare, though the father always assumed the airs of a gentleman. I'm surprised they didn't all starve long ere this."

"It wasn't starvation, but consumption, that carried the parents off and left the boy an orphan on the parish. He attended a charity school in Waterford, and later a local subscription was raised to see him through Trinity. He went on to study at the Inns of Court in London, and practised his profession there for a year or so before returning to this district. To my certain knowledge, Ruan drew up Sir Andrew Ivory's will."

"And has dispensed legal advice to the daughter since her bereavement?"

Thomas nodded. "The expectation of an interesting announcement from Dromana House was high a year ago, before the baronet's death."

"Your knowledge of local gossip amazes me, Thomas — you'd make an excellent spy. Tell me, are you so well informed about Lady Ivory? The second one, that is."

"I know almost nothing about her, except what gossip reported, but she was a very lovely creature," the other man said reminiscently. "Sir Andrew met her in Dublin while on a visit to his elder daughter Rosamund — who was married right out of the schoolroom. After only a few years of wedlock, Lady Ivory separated from her husband and eventually left Ireland for good."

"That family is plagued by matrimonial scandal," Torin mused. "It's no wonder that poor girl looked so deuced uncomfortable when I said I hoped to meet Lady Ivory!"

"I imagine she might well," his cousin agreed. "But to her everlasting credit, Garia has never maligned her stepmother, although I gather she might have cause to do so."

The following morning Torin decided to read through his grandfather's private papers. After breakfast Thomas Montrose handed over the key to the late Earl's desk and together the two men went to the study, where a fire had been kindled against the September chill.

The first drawer contained the voluminous correspondence that had come from Torin's own pen during the previous ten years; he removed the collection of letters, thinking it would be enjoyable to relive his experiences in other lands. Most of the other drawers were crammed full of notes and memoranda, which he would reserve for sentiment's sake. One compartment contained a number of curiosities: several drawings, obviously created by the hand of a talented child, some verses, and a bird's nest constructed of moss held together with bits of straw. Torin recognised it as the inverted, dome-shaped dwelling of a long-tailed tit.

He picked up the nest carefully, to prevent any disintegration of the materials, and glanced over at his cousin. "Can you explain the significance of all this?"

"Birthday gifts to Uncle Matthew," Thomas replied. "The drawings and poems are from Egan Howard, and the tit's nest from young Bennet."

"A fine specimen. Am I wrong in guessing that it was poached from my grandfather's own woodlands?"

Here was the opening Thomas had been seeking for two whole days. He cleared his throat by way of preamble, then said, "Well, Torin, the Howards have been used to roaming freely about the estate. Uncle Matthew permitted them to ride, shoot, and fish here whenever they pleased." And then he raised the ticklish question of whether or not the new master of Cloncavan was prepared to continue this generous policy. He held his breath, for he dreaded seeing the faint lines deepen around the sharply chiselled mouth, as commonly occurred whenever his noble cousin was displeased. To his great relief, Torin smiled.

"You may inform the boys that they may continue to ravage my birthright. Jeremy Howard looks a promising lad — we should have him over to shoot with us one of these days."

Then he turned his attention to the final drawer, which held only some rolled-up parchments. He untied them and gave the one on top a cursory inspection. His interest was roused when he spied his own signature at the bottom. "What the devil is this?" he said, then submitted the contents to a more thorough review.

Glancing over his cousin's shoulder, Thomas asked, "What have you found there?"

Torin looked back down at the page he had been reading, his expression one of perplexity.

"This appears to be the betrothal contract between myself and Miss Ivory, drawn up ten years ago for a marriage that never took place. What do you make of it, Thomas? I would have expected these documents to have been destroyed, and long ago!"

"So should I," Thomas admitted, holding out his hand.

"Grandfather was more than generous in the settlements he proposed making my bride," Torin observed. "Not only money, but property too."

Thomas shook his head in amazement. "Torin, do you realise what it means — the fact that this contract still exists?"

"If you are about to tell me that Miss Ivory and her attorney might drag me into the law courts on a breach-of-promise suit, you may as well hold your tongue. I wouldn't believe it of her."

"Nor would I think it of her," Thomas said, "although it would be well within her rights. It's worse than that, Torin, if you would be serious for a moment."

"But both parties to the agreement are dead, which surely nullifies it."

Thomas pointed to the bottom of the paper. "But *you* were one of the those parties, Torin, and you are not dead. You signed your name to this promissory paper on May 12, 1802, signifying your intent to wed Berengaria Elizabeth Ivory, younger daughter of Sir Andrew Ivory, Baronet. She was underage at the time, but you were twenty-two, past the age of majority. The marriage was agreed upon by you and her father — your grandfather was only a witness to the pact, in addition to Horace de Lacy, Esquire, and Sir John Neale. I'm afraid Ivory's death in no way alters your obligation to his daughter. You'd better destroy this at once — I don't understand how Uncle Matthew neglected to do so himself."

"Don't you? Maybe he was planning to hold me to that promise. He was a crafty old weasel and as stubborn as the day is long, and I daresay he's laughing his head off, wherever he may be now." Torin rubbed his chin thoughtfully. "So, Miss Ivory is still betrothed to me."

"It is more that you are betrothed to her." Thomas exhibited the thick parchment yet again. "Although you could say that she is in some way bound to you. It makes no difference. You won't want to tell her of your discovery."

"No. No, I don't think I do." Torin took the papers from his cousin and began to roll them up again. When he had tied them together, he replaced the papers in the bottom drawer and turned the key.

"What do you think you're doing?" Thomas cried in alarm. "You should set those documents on the fire — you'll regret it if you don't!"

"Calm yourself," Torin advised him. "Grandfather kept them hidden away for a decade, so why should I not do the same? I am content to let them gather dust and cobwebs, for they will be my talisman, a reminder of past indiscretions." As he said this, his eyes hardened, and the lines about his mouth were suddenly quite pronounced.

This was the very expression Thomas had feared to see earlier. Nevertheless, he renewed his plea. "Now, Torin, listen to me, I beg you — "

"I thank you for your advice, dear coz. It is duly noted, but I have chosen to disregard it."

"Just what are your intentions?"

"Don't be absurd. I have none."

"Then do as I ask and destroy those documents. I cannot in good conscience stand by and let you preserve something that might distress Garia. You slighted her once — and her family. Surely you would not do so again!"

"Come, come, my dear fellow, there is no need for these histrionics. Miss Ivory is nothing to me — nothing except, as I have just learned, my promised bride. Still, the very fact that I have neither a need nor any desire for a bride renders those papers perfectly harmless." Torin laughed softly as he walked over to the window. "My needs have always been of a vastly different sort, I assure you."

Thomas went rigid, and his face was suffused by hot colour. "Surely you would not take advantage of Garia's unfortunate lack of male protection! You are mistaken if you think I'll stand silently by and let you entice her into — into a liaison of some sort."

"I ought to call you out for that," Torin said angrily, turning away from the window. "However, since my reputation has preceded me and may be somewhat deserved, I will let the insinuation pass. What I said a moment ago was a bitter jest, and you jumped to the wrong conclusion. I must assure you that I haven't returned to Ireland for the purpose of seducing any of the Betty O'Brians of the district, much less ladies of quality like Berengaria Ivory. Cloncavan is my home. I am content to live here for the present, and in time I trust all the worst gossip about me will die a natural death."

"Of course it will," Thomas agreed hastily.

"Now, if you will be so good as to grant me some time to myself, I must write some letters to England. I daresay when my friends there learn my intentions, they will suppose I've taken leave of my senses. Certainly I've begun to have my own doubts that I'll ever fit comfortably into this insular, hopelessly provincial corner of the world."

4

I cannot hide it:
He was my heart's love.
— Irish Poem

The morning after the Assembly, Garia
couldn't dismiss the Earl of Lindal from her
mind, not even as she bent her dark head over
a letter to her sister in which she deliberately
omitted any mention of his lordship's return.
Every now and then she laid down her pen
to dwell upon the encounter of the night before. Nor could she keep older, less pleasant
memories at bay. As she considered these, she
recalled the Earl's claim of having changed.
It could be as true for him as it was for her.
Certainly she was a decade older and centuries
wiser than that dreamy Garia who had
founded her hopes for love upon a false impression of an unknown youth.

In her childhood she had often begged her
gentle mother to tell her of the origins of her
unusual name. She had never tired of hearing
the sad but romantic history of Berengaria of
Navarre, the beautiful, neglected wife of Rich-

ard the Lionhearted, or that of the lady Rosamund, mistress of Henry the Second. They had sparked an imagination that had been further fuelled by Nurse's Irish folk stories and legends.

Throughout her girlhood Garia made up stories about herself, in which she alternately figured as a princess and a beggarmaid, but was always courted by a golden-haired and gallant prince, sometimes in disguise and sometimes not. So when the match with the Viscount Melbury was first proposed to her, it seemed the fulfillment of all her longings. At sixteen she had known virtually nothing of marriage and even less of men, but rumour told her the Viscount was handsome, her chief requirement in a husband. She filled in his blank face with that of her favourite fairytale prince and did not doubt that he would fall in love with her on sight. After the marriage they would live at Cloncavan Castle — no more suitable dwelling for the heroine of a romance could be imagined.

As she sat there in the silence of the drawing room, Garia could still recall with perfect clarity the day she had been summoned to that same room. And she let herself re-live that heart-shattering moment when her father had apprised her that the marriage was off and the Viscount gone, perhaps forever. She would never be a Viscountess nor even meet that paragon of manly beauty about whom she had dreamed.

She had gone into hysterics — her novel-reading had taught her that this was *de rigueur* when faced with disappointment in love, and for two days she refused to leave her room. But despair of that magnitude was difficult to sustain, and on the third day she rose from her bed of tears and returned to the school-room and her lessons.

The scandal faded with time, and eventually Rosamund, by then a matron of several years' standing, made a push to introduce her sister to Dublin society. But the merry, romantic schoolgirl had developed into a quiet young woman who discouraged one promising suitor after another and returned to Dromana un-dismayed by what her sister regarded as her unfortunate failure to snare a husband. Her exposure to her father's unhappy second marriage set the seal upon her determination never to marry where she did not love.

Which meant that she had better learn to love Charles Ruan, and very quickly, she warned herself, picking up her pen once more. Now that her year of mourning was over he was bound to broach the subject of marriage. She liked him very well; he was always eager to advise her on the running of her estate, which indicated he was willing to take on the management of Dromana. He was wealthy, and he had lately purchased a fine house in Waterford. But despite his manifold attractions, she balked at committing herself to marriage. Independence was now a habit with her, one she was not certain she was willing to break.

It was Mr. Ruan's habit to call upon her once a week, so she was not greatly surprised when her butler announced the lawyer a little while later.

"I bid him wait on the doorstep," McCurdie told her, "lest you were after wishing to turn him away."

"Of course not!" she cried in exasperation. "Show him in here at once." Ever since his master's death, McCurdie had taken to discouraging male visitors. Garia set aside her letter to Rosamund and, after straightening her writing desk, cast a nervous glance around the drawing room to make certain nothing was noticeably out of place.

She rose as a good-looking gentleman with chestnut hair entered the drawing room. "Why, Garia," he cried happily, "you have put off your mourning! And such a becoming gown!"

She had to distrust this compliment, for she and her aunt had agreed that this particular shade, a dull gold, did nothing to enhance her looks. "I fear you are too kind, sir," she replied.

"Surely it is no secret that I think you look well in anything!" he declared, smiling at her.

They sat down together and chatted over the teacups with ease, until Mr. Ruan chanced to mention the Earl's return. Garia assumed he knew nothing of her long-ago engagement, for he had never mentioned it.

She said, with the faintest hint of constraint, "I can't imagine his lordship will remain long in our midst."

"Certainly for no longer than it takes to raise the rents," the lawyer said grimly, "which might well cause discord and distress among the tenantry."

"Oh, I do hope not," Garia said, frowning slightly.

"His lordship's predecessor may have chosen to live on the estate, but it would be madness to expect this Lord Lindal to be anything but another absentee landlord," Mr. Ruan continued. "Given his previous lack of interest in his inheritance, I can only assume he has come to Cloncavan only to wring money out of it, or else his visit is the result of some whim. I agree with you that he will soon be off on some other spree. I knew him years ago, before his grandfather shipped him off to Eton."

"Did you? I had never met him until yesterday."

"He was a toplofty, imperious little fellow then," said the lawyer. "Thomas Montrose idolised him and was ruled by him, but I was not so inclined."

Garia's impression of the nobleman's affability made it hard for her to accept this portrait of him as a spoiled neighbourhood bully. But she was prevented from quizzing her friend further on the subject of the Earl, for he was eager to learn if the winter wheat had been sown yet. As always, when he discussed estate business, it was evident that he had every expectation that Dromana would belong to him someday.

"You would scarcely believe how I envy you, living in this remote, pastoral place," he acknowledged, leaning slightly forwards. "It did not take me long to discover that there are more important things in this world than money."

Garia laughed softly. "You are fortunate in having enough money to disdain it!"

"Fortunate?" he echoed, then shrugged. "I am not so sure. My labours grow more wearisome daily as my clients increase in number. I am besieged with invitations from Waterford society. That puts me in an awkward position with regard to reciprocating, for at present I have no hostess to receive for me. Although that is something I hope to remedy in due time."

Garia experienced a frisson of alarm at this statement and the smile accompanying it, for she supposed the proposal she had expected and dreaded for the past two years was about to be made. But before she or Mr. Ruan could utter another syllable, McCurdie's spare figure materialised in the doorway.

"The Earl of Lindal," he intoned impressively. In the face of his mistress's bewildered expression, he added with an air of injured justification, "Well, Miss, if you was wishful of entertaining *one* gentleman, to my mind 'twas likely you'd not turn up your nose at another!"

Garia blushed furiously as she welcomed the new arrival, and extended her hand with a self-consciousness that she feared wasn't lost on the Earl. He bowed over it, and when his green eyes met hers she fancied she read amusement in their depths. A foolish conceit, for he could have no idea of the scene he had interrupted nor of her own overwhelming gratitude for his doing so.

He turned from her to greet her startled guest, who had also risen, saying smoothly, "Charles Ruan, isn't it? My cousin has told me something of your successes, and I offer my felicitations." After a sweeping glance about the room, which took in the worn, out-of-date appointments, Torin enquired of his

hostess whether her aunt was at itors. "I was disappointed not to b to Miss Laverty last night at the and as I was on my way to the seemed the perfect opportunity to p self. I hope I don't intrude."

"Not at all," Garia told him. " afraid my aunt and my brother E out on a blackberrying expedition, al I expect that they will return shortly are not in too great a hurry to wa her, I trust?"

"Why, no, I am in no hurry at all," he sured her with a smile.

She bid both gentlemen be seated, a stepped into the hall to ask McCurdie to brir up a bottle of the fine Madeira her father ha laid down on the occasion of his second mar-riage.

When she returned, Mr. Ruan said, "His lordship mentioned an Assembly at Cloncavan. You did not tell me that you had attended it."

"Didn't I? It was rather a squeeze for our village hall, but a pleasant evening despite that."

"For you, perhaps, Miss Ivory," Torin re-marked, "but the gentlemen present, my cousin and myself included, were desolate that you chose not to dance."

Charles Ruan chose to make the most of

opportunity to reveal his superior knowl-
e of the lady's circumstances. "Miss Ivory
lately been mourning her father," he said
ressively. "And having suffered a similar
s yourself in this past year, I wonder that
u should be desirous of taking part in the
nce, my lord."

"But my circumstances are rather different,
or as you are no doubt aware, my grandfather
nd I had not met one another for several
years. But had he been able, I feel sure he
would have strongly urged me to partner Miss
Ivory. In the dance," he added audaciously.
"But it cannot be unknown to you, sir, that
I might have formed a more lasting partner-
ship with the lady."

Garia went rigid as she realised the implica-
tion of what he had said. Since she would
rather explain herself and make as light of the
situation as possible, she quickly turned to the
lawyer. "My father and the Earl's grandfather
put their heads together and tried matchmak-
ing once, but nothing came of it." She prayed
that Lord Lindal would corroborate her explanation; essentially it was a factual one.

"It is true that our elders' plan did not prosper," he conceded, "but not because they were
at fault."

Garia had never been happier to see her aunt
and her brother as she was at the moment

of their entrance, which she judged most timely. She performed the introduction Lord Lindal had sought, then greeted Egan, whose mouth was decorated with telltale blackberry stains.

Breathless with excitement, he informed her, "There was a fox in the wood — at least, I'm very nearly certain it was a fox, although Aunt Judith says it may only have been a squirrel. Won't Bennet be sorry he missed it? I shall draw it for you, Garia, and tint the sketch with my new watercolour paints if you like."

She put her arm around the exuberant child and declared, "I would like it very much. But you haven't greeted Mr. Ruan yet, and here is Lord Lindal, whom Jeremy and Bennet met in Carrick the other day."

The boy drew even closer to Garia as the two callers were brought to his notice. Stumbling over the words, he managed to say all that was proper to Mr. Ruan, and bobbed his head wordlessly in the Earl's direction. Then he took a corner seat and from its seclusion eyed the company with his usual detachment.

Torin, who had noted Egan's withdrawal, said invitingly, "Come here, young fellow, and take this place beside me. I'm pleased to meet the artist I've heard praised so highly."

"Egan is our family poet as well," said Judith Laverty with a fond smile. "We are very proud of him, Lord Lindal."

"With good cause," he said promptly. "I've seen the fruits of Egan's labours among my grandfather's personal effects. Didn't you make some drawings for him?"

"Yes," the child replied cautiously.

"He obviously treasured them highly."

"The other Earl let me visit his library whenever I pleased," Egan informed the imposing stranger. "Will you do so, too? If you please," he added as a polite afterthought. He shifted in his seat, for it suddenly dawned upon him that he was the object of all eyes. Garia had broken off in the midst of whatever she had been saying to Mr. Ruan, who looked annoyed. Aunt Judith continued to smile, but wonder of wonders, the Earl appeared to be giving the request due consideration. To improve his chances, Egan smiled up at him. This was always his younger brother's most successful ploy, for Bennet could smile with devastating effect.

It was not his facial expression, but the longing in his brown eyes that struck Torin, who had already sized up his supplicant as a shy, reserved child, unaccustomed to asking favours. But young Egan, it turned out, had pluck — perhaps as much as that imp Bennet. It was clear that he would submit to any kind of torture, even that of addressing a stranger, to regain access to the Castle.

"You may certainly continue to use my library," Torin informed him, "but do you think you might make yourself useful there on occasion?"

"Useful?" Egan repeated, to make sure he had heard properly. "In what way, sir?"

"My book collection is about to be catalogued, and I'm of the opinion that this Mr. Dickinson who is coming down from Dublin to undertake the job might require an assistant. Someone already familiar with the contents, which I, alas, am not. Would you be interested in the position?"

Egan stared up at the nobleman, his leaf brown eyes wide with wonder.

"You will have to work very hard, Egan," Mr. Ruan interjected. "In the past you have not been inclined to exert yourself, you know."

The child flushed but said staunchly, "I can do it." He turned to his sister for confirmation. "Can't I, Garia? Tell the new Earl."

Garia cast an anxious glance at her visitor. "Are you serious about this, my lord?"

"I'd not have asked it otherwise, Miss Ivory."

"No, of course not," she said hastily. "Egan is certainly a capable boy, and I think he would be particularly suited to that sort of work."

"Then we will consider it a settled thing,"

said Torin, and he looked down at Egan. "But you must promise me that you'll not neglect your drawing and verse making."

"As if there were any fear of it!" said Judith, ruffling the boy's hair. "Egan, you haven't yet thanked his lordship."

"Oh, that is quite unnecessary," Torin said airily, "for it's I who am in his debt. Mr. Dickinson is due to arrive at the Castle next week, and I'll send a message over as soon as he is ready to begin his assignment."

"Yes, sir. Thank you. I — I shall be waiting to hear from you!" With Garia's permission Egan bid goodbye to the guests and almost ran from the room.

When the Earl took his leave a little while later, Garia accompanied him to the front door and tried to make up for any insufficiency in Egan's thanks. "I appreciate your kindness to my stepbrother," she told him. "And though I suspect your man has no need of a little boy's assistance, I do know it means a great deal to Egan to be asked."

"He will be a considerable help, but it's more important that he enjoy himself. Thomas tells me the child is hard of hearing."

"Yes, he's deaf in one ear," Garia stated sadly, "the result of a fever. As a consequence, he has an unfortunate habit of withdrawing and keeping to himself." Despite the fact that

70

she and the Earl were out of earshot of her aunt and the attorney, she lowered her voice to say, "And I must thank you on my own behalf as well. For not — for not refuting what I told Mr. Ruan about our — concerning our . . ."

"*Dis*engagement?" Lindal supplied helpfully. "How could I do otherwise, when I exposed your dark secret?"

"Perhaps I ought to have told him about it, but it always seemed such an inconsequential bit of ancient history."

"Inconsequential?" he quizzed her. "Not that, surely!"

She bit her lip, then said, "You know what I mean."

"No, I'm not sure I do. What I did ten years ago was perfectly brutal, an insult to your father and potentially ruinous to an innocent girl like yourself. Even worse, I'm afraid I never experienced sufficient regret, although the instant I met you, I began to deplore the folly of my younger days." Taking her hand, he said softly, "Pray, do not hold me accountable for the actions of a thoughtless, selfish youth, bent on cutting a dash. Do set my conscience at ease and tell me you forgive me for the most shameless act of my life!"

"Of course," she said a trifle breathlessly, and gazed down at the floor.

"I don't mean to embarrass you by constantly referring to the past — in fact, I would prefer to put it behind us forever."

"Indeed," she murmured, drawing her hand away in confusion. "That is, I did so long ago, my lord."

With a bow, he left her, and she returned to the drawing room, her face a study in thought.

Mr. Ruan did not long outstay the Earl, and when he was gone, Judith Laverty commented brightly, "Well, you must have had an interesting morning, my dear."

"It has certainly been an eventful one!" Garia agreed. "Usually the knocker is silent for days on end."

"True, but I suspect those days are done. I shouldn't be surprised if Lord Lindal becomes a regular caller, and there is no mistaking Mr. Ruan's purpose. That one will be back sooner than you may wish." With a playful smile, Judith declared, "I'll not soon go blackberrying again during the visiting hour, for fear of missing all the fun!"

"I don't know that I would call it that," was Garia's weary reply.

The sudden crash of the front door heralded the return of Bennet, effectively banishing all thoughts of her suitor and her nearest neighbour.

The youngest Howard raced into the drawing room, shouting, "Garia, Garia! You'll never guess what happened! Jeremy and I met that new Earl on the road — he'd a capital pair of greys between the shafts of his curricle — and he invited Jeremy to shoot with him and Mr. Montrose tomorrow. What do you think of that? And," he said, taking a deep breath that expanded his little chest to its limits, "*I* am to go along and carry the game bag for them!"

5

*A powerful, muscular, handsome pup,
healthy, well-fleshed, hard and fiery!*
— Brian Merriman

One rainy day McCurdie interrupted Bennet's
recitation of his multiplication tables to inform
Garia that a "rascally, red-haired creature"
had come to Dromana asking after the mistress
of the establishment. He added that the man
bore an astonishing resemblance to the
O'Patricks, tenants at Dromana for generations.

Bennet's eyes were bright with the hope of
liberation, but Garia told him to await her return. She hurried to the library, where she
commonly received those who came to her
with grievances or requests, and she also recognized the "creature" as one of the O'Patrick
clan. But she failed to see why McCurdie had
put his nose up at the man who introduced
himself as Con O'Patrick, for his rough clothes
were as clean as any she had seen among the
labouring class, and his bow more deferential
than she had any right to expect. His frame

was slight and thin, but his eyes were bright with health and good humour and his shaggy red head had a proud tilt to it.

"I have no need for a labourer," Garia told him, never doubting he had sought her out for employment. "The harvest is complete, what there was of it, and I have plenty of men and women to see to the sowing."

"Oh, aye, me cousin Robbie was tellin' me that — just before the she-wolf he wed was after throwin' a jug at me head. But I dodged it, sure, and she missed me!"

Garia smiled at this accurate description of the tempestuous Bridgie O'Patrick. "You are a cousin of Robbie, then?"

"In a manner o' speakin', your honour, ma'am. Robbie O'Patrick is the youngest nephew of me own father's father, but we never laid eyes on each other till yesterday when I reached his door."

"What brings you to Cloncavan, Con O'Patrick? Just this visit to your cousin?"

"Not that entirely, ma'am. Not for that am I sleepin' in the stable with me cousin's horse, and all because that vixen Bridgie refused me a bed. Me aim in comin' was to find employment, which ye guessed right off."

"I'm sorry, but I've none to offer you. Dromana is but a small property, and in any case, my bailiff Mr. Doyle would be the one

75

to ask, not myself. What sort of work are you seeking?"

The man grinned disarmingly. "Oh, any and all work. Lastly I was a fisherman, but I thought to get drier employ."

Garia knew that if he'd been involved in smuggling, that lucrative offshoot of the fishing trade, he would never have given it up. He seemed to be an honest man, and she deeply regretted that she had no work for him.

"I've a good hand with the horses," O'Patrick continued, "I do indeed."

"My stables are fully staffed. We have a coachman and two grooms already," she answered.

"'Tis good I am with wee growin' things."

"I require no under-gardener, either. There are only the kitchen garden and the rose beds, which are not extensive."

"Robbie said you might offer me a shilling to drive the pigs, but the man's a dreamer like his father afore him."

Garia doubted that he had ever known her tenant's father, for Robbie O'Patrick was fifty years old if he was a day, and this man certainly no more than thirty. She supposed there was a chance Mr. Doyle might use him as a stone picker, but Con appeared to be too capable a worker to be wasted in such a lowly occupation. For one mad instant she wondered if she might hire him on as a manservant, but had to reject the notion at once. McCurdie would doubtless resign his post in high dudgeon if she did, and he had been with her family for longer than her lifetime. As much as she liked Con O'Patrick, she was on the verge of dismissing him when it occurred to her that he might have better luck at the Castle. Mrs. Tobin, the housekeeper, was frequently heard to complain that few servants remained there for longer than a fortnight. With so many comings and goings surely there would be a vacant place for this fellow.

She folded her hands on the desktop, and the man eyed her expectantly. "Mr. O'Patrick, I suggest you go up to Cloncavan Castle, two miles from here. Mr. Montrose is the gentleman to ask for, and you may tell him I sent you. In fact, I shall write a note to him."

Con clutched his wool cap and bobbed his head up and down. " 'Tis that thankful I am, your honour, ma'am. That dreamish Robbie ne'er uttered a breath about no castle, divil take him! Are you thinking there's a chance for me, then?"

"I cannot say. But in the event Mr. Montrose has nothing for you either, come back to Dromana. You can pick stones in the south field, but I must warn you the wage won't be very high. And if you need a lodging, I can always have a word with Bridgie O'Patrick."

"Robbie spake true when he said ye're as fine a soul as ever walked this earth!" the man said reverently. "May the blessings of Mother Mary be heaped on your honour. And if 'tis in my power to do you a good turn in kind, 'tis glad I'll be to do it!"

"Did Bridgie give you breakfast?" she asked by way of diversion; his effusive thanks, however sincere, would not soon end, for he was as typical an Irishman as she had ever met. When Con shook his head, she told him to go to the kitchen for some food before he set out for the Castle. Then she reached for a sheet of writing paper and began her note to Thomas Montrose.

When she had completed the task to her satisfaction, she returned to the drawing room. To her astonishment, her pupil still waited for her, just as she had bid him. "Why, Bennet, what a good boy you are!" she said approvingly.

The child turned reproachful eyes upon her. "You *told* me to wait."

She laughed at that. "Turning me up sweet, are you? Now what would you be wanting, I wonder."

"The dog, of course!"

"And what dog might that be?"

"The one at the Castle. Oh, Garia, it is *the*

dog — my dog! You'll see — oh, you must agree to it!"

She sat down and said calmly, "Perhaps you had better explain everything, Bennet, for I confess I am at a loss."

"Well, when I was at the Castle the other day with Jeremy and Egan — the day we went shooting — we stopped at the gamekeeper's cottage. The new Earl said there was a litter of pups I might like to see."

She took advantage of his intake of breath to observe, "But I thought you had decided against a gundog."

"The pup I want is nothing so paltry — it's a great hound. You know, an Irish wolf dog, like in the *legends!*" He paused to let this impressive fact sink in.

"Good heavens."

"I knew you would understand! There aren't any wolves in Ireland any longer, so a wolf dog is a very rare and special sort of dog — almost nobody has one. And Agamemnon is descended from the wolf dog that belonged to the Lords of Lindal centuries ago. Well, at least a couple of centuries ago," he amended. "The new Earl explained it to me."

"Did he indeed?" Garia asked hollowly. "And who, pray, is Agamemnon?"

"My pup — the one that will be mine when

you say I may have him. The new Earl says that I must have your permission."

"But why did you wait so many days to ask for it?"

"So I could prove to you that I *deserve* to have Agamemnon," Bennet replied impatiently, as if it should have been perfectly obvious to her. "Did you not notice how I have eaten my beans, which I quite detest? And I didn't ask for a second piece of cake last night, though," he added darkly, "I wanted one. And yesterday when it was so sunny, and I knew Jeremy was to be fishing over at the Castle, did I not sit for Egan so he could draw my profile?"

"Yes. Yes, you did," Garia agreed solemnly.

"And today I did my sums and my twice-times and thrice-times almost perfectly, and then I waited for you when you told me to. So now you can't refuse me Agamemnon!" he concluded triumphantly.

Garia stifled her impulse to hug him to her breast, for he was old enough to reject her displays of affection, just as Egan had done at the same age. Could this lively, eager boy really be that laughing infant she had bounced on her lap some six years ago? The eyes were the same startling violet blue, the cherub mouth had not changed, nor the coppery curls. But he was growing so quickly that she fancied she could see it happening before her eyes. Egan too, and Jeremy was nearly a man at fourteen.

"No," she said at last, "I won't refuse you your pet, Bennet. But it's because I had already promised you a dog, and not because you behaved so well this week. You were thinking more of the reward than you were of pleasing me and Aunt Judith. Oh, dear, I sound like my old governess, and that is a horrid thought."

"But I don't mind. Jeremy always says you're entirely too easy with me'n Egan, so if you think you should scold us more often, you may," Bennet said handsomely.

"Thank you, sir, but I had rather see you and Egan act like the gentlemen I know you to be, and then I won't need to scold. That's enough preaching for now! Tell me all about Agamemnon. Wolf dogs are — are rather large, are they not?" She tried to sound as if great size was an admirable quality, all the while glancing dubiously at a spindly-legged table. Prudence dictated that she remove the delicate china ornaments resting there.

"Larger than spaniels or foxhounds," Bennet chirped, "for they are bred to catch wolves, and a wolf is larger than a bird or a fox. Empress, Agamemnon's mama, is only a little larger than a sheepdog. But Agamemnon will not be big for quite a long time," he said seriously.

This was only mildly reassuring, but Garia managed a smile. "When do you take possession of your property?"

"I've but to send word by Egan, and someone will bring Agamemnon from the Castle. That," he said as a clincher, "is what the new Earl said."

The someone who brought Bennet's new pet to Dromana turned out to be the new Earl himself. He arrived the next day in his curricle, and at the sound of its approach, Bennet rushed down the front steps. The gentleman handed him an armful of wriggling dog, which the child clutched to his chest.

"Oh, thank you, sir! Come into the house now," Bennet demanded, with a blithe disregard for good manners, "for Garia will like to thank you as well!"

But Miss Ivory looked more chagrined than thankful when Bennet, followed by the Earl, bore his new pet into the library. She had just embarked on a search for one of Egan's missing drawing pencils and was on her hands and knees, peering beneath a pedestal writing table.

She heard Bennet say, "Garia, *do* get up from the floor and have a look at Agamemnon. The new Earl has brought him here, and in his curricle, too!" Turning her head, she was stunned to find a pair of highly polished black boots. She shoved a wayward lock of hair back from her face and ventured an upwards glance.

"May I help you up?" his lordship asked gallantly.

She accepted his offer as graciously as possible for someone who had been discovered in such an undignified position. Her face was hot, her hair dishevelled, and her gown so old and faded that the original colour was a matter of guess. But the gentleman's smile was warm and friendly, not at all mocking. She received another unpleasant shock when she looked towards Bennet and saw him straining beneath the weight of the young dog. This was not the soft ball of fur that she had expected, but an animal fully half her brother's size, shaggy and grey.

"You may be the first to hold him, Garia," he said with the air of one bestowing a great favor.

She had little choice but to sit down on the sofa with the heavy dog sprawled across her lap. Lord Lindal took an armchair across from her, while Bennet plopped down on a footrest. "So this is Agamemnon," she murmured, as the creature leaped to the floor, all awkward body and long, long legs. She looked over at the Earl and murdered him with her eyes, although she ship to bring him. You might just as easily have sent a groom, or let Egan bring the dog."

"True, but I had a strong desire to see Agamemnon safely bestowed upon his new owner. I hope you don't disapprove of this addition to your household?"

"Not in the least," she assured him mendaciously, watching the ungainly animal gambol across the floor, sniffing at the chair legs. "I only hope I can prevail upon my brother to shorten his name into something a little more manageable. For if I must be forever calling a dog rejoicing in the name Agamemnon, I shall be bound for the madhouse within the span of a week. Although I don't doubt he will grow into it — all too soon!"

"Aga-mem-non," Bennet said slowly, enunciating each syllable. "I have it, Garia — I shall call him Nonny!" He looked to the Earl for approval of this diminutive.

"Hey-nonny-no," his lordship said with a smile, tickling the pup behind its ears. "*No*, you rascal, you may not climb upon my boots!" He set Nonny aside carefully, and the dog scampered back to his new master.

Torin hoped the lad and his pet would take themselves off now, for he had come with every intention of speaking privately with Miss Ivory. During his last visit to Dromana, she had been preoccupied with Mr. Charles she had been preoccupied with Mr. Charles Ruan, and now her little brother and the pup were rivals for her attention. "Thomas sends a message of thanks to you," he told her, "and I must second it. You served us well by recommending Con O'Patrick. His arrival was timely, in fact, for my former groom suddenly decided that Ireland doesn't agree with his constitution."

"I'm relieved there was a vacant place at the Castle. The man impressed me so, yet I couldn't afford to — that is, we had no work for him here," she amended, too late, and a wash of colour stained her cheek.

Torin narrowed his eyes, but he merely observed that Con had a way with horses and proved a welcome addition to his stables. Then he asked, "Will I have the pleasure of seeing you at the Duke of Devonshire's ball tomorrow evening?"

"Is there to be one? I'm afraid I don't move in such exalted circles," Garia declared. Not wishing to seem peevish, she continued, "Naturally I have heard that His Grace is making his first visit to Lismore Castle, but I am not acquainted with him. I believe he is a very young man."

"Oh, the veriest child," Torin said gravely, although his eyes danced to hear her speak as if she had one foot in the grave herself.

"He turned twenty-two on his last birthday. And like your brother Egan, he is partly deaf."

"That I did not know." Garia looked down when Nonny placed his muzzle on her knee, and she stroked it tentatively.

A little while later, as Torin tooled his curricle along the muddy, rutted drive, he pondered the many unanswered questions about the state of affairs at Dromana. To begin with, he couldn't imagine why the unmarried Ivory daughter should have inherited her father's property. He could only suppose that the Baronet had died in the expectation that she would be wed to her Mr. Ruan in due time. But both of his visits to Dromana had convinced him that the house had seen better days. This was unexpected, for to the best of his recollection Sir Andrew had been a man of moderate fortune. Yet he must have experienced a reverse of some sort if his daughter had been unable to hire Con O'Patrick, a labourer whose wages amounted to no more than a few pounds a year. Miss Ivory's house was neat and well tended and tastefully furnished, with a preponderance of the dark, bog-oak furniture so popular in Ireland. But today Torin's sharp eyes had seen how sun-faded the library draperies were, and on his last visit he had noted that the drawing-room hangings and upholstery were far from new.

That it was a happy home he did not doubt, but the three boys must be a shocking drain upon the lady's purse. He hated to think that financial worries were the reason for that occasional crease of worry on Berengaria Ivory's fine brow.

Torin, who had never counted the cost of anything in his life, remembered hearing that the union with England eleven years before had adversely affected Ireland's economy, yet had never guessed that any of his neighbours might have suffered. And he had to wonder if perhaps Mr. Ruan's fortune was the reason she favoured his suit.

Although he had never observed the gentleman in question around Bennet or Jeremy, his treatment of Egan did not augur well. It was a pity the lawyer failed to appreciate that shy, serious child, who so needed to be drawn out. Torin had begun to know Egan pretty well, and had heard Mr. Dickinson praise his young assistant, not only for his industry but also for his talents.

Young Jeremy Howard was harder to fathom than his little brothers. He wasn't secretive, precisely, but he had a certain reserve about him. He was a good shot, a fine horseman, and according to Reverend Ashgrove, an able scholar. But he had once admitted to Torin that he felt he was a burden to his stepsister. He hadn't elaborated on this, nor had Torin pressed him; it had been clear enough that the boy chafed at being on the receiving end of what he must regard as charity.

Young Bennet Howard was as lively and as unformed as the pup Nonny, but already he possessed a charm that was difficult to withstand. He resembled his brothers neither in looks nor in disposition, little devil that he was. Torin didn't envy Miss Ivory her guardianship of that young rascal, but it was evident that Bennet held a special place in her heart.

That evening, as he and his cousin sat down to a friendly game of chess, he was careful to phrase his thoughts in as disinterested a fashion as possible. "I am curious about our old play-mate Charles Ruan, and why Miss Ivory has settled upon him as a life partner."

"There's nothing objectionable about him," Thomas replied. "To be sure, he is a professional man, but his forebears are supposed to have been gentry." He looked up from setting out the chessmen to ask, "What business of yours is Miss Ivory's choice?"

"I can't help but feel a certain responsibility towards her."

"I think you're just being a dog in the manger," was the other gentleman's assessment.

"Well, we both know I can lay my hands on a certain paper. Perhaps before I relinquish whatever claim I might have to the lady, I should satisfy myself that this fellow is worthy of her."

"You have no claim at all so far as Garia is concerned," Thomas pointed out, "for she knows nothing about that betrothal contract."

Torin shrugged, but said nothing further. In his opinion, his cousin was undoubtedly the more deserving gentleman, and he and Miss Ivory appeared to be excellently suited. Both were staid and reasonable, and neither was the sort to care how little money the other might bring into marriage. But, he reminded himself, Thomas had disavowed any intention of offering for that intriguing young woman a third time. "Well," he said aloud, "I wish you would take it upon yourself to renew your courtship, for I'd give *you* my blessing, dear coz. But playing at matchmaker is the preserve of females, and I doubt I have any talent for it."

Torin directed his thoughtful gaze toward the massive chimneypiece decorated with a carved representation of the Montrose coat of arms. Inscribed in Latin upon the banner beneath the stone shield was the family motto, which expressed the bellicose sentiment that preparedness for battle was the surest path to victory.

6

These young men assembled here,
These boys shall be a hero flock.
— Lochlann O'Dalaigh

Michaelmas Day at Dromana House was celebrated with the traditional goose, redolent of sage and onion. The servants and farm labourers were granted a holiday, and the Howards had no lessons that day. In the afternoon they persuaded Garia to join them for a rollicking cross-country ride. By the time it was over, Bennet's fat pony was exhausted, Egan had spied what he claimed was an eagle, and Jeremy had suffered a trifling fall that bruised his pride greatly and did only slightly less damage to his new riding coat.

"A roaring great fall!" was how Bennet described his brother's toss to Judith Laverty at teatime. "Poor Jeremy knocked a groan out of the road when he struck it — that's what Erris said."

With unwonted severity she told him that if it was his ambition to grow up to be an Irish groom, then he would do well to ape

Erris's mode of speech. "But if you aspire to be a gentleman, Bennet, then you'd do better to study Lord Lindal or Mr. Montrose."

"Or Mr. Ruan," Garia added, but as she was occupied with pouring the cups, she missed her brother's fleeting expression of distaste.

The evening was spent in noisy games such as spillikins and jackstraws, until it was time for the younger boys to go to bed. Jeremy went upstairs not long afterwards, and Garia admitted to Judith that she, too, was thinking of her bed. "I'm fair exhausted," she told her aunt.

"It's not to be wondered at, when you persist in careening about the countryside after that pack of wild Indians," Judith observed. "Not but what I can tell that your day on horseback has done you a world of good — much more than occupying yourself with matters you would do better to leave to me. Why won't you let me take over the running of the household, Garia? I can't sit about endlessly embroidering altar cloths or new chair covers while you wear yourself to a bone day in, day out."

"But Aunt, you didn't come to us to be a drudge. I will be thankful for your company for as long as Grandfather Dunlaven can spare you. But if you find it dull here, you must return to him. At my age I hardly require a chaperone," Garia added diffidently.

Judith cut a thread with her sewing scissors. "I had far rather remain at Dromana, for I'm convinced I can be more useful to you than to my father. But I vow I'll pack my bags tomorrow unless you give me your word that from now on I shall be in charge of running the household."

Laughing, Garia asked, "And what do you expect me to do with myself all day?"

"Whatever pleases you. Go to Rosamund for a visit — she and Lord Kelsey are in the thick of Dublin society. You needn't scruple to leave the boys in my care, nor Dromana. You might benefit from a holiday, my love, and it would give you time to think over your answer to Mr. Ruan. And you never know what might come of it."

"Dearest Aunt, I don't pine for high life, I promise you. And I had my fill of the Dublin beaux when Rosamund brought me out so unsuccessfully. If you demand more responsibility here, you are welcome to take charge of the household. Tomorrow I'll inform Mrs. Aglish and McCurdie and Cook that they'll be receiving their orders from you. And I warn you that instead of junketing to the city, where Rosamund would keep me busier than I could ever be here, I'll probably ride out with the

Cloncavan pack at every opportunity."

"That possibility crossed my mind before I made my offer. I would be glad to see you enjoying yourself again."

When Garia bid her goodnight a little while later, Judith took one smooth, slim hand in her own plumper one and said, "Dear child, I want to see you happy! Don't think me a meddling old woman — I had rather you sent me packing than be considered so."

"You are not the least bit old, and I acquit you of meddling, though I feel positively brutish letting you take on the headaches of running this house."

The next morning, when Garia's eyes flew open at a typically early hour, it was all she could do to remain under the bedclothes. She forced herself to nestle back against the pillow and tried to plan out this first day of liberty. A peek at the sky showed the promise of a fine day, and she regretted that she'd had no word when the Cloncavan hunt would be meeting.

She gave Egan and Bennet their lessons as usual, and when she dismissed them she concealed her strong desire to ask where they were bound. They wouldn't appreciate an adult sister, however well loved, tagging along with them. Complete idleness was so abhorrent to her that she was happy to discover that some jars of currant jelly promised to Mrs. Ashgrove had not yet been delivered. She decided to walk to the rectory — it was the perfect opportunity for exercise and she was eager for a visit with her friend, Frances Ashgrove. So she donned her new claret-coloured pelisse and set out with a basket on her arm.

On her way to the village she passed the small white-washed cottages that housed her tenants. She felt fortunate compared to Bridgie O'Patrick and Sally Murrow, and especially poor Molly McEvoy. They had many more than three children to provide for out of their small cottage gardens and single cows or pigs, and their husbands laboured long and hard. Garia owned the roof over her head and she always knew where her next meal was coming from.

But she had money troubles of her own, even though the estate was out of debt for the first time in many years. Some of the modest income she derived from rents and wool and flax went towards buying more sheep, or preparing a new field for planting. She hoarded the rest, every spare pound and shilling, and since her father's death she had practised stringent economies, going without little luxuries like a second hunter for herself or new draperies for the downstairs rooms. And at every quarter-day she met with her banker in Waterford to turn over to him whatever amount she had saved. Her sole ambition, the one thing that ruled her every decision, was to make her stepbrothers her wards, legally. Sir Andrew had always intended to adopt the Howards, and his daughter was determined to carry out his wishes. But no one knew about her plan, for she had never discussed it with anyone, not her Aunt Judith, not Charles Ruan.

Fear of losing her stepbrothers stalked her day and night, for at any moment Josepha might descend upon Dromana. And because it was well within her rights to take her sons — and claim the small legacies left to them — it was imperative that Garia make them her wards as soon as possible. Whether or not the courts would grant her the guardianship of three boys who were not of her blood, and who had a living parent besides, was an unanswered question. But her lifelong exposure to the system of Irish justice had taught her that anything might be accomplished if one had enough money. And when she thought of her ever-growing fund, she saw a ray of hope amid the clouds of uncertainty.

As she walked along the crooked lane leading to the village of Cloncavan, she shifted her basket to her other arm and sighed over the dilemma that Mr. Ruan presented. Although she suspected the courts would favour the suit of a married woman, she was undecided about the wisdom of marrying him, for he deserved a better wife than one who wed him because she was desperate to provide for her brothers. He might well refuse to adopt the Howards himself; he would quite naturally expect to have children of his own someday. And because she had witnessed the unhappy results of a loveless marriage, she could not accept her suitor until she felt something rather stronger than respect for him. Despite Mr. Ruan's many fine qualities, he drew not a single spark of passion from her breast, and she feared it might always be so. It was her failing more than his; quite possibly it stemmed from the disappointment she had suffered as a girl, as much as from her father's misalliance. But honesty compelled her to admit to herself that Mr. Ruan was not particularly warm-natured, whereas she was capable of showing her affections where they were felt.

As she approached the front door of the Rectory, she shoved the vexing problem of Mr. Ruan to the back of her mind. Her knock was answered by Miss Frances, a tall, large-boned girl who resembled her father far more than she did her pretty mother. The Ashgroves joked that Frances ought to have been a boy, but they were already blessed with four sons, all at school in England, and they wouldn't have exchanged their only daughter for the world. It was said in the neighbourhood that no one behaved less like a parson's daughter than Frances Ashgrove, but she was well liked for all that — or perhaps because of it. Her frank, open manners and lively disposition were valued by her host of friends.

"What a delightful surprise," she said, leading Garia into the neat parlour. "Mama went out an hour ago and I am bored to death without her. She'll be sorry to have missed you, but this morning Lord Lindal sent all the torn and threadbare linens down from the Castle to be given to the poor. So Mama took them over to the village hall, where her sewing girls have gathered to do the mending." Frances stood back a little to inspect Garia's attire. "Just look at you! Is that a new pelisse? The colour is vastly becoming! I'm envious, for the last new things I had were a pair of Limerick gloves and some ribbons."

Garia handed over the preserves and apologised for the delay. "I'm afraid it slipped my mind that your mother had asked for them, but I brought them as soon as I remembered."

"Never mind that. Give me your basket,

and I'll bid Cook fill it with some of our apples. They've just come in, more than we can ever use, and your brothers will dispose of them quickly enough!"

When Frances returned from the kitchen, the basket was filled to the brim with ripe fruit. Taking a seat, she asked her visitor for all the news from Dromana.

"There isn't much," Garia replied. "Aunt Judith staged a palace revolution and has supplanted me as mistress of my household — and while it seems odd to be a lady of leisure I am content with it for a while. Bennet has his dog at last, a wolf dog, no less. Our housekeeper loathes him and our cook adores him — she persists in plying him with the most delectable of our table scraps. I don't doubt Nonny will be the largest dog in the parish before long! Jeremy takes his gun out most days, and Egan is busy at the Castle, helping Mr. Dickinson to catalogue the book collection."

"Yes, I met Mr. Dickinson at church on Sunday. Mr. Montrose introduced us." Frances paused, and for a moment her expressive face wore a slight flush. "Both gentlemen speak highly of Egan's aptitude for the work."

"We are grateful to the Earl for suggesting it. As you know, I've been at my wit's end trying to interest that child in things other than writing and drawing, and I could never have hit upon anything so well suited to his disposition."

After a pleasant half hour, Garia took her leave, and Frances promised to return her call very soon. She said merrily, "I vow, I learned nothing from you this morning, for I have been such a good girl! I didn't even ask about Mr. Ruan, for all I heard he was in the village not so long ago. And you needn't deny that he called at Dromana House, for our own Nellie saw him turn in at the drive when she was walking out with Brian Cady. Nor did it escape my notice that Lord Lindal was hounding you at Cloncavan Assembly! But I'm the soul of forbearance and won't tease you about either circumstance."

"Oh, no — you would *never* be so unkind as to tease!" Garia retorted. "Knowing I could respond in kind, and quiz you about the flirtation you were carrying on with one Mr. Ralph de Lacy at the same Assembly."

"Horrid creature, I never flirt. It was all on his side!"

With a disbelieving laugh, Garia departed. She was not yet ready to return home, so she walked the short distance to the village proper just for the pleasure of peering into the window of the dressmaker's shop. She found it shuttered, which was more often the case than not.

There was nothing else to keep her, so she started for Dromana, oblivious to the curricle that was overtaking her. But upon hearing her name, she looked up and saw Lord Lindal hand his reins to Con O'Patrick, who sat beside him attired in a neat blue livery. The Earl climbed down from the carriage and made his way to Garia, dodging a turf-laden horse cart and several of the carter's scraggly offspring to reach her.

"May I offer you a place in my carriage, Miss Ivory?" he inquired. "It would be my pleasure to take you wherever you may be bound."

"I prefer to walk home, though I thank you," she answered. "It is but two miles to my front door, and chasing after little brothers all these years has built up my stamina!"

Smiling down at her, he said he didn't doubt it. "Might I join you, then?" he asked. She nodded, and he called over his shoulder, "Drive on to Dromana House, Con, and I will meet you there."

The groom set the horses off at a trot. "What lovely creatures," Garia said as they passed by. "You must know my brother Bennet has praised your skill with the ribbons night and day since you took him up in your carriage last week."

"How very boring for you! In future I'll take care not to excite him. How is Nonny?"

"Thriving," she said with a laugh as he fell into step beside her. "Mrs. Aglish predicts he'll devour us in our beds before he's very much older, for the truth is he's an indefatigable chewer. The only way to ensure the safety of the table legs is to give him an endless supply of mutton bones. I only hope they don't give him a fancy for the taste of sheep."

"Miss Ivory, had I known I was foisting yet another charge upon you, I would never have given him to Master Bennet. My only excuse is that your imp of a brother assured me a dog in the house was of all things what you would most like!"

"Oh, but I do like it! Nonny makes a delightful pet, and we have all grown fond of him. Even Cook spoils him dreadfully, and she has never liked dogs."

He offered to carry her basket, and although at first she declined, he persuaded her to surrender it to him. As they strolled along the quiet lane, Garia cast about in her mind for some unexceptionable remark that might inaugurate conversation. Although she was curious about the Duke of Devonshire's ball at Lismore Castle, she had too much pride to beg for details of what must have been a glittering affair.

But Torin addressed her first, raising a topic on which she was always ready to speak. Said he, "I flatter myself I have become rather friendly with your stepbrothers, ma'am. You are to be commended for bringing them up so admirably."

"The credit for that belongs to my father," she told him.

"Some of it, perhaps, but certainly not all. I confess, I am curious about their origins."

"Whatever their lives were before their mother brought them here, only Jeremy is of an age to recall, and he has never told me much," Garia said. "I think it must be an unpleasant subject. My stepmother was a widow when my father met her in Dublin. Josepha Howard was her name then."

Torin came to an abrupt halt. "Josepha Howard?" he repeated.

"Mrs. Howard, yes."

"And a widow — so Howard died, did he? Of course it must be the same lady I met in London some years ago. Bennet is very like her, isn't he? His eyes, even the colour of his hair."

Garia stared up at him blankly. His words had conjured the specter of her auburn-haired, violet-eyed stepmother, and a familiar apprehension gripped her. "Can you really be acquainted with her?"

"I think I must be," Torin acknowledged ruefully, "for I knew her husband. He was

102

a remote connexion of the Duke of Norfolk's family, and heaven only knows where the lady sprang from, or how she contrived the match. Although I could hazard a guess. Young Jeremy must have been born soon after the ring was on her finger."

"He and Egan may be Mr. Howard's sons," Garia said in a low voice, "but I doubt that Bennet is."

"Exactly how old is he?"

"Seven years — and some months. His birthday is March fifteenth — the Ides of March."

"Your stepmother was quite popular with the town bucks. Howard, poor fool that he was, either knew not or cared not how she spent her days — or her nights. He was a sickly fellow, but good enough for all that. I seem to recall one of the lady's liaisons of eight years ago," Torin said ruminatively. "Her most notable conquest, in fact."

"Lord Lindal, will you tell me about that admirer? I don't ask his name, but I should like to know what manner of man he was. For he may have been Bennet's father," she added softly.

"Miss Ivory, he was a younger son, charming and well liked. His family pried him from the clutches of the fair Josepha by purchasing a commission for him. He became a credit to his regiment, a part of the Peninsular Army, and perished at Ciudad Réal."

Garia clasped her hands together. "A soldier — how Bennet would like that, and he can never know. As you say, he favours Josepha, at least as she looked when I last saw her, which was fully three years ago. But I ceased to think of him as her son when she went away." She paused, then made the observation, "What a small world it is — to think that you actually knew Josepha. Did you — was she ever your — ?" She hesitated, unable to phrase the question to her satisfaction. And then, when she realised what she was asking him, she clapped one hand over her mouth in sudden shame. "My wretched tongue! What must you be thinking? As though *that* were any business of mine!"

But her companion was more amused than shocked by the unfinished question and her obvious discomposure. He struck his forehead with his fist in a gesture of comical dismay and intoned, "My reputation, Iago, my reputation! My dear Miss Ivory, I swear to you I never knew your stepmother in that way. La Howard was never to my taste at all," he added outrageously.

"Oh, I'm so thankful! Not that I mean to imply that you couldn't have a — dear me, now I'm tangled again!" She took a deep breath and continued, "Well, a lady doesn't reach the age of six-and-twenty without discovering that gentlemen do have their *chères amies*. But I'm relieved to know you didn't admire Josepha. I don't think I could have borne that."

She gazed at the roof of Dromana House, which lay just ahead of them, and said reflectively, "She was always a supreme actress, and when Papa met her up in Dublin she must have played the part of widowed mother of fatherless sons to admiration. But she would not have needed to dramatise her plight, I suppose, because within a span of a few months she had moved to Ireland, borne Bennet, and buried her husband. Rosamund — my sister — maintains that she had found and lost a protector as well, and pursued Papa because he was a real gentleman who might marry her. And she judged him rightly, more's the pity."

Torin asked gently, "Did you not try to dissuade him from marriage?"

"I was not there to do it, nor would I have succeeded any better than Rosamund did. I like to think it was the boys who won his heart, and not their mother. The match was not a real *match* at all and was a disaster from the first. Josepha was disappointed in Dromana — although it was less shabby in those days, it wasn't nearly grand enough to suit her. She might have made real improvements, but she cared only for new gowns and carriages and jewels — oh, the debts she ran up! In Waterford and in Dublin!"

"I can well imagine," Torin said.

"I think the only ones who didn't suffer from the marriage were the boys," Garia continued. "Jeremy was eight, Egan four, and Bennet a year old when Josepha brought them to Dromana. She was only too happy to leave them in my care, and I soon learned to seek refuge in the nursery — it was the one room in the house that she never entered. No, that's not entirely true," she said, determined to be fair. "I suppose she was fond of the children in her way, but it wasn't my way. I shall never like her, but I do love her sons. They need me — and I suppose I need them, too."

This was the first time she had spoken so freely about Josepha. She had not suspected that Lord Lindal could be so sympathetic a recipient of her confidences. And although she had at first been dismayed to learn he knew her stepmother, that fact permitted her to speak quite frankly. It was true, she told herself, what everyone said about confession being good for the soul, even if the sins confessed were not one's own.

"And you have never heard from your stepmother since she left Ireland?" he asked her.

"No. She ran off, you see, with a man in

the East India Company, and with no more thought for us at Dromana than for a pair of discarded dancing slippers." And then Garia voiced her greatest fear, the one that often disturbed her sleep in the middle of the night. "Although I worry that she will return one day."

"I wouldn't let that possibility concern you too much," he said soothingly as they approached the faded, red brick facade of Dromana House. "I should think India suits your stepmother down to the ground — an abundance of gentlemen starved for female companionship, and a set of people whose lax conduct will not permit them to censure hers."

"But if she receives Mr. Ruan's letter informing her of Papa's death, she might come back, especially if she thinks she can gain something by it. She's very greedy, and the boys were left legacies in my father's will. That is why I — " She broke off, then shook her head. She had said too much already and could never explain to this man, so nearly a stranger, that she planned to make the Howards her wards.

"Why you what?" he prompted.

"It is of little importance. There's nothing so dull as being forced to listen to others drone on about family affairs."

"As you may recall, it was I who drew you

out on the subject," he reminded her. But she would not permit him to draw her out further, and she appreciated his gallantry when he subsequently changed the subject by saying, "The Cloncavan pack will be running two days hence. Shall I expect to see you? Jeremy describes you as a hard rider to hounds."

"Is that the character he gives me?" she cried in mock despair. "I must contradict him — I generally go no farther than the first few fields and take care never to be in at the kill. You mustn't believe everything my brothers say, Lord Lindal!"

She regretted the necessity of parting from him, but the curricle and pair were standing ready. He bid her good-day and drove off, and as she watched him go, it seemed to her that he had carried with him a host of her personal demons — and willingly, at that.

Along the road home, Torin sorted through everything he had heard. So, he thought, the spendthrift Howard woman was responsible for Miss Ivory's money woes, and doubtless for other woes as well. He urged his horses into a swifter pace and summoned up every dim, fleeting memory of Josepha Howard. Her opulent beauty had stirred the hot blood of his peers during her one season in London, but Torin had considered her too cold and too calculating. Young Bennet, it seemed, was the product of her liaison with that handsome, besotted soldier who had enjoyed her favours for a time.

But his reflexions were short-lived, for Con O'Patrick, unlike a wooden-faced English groom, considered it his place to converse freely with his master. And at every opportunity he sang the praises of Miss Ivory, whom he regarded as his benefactress. It was beyond Torin's power to check Con's flow of blessings upon that lady's head, and he smiled to hear for the tenth time how Miss Ivory had saved Con from the dreadful fate of being forced to endure Bridgie O'Patrick's uncertain temper and ill-cooked meals.

7

Ah, now a gentler fall . . .
— Gerald Fitzgerald,
Earl of Desmond

The day of the hunt dawned cool and damp, and the morning mist had barely begun to dissipate when Garia and her brother left Dromana. She was riding Brutus, a strong if not showy animal, capable of jumping any obstacle, be it ditch, wall, hedge, or stream. But Jeremy's new hunter was the finer of the two, and he was justly proud of it. The hunt met at the gates of Cloncavan Castle, and as soon as they arrived there, Garia saw that two of the Misses Neale had accompanied their papa, who was the local Master. If Jeremy was relieved to be able to leave Garia with her friends, he was too well mannered to betray it.

Although no novice at hunting, Garia was experiencing an unwonted self-consciousness. Her father's absence was partly responsible, but that this would be her first time hunting in the presence of the Earl of Lindal also disturbed her. He, no doubt, had ridden with the famous packs in England — the Quorn and the Melton. She glanced over to where he stood conferring with the earth-stopper and Mr. Doyle, one of the whippers-in, and received a nod and a welcoming smile. Suddenly she wished her habit were smarter and newer and a more dashing colour than plain, dull black. She wore a hat of chip-straw tied behind her curls; its jaunty, russet plume was the only bright note to her ensemble.

Of the twenty pairs of foxhounds led out from the hunting kennel Garia knew many by name, and she admired the younger dogs who were being entered for the first time. The small neat heads were indicative of the Cloncavan strain.

"There is a west wind today," she remarked to the Misses Neale. "That should favour the scent."

"Aye, Papa said as much," Katy replied, stroking her pony's neck.

But her sister Eliza was more interested in the hunters than the hounds. "Doesn't his lordship look fine in his hunting rig?" she asked. "The other gentlemen are nothing to him."

"Not even Ralph de Lacy?" Garia teased, for her young friend's preference was well-known.

When the hunt set out for the first covert, the three ladies kept to the rear. But because the hounds picked up a scent almost at once, they were forced to pick up the pace. Jeremy, who had been near the front, held his horse back until Garia came abreast of him.

His face was alight with excitement as he called out, "They've found already! 'Tis a dog-fox as big as a collie and as red as Bridgie O'Patrick's head! You must come forwards, Garia, for if you're not there when we run him to ground, you'll be sorry!" And he rode off at a canter.

With a gesture of apology to her friends, Garia put her heels to Brutus and followed her brother's lead. She was amused to discover that nearly every grubby boy in the parish was running on foot behind the host of blue-coated horsemen galloping *ventre à terre*. And, as usual, some members of the labouring class had mounted their plowhorses to join the hunt. There was even one man riding a donkey.

All halted when the hounds gathered around a promising tunnel in the damp earth, but Garia saw some of the gentlemen shaking their heads in disappointment. Thomas Montrose rode back and forth, producing ear-splitting notes from his horn, but the dogs paid no heed to his summons and continued to paw at the ground in frustration.

"Ferrets," said a familiar voice at Garia's

side, and she looked over to see the Earl on a black-tailed chestnut. "Only, look — the hounds have discovered their mistake and are now halfway over the hill. Do you follow?"

She gathered up her reins quickly. "Oh, yes!"

"It may be rough going farther on," his lordship warned, "and heaven knows how far the fox will take us. Has your mount staying power?"

"A wealth of it — it will be many miles yet before Brutus is blown." Wholly caught up in the excitement, she followed the big chestnut. At the summit of the hill she reined in, entranced by the vista of blue sky and gently rolling land intersected by the distant river. "Oh, how lovely!" she cried involuntarily, turning to Lord Lindal, who was still beside her.

But Torin was concerned with the enterprise at hand and asked her, "Wherever did those scruffy youngsters spring from? Do they always follow the hunt?"

Garia smiled at his aggrieved tone. "Generally they do."

With his whip he pointed at the hounds, which had checked once more. "I'm afraid they must have picked up a stale scent. I've never seen such disoriented — but wait, they're off again."

"And running in opposite directions!" Garia laughed to see the dogs' confusion. "Poor Mr. Montrose — shouldn't you go to him?"

"If you'll accompany me. Take care, now, this hill is quite steep on the descent, and there are many rocks."

But Brutus was surefooted and skirted the obstacles in his path with little difficulty. Mr. Montrose rode to meet his cousin, grinning sheepishly, and stated that the hounds were tracking two foxes. "We caught a glimpse of one of them earlier," he said. "Sir John and the de Lacys will follow that line, and I the other, with Jeremy Howard and Brian Doyle. You may take your choice, Torin. Like as not we'll end at the edge of the sea before all's done, and with a host of drowned foxhounds on our hands! Those dogs are wild as be-damned — beggin' your pardon, Garia."

Torin said wryly, "Too many young hounds entered at once — I told Doyle as much. I believe I'll follow our Master. Miss Ivory, do you care to wager that we'll catch a glimpse of the fox's brush before Thomas and your brother do?"

She shook her head. "I'm no gambler, my lord, and seldom trust the vagaries of chance."

"But you must, just this once, and permit me to set the stakes. A dance at the next Assembly?" He took her laughter for assent.

"There, Thomas, you are witness to our bargain, and it's a good thing, as we have no betting book by us. Be off now, and take care you don't break your neck!" As his cousin rode on, Torin looked over at Garia. "Come along, ma'am — it will go hard with me amongst the locals if I cannot keep with my hounds, you know."

They covered the ground at a clip as they tried to catch up with those who had already ridden ahead after the dogs, and Garia was pleased that Brutus was proving her earlier claim about his stamina. The hounds they followed scrambled through brush and furze, drawn once again by a scent that Garia had nearly begun to hope was not stale after all. A sudden, piercing cry from one dog caused her to fear it had been trodden on by a horse, but when the whole pack began baying in concert, she knew they had sighted their quarry.

There was a low stone wall ahead. Garia gave Brutus his head and felt his stride lengthen. Then she knew the familiar, floating sensation as the animal tucked his legs under him and vaulted over the obstacle. It was a clean jump, but Brutus tangled a leg in the brush on the other side and lurched so sharply that Garia lost her balance. As she pitched sideways, she kicked her foot free of the stirrup and fell, hitting the soft, soggy ground with a thud.

She sat up and rubbed her shoulder, but the horse was her greatest concern. Brutus was cropping grass only yards away, and as he walked she was pleased to note he did not favour any of his legs.

Torin, a witness to her fall, was running towards her. "Don't move," he cautioned as he knelt down beside Garia. "Have you sprained your shoulder?"

"I don't *think* so," she told him, "only I do feel a trifle shaken."

"And no wonder." He fumbled in his coat pocket and brought forth a silver flask. "This will steady you." When she shook her head he said firmly, "Drink, Miss Ivory — but not too much at once. Best to take small sips, or you'll regret it."

"I know," she said. "My father taught me." She held the flask to her lips and let the brandy slip slowly down her throat. It felt like liquid fire and warmed her to her toes.

"That's a good girl," Torin said encouragingly, and placed his arm around her shoulders for support. "Once more now."

She obeyed, then handed the flask back to him. As she did, she made the mistake of meeting his eyes, as green as the fields they had ridden together and only inches away from her own. In them she read concern, and something else that she could not identify. But his penetrating, unfathomable gaze made her breathless in a way that two hours in the saddle and miles of rough ground had not. He seemed to be in no hurry to withdraw his arm, and she wondered if perhaps he meant to kiss her. Her heart hammered against her ribs, and she murmured, "I am perfectly fine now."

He further alarmed her by grasping her by the wrist. "Flex your fingers," he commanded, and she did. "See, you are trembling. And far too pale to suit me."

It was all his fault, although naturally she would have died before admitting it. She pulled her hand away and brushed her hair out of her eyes. "I've lost my hat," she realised.

"And not a few hairpins, I should think," he said, smiling. He reached out to touch a curl that had tumbled onto her shoulder, then, as if he had done nothing out of the ordinary, he said, "Wait here, and I shall hunt down your property for you."

As soon as he turned his back, Garia drew the deep, desperate breath she had been holding for so long and climbed to her feet. She brushed the dirt from her habit as best she could, and went to check Brutus.

"I've found your hat in this ditch," Torin reported. "But I fear it is a ruin."

"Never mind. No one will see me as I am, for it is high time I went home." Inspecting the obstacle that had been her undoing, she said, "How humiliating — that wall is but two feet high!"

"A tumble is no reflexion upon your skill, for the best of riders takes a toss now and again. Your father must have told you that, for he was a great horseman. I have never seen a lady with lighter hands than yourself, nor have I witnessed so graceful a fall. To think I'd have missed it had I not been looking over my shoulder!"

"I wish you hadn't been!" she said with a flash of spirit. "As you see, I am still in one piece, and ready to mount, my lord."

But Torin was gazing beyond her, to a copse a little farther on, where the other riders had paused. "Surely they cannot be waiting for us!" he exclaimed. "But, no, they've actually cornered the fox! Don't look now, it may be a bloody sight. You have your tumble to thank for not being in at the kill, you know." He looked down at her, and his voice was soft and caressing as he added, "But pray do not resort to that trick ever again, I beg you." In a more normal tone he said, "Wait here but a moment, my dear, while I put in my appearance at the scene."

Garia was seized by a wish to rush headlong

back to the sanctuary of Dromana, for her tumble hadn't frightened her half so much as his lordship's gentle words and warm smile. No, no, she told herself, this could not, it must not be. For Lord Lindal had a past — and a position — that precluded his ever making her the object of any serious intentions.

He soon rejoined her and as he threw her into the sidesaddle, Garia found that she could no longer meet his eyes. She busied herself with arranging her trailing skirts and adjusting her reins. She was reluctant to let him escort her home, and asked, "What about the other part of your pack?"

"Heaven knows where my hounds are now," he replied. "I've had my fill of hunting for one day, and my sole desire is to see you safely to your door."

"But you will miss the hunt breakfast back at the Castle!" she protested.

"It will last for hours, and my late arrival won't be noticed — or remembered. Have you any knowledge of where we are now, or in what direction we must ride?"

She couldn't help but laugh and felt better for it. "As a matter of fact, I do. You should be mortified, not knowing your own country!"

"You'd not dare to hold it against me, Miss Ivory," he said with a wicked grin. "Only re-call how magnanimous I have been over the matter of that little toss you took!"

She led the way to the narrow, winding lane that separated his property from the bog land she had recently purchased. Her mind was a whirl of confused thoughts, and she said very little as their horses ambled along side by side. Had she misread the warmth of his expression and intonation? she wondered, still occupied with all that had transpired immediately after her fall. Perhaps she refined too much upon his gallantry.

Just before reaching Dromana, they met Con O'Patrick, who was riding a lean pony and whistling a gay tune. As he spied his master, he waved his cap and cried, "Your lordship's honour — and Miss Ivory too! Such goings-on as you'll nivver imagine!"

"Have you news of my hounds, Con?" Torin asked him.

"Aye, that I have. Them little dogs just ran the wee foxie into the Manahans' henhouse at Smallridge and caught the poor beast right enough. They managed to ate a couple of chickens besides. But Mrs. Manahan, she's a lovely, grand lady, she is, and is after servin' the gentlemen a handsome breakfast for all that! Such a run as they had, too — the poor horses' hooves was droppin' off at the end of it!"

"I must confer with my cousin to learn which of us found first," the Earl said to Garia.

"For I have not forgot our wager — and intend to claim my prize."

After Lord Lindal rode off to the Castle and his breakfast, Judith Laverty asked her niece if she had enjoyed the day's run.

"I suppose so," Garia responded, but she was not inclined to elaborate. It was not quite noon, yet she was exhausted. She excused herself and went upstairs to her bedchamber, where one of the housemaids helped her remove her riding habit. While Cora was doing her best to brush away the mudstains, she said merrily, "Nivver will ye guess what has been going on at Dromana today, Miss Garia."

"Probably not, so you may as well tell me," her mistress replied, taking up her comb.

"Oh, 'twas the divil of an uproar!" Cora declared. "Molly McEvoy caused it all, not but what I don't disbelieve her, meself." She paused, savouring the importance of being the bearer of interesting news. "Not two hour ago she came to the kitchen door a-wringin' of her hands and moanin' fit to die, and said Bridgie O'Patrick has put a curse on all her geese. Sure, and they were droppin' like hailstones at Molly's feet in the morning when she went to feed them."

"Dead?"

"Entirely! Molly has got geese dyin' that

has nivver died before, Miss Garia, and powerful angry is she. She vows to have her revenge on that witch Bridgie."

Garia sighed all the way to her toes, for accusations of this sort were not uncommon in the neighbourhood. Her only recourse was to go to the McEvoy cottage and try to convince Molly that something besides the ill-will of Mrs. O'Patrick had caused the geese to sicken. She would do so that afternoon — or on the morrow — but for now all she wanted was a bit of solitude for peaceful reflexion.

It was not to be granted her.

She had just stretched out comfortably upon her bed when Cora mentioned Nonny's mysterious disappearance. "And not long after we discovered it, Master Bennet went missin' as well."

"Since when?" Garia asked, rousing herself.

"Oh, these two hours or more," she was told.

"I wish my aunt had told me," she declared, pinning up her hair again.

"'Tis likely she didn't want to worry you," Cora said blithely, having done that very thing.

Bennet's failure to return home in time for his supper alarmed both Judith and Garia, who set out with the groom Erris to search for him. They visited several of the neighbours before turning up boy and dog in the kitchen of the

Doyle house, where Bennet was happily chewing on bread and cheese. And although Garia managed to keep her temper in the presence of the bailiff's wife, on the way home she gave her errant stepbrother a rare scold for causing herself — and Mrs. Doyle — so much trouble. As soon as they returned home, Nonny was banished to the kitchen, where Cook plied him with the choicest viands at her disposal lest the "poor creature" be hungry after his adventures.

Jeremy, too, was late in returning home, and he had much to say on the subject of the first-rate run he'd had. Thomas Montrose had even presented him with that honourable trophy, the fox's brush. Just as Jeremy finished describing his day, Egan arrived from the Castle, where he and Mr. Dickinson had discovered an exceedingly rare volume of Ovid that had excited their enthusiasm.

When at last Garia was left alone with her tumultuous thoughts, it was late at night and she was tucked into bed. From the warm security of her blankets, she looked back at the morning as if from a great distance.

She couldn't deny that she was strongly attracted to Lord Lindal. Oh, irony of ironies that she should tumble into an infatuation with the very gentleman who had cut up her peace so long ago. To her credit, she had given no hint of how his warm smiles unsettled her or how his slightest touch made her pulse quicken, but that was cold comfort. She reminded herself that he was quite above her touch and far beyond her reach. Lord Lindal was wealthy, titled, and experienced. He was a handsome butterfly, flitting hither and yon from one bright and lovely flower to the next, sampling each and lingering at none. And there wasn't a chance in the world that he would think twice about a young woman past her first youth, saddled with three boys and a property that was barely profitable. At most she could aspire to be his partner in some mild flirtation; to expect anything more would be arrant foolishness. She would do well to accept the truth, painful and disappointing as it might be.

She supposed she faced a long and treacherous autumn—unless he should go away as suddenly as he had come. But there was no solace in that, for the very thought of his leaving Cloncavan was even more disturbing than the possibility that he might remain. Well, she must simply do her best to concentrate on other things, namely looking after her stepbrothers and managing her estate. Before she closed her eyes and courted sleep, she told herself that the afternoon had been proof enough that she did not lack for distractions.

8

She is the pearl and being of all Ireland.
— Turlough O'Carolan

Two days passed before Torin set eyes again on Miss Ivory, but from time to time she stole into his thoughts. She had charmed him from the moment he had met her at the Cloncavan Assembly. In subsequent encounters he had been increasingly captivated by her wit, her humour, and her beautiful sense of calm. The wealth of love she showered upon her step-brothers commanded his admiration, as did her skill on the hunting field and her gallant recovery from her fall. But she delighted him most of all on those rare occasions when she became flustered by some unconventional outburst of his — or her own. In such instances he was able to see through that veneer of propriety to some other, more elemental part of her, one he liked to believe was known only to himself.

However, he had no idea whether or not Miss Ivory would care to know how well he liked her, and how much he would like to know her better. Possibly his lamentable conduct ten years before made it impossible for her to regard him with anything other than indifference. And in his heart he knew that he deserved no more, if as much.

Mr. and Mrs. de Lacy invited a small party for dinner and dancing, and Torin was pleased to find Garia among the company. As soon as a set began forming for a reel, he invited her to be his partner; when she hesitated he announced that he had won the wager they had made on the hunting field. "As best we can determine, we trapped our fox a good quarter of an hour before Thomas did his. It is within my rights to claim my prize, you know," he said.

The smile he gave her was the very one that made Garia's heart skip two beats. "I — I am honoured, my lord," she stammered, and permitted him to lead her onto the floor. They were the lead couple, so when the musicians struck up the lively tune she immediately skipped forwards to make her curtsey. But her heart was not nearly so light as her feet. At least, she thought thankfully, the exertions of the dance rendered conversation impossible. Despite her resolve not to respond to Lord Lindal's overtures, within moments his very smile had swayed her and she had violated that resolution. This did not augur well for the future.

During the final measures of the dance she decided she would fob him off by pretending she had torn her flounce, or by some other stratagem, but his lordship offered her no opportunity.

"You will want some lemonade now," he hazarded as she rose from her final curtsey and he straightened from his polished bow. "I do myself."

He obtained two cups from a passing footman, and Garia accepted hers with a smile. She realised it had not been a very convincing one when he asked gravely if he had done something to offend her. "Why no," she said, too brightly. "Not at all."

"Is everything well at Dromana?"

"As well as it ever is," she said with a flash of genuine humour.

"I feel sure your inheritance must present some vexing problems," said Torin. "You may tell me if you like. I, too, am learning the business of running an estate. What is it that troubles you?"

His gentle, persuasive words prompted Garia to confide one of her problems that did not involve him. "Today my bailiff informed me that we've lost a prize ewe to colic. She will be missed, for she was an excellent and proven breeder." Her cheeks pinkened in response to the frankness of her own remark, but the Earl's expression was interested, nothing more. So she added, "I had hopes of improving my stock, you see, and she was indispensable in that regard."

"It so happens that I could spare a ewe — or two."

At a loss, Garia sipped her punch, then said, "Perhaps I should send Mr. Doyle to the Castle to discuss the matter with Mr. Montrose."

"I had far rather discuss it myself, and with you," Torin declared. "Will you be at home to visitors tomorrow?"

She felt her palms go damp inside her kid gloves, and at the same time her colour receded. "I'm afraid not, my lord. That is, I expect to be very busy." It was a feeble explanation — none at all, really — so she was rather surprised when he accepted it without comment.

The Earl did not invite her to dance again that evening, and he took Frances Ashgrove in to supper.

But she hadn't lied to him, she reminded herself as she made a pretense at flirting with young Mr. de Lacy over the cold collation Mrs. de Lacy had provided her guests. Earlier in the day she had received a note from Mr. Ruan, announcing his intention of calling at Dromana the next day, and she had every expectation of receiving an offer of marriage from the man she could admire but did not love. But thinking about it made her head ache; pleading infirmity, she induced her aunt to leave the party shamefully early.

The ladies returned to Dromana to find Jeremy in the library, his head bent over his Latin book, and a sleeping Nonny stretched out at his feet. "I didn't expect to see you home so soon," he told his stepsister after Judith Laverty went up to bed.

"It has been a fatiguing sort of day," Garia replied, dropping into the nearest chair and massaging her temples.

Jeremy went to close the door, and in a low voice he said, "There's something I must ask you, and I hope you won't take it amiss, or think me impertinent."

"I hope not, too," she said, with a faint, fond smile.

"We all know Mr. Ruan is calling here tomorrow. And it's useless for me to pretend I don't know his purpose. Will you wed him, Garia?"

"Do you have any advice to offer me?"

"Advice? How should I presume to advise you on such a matter? I thought you must know your own mind by now."

Meeting his eyes, so fine and brown, so trusting, Garia did know her own mind. There was only one possible reply to Charles Ruan's proposal, and it was that which would most benefit Jeremy and Egan and Bennet. Their future was the single most important consideration, and she would do anything to ensure that it would be a happy, secure one. In Charles Ruan lay her best chance for keeping the boys should Josepha ever claim them. Love him she did not, but wedding him would put an immediate and expedient end to her hopeless love for Lord Lindal as well. Marriage would be a refuge from the muddle of emotions that had made her miserable ever since the day of the hunt.

She took a deep breath and said firmly, "Yes, Jeremy, my mind is quite made up, and I have decided to accept Mr. Ruan." Did she imagine it, or did he seem troubled?

"Oh, Garia — are you *quite* sure?"

"Quite, quite sure." And she was. "Does it please you?"

"It must, if that is what you want. I always hoped Egan and Bennet and I would not affect your decision to marry or prevent you from making a life of your own."

"But the three of you are part of my life," she told him. "I daresay Mr. Ruan will become your legal guardian, just as I have wanted to be ever since Papa died. Only think, Jeremy — It will mean a fine school for you and a proper education for Bennet and drawing masters for Egan. And in a few years you shall go to Trinity College in Dublin. If you wish to study the law, Mr. Ruan will see that you go to England, to the Inns of Court as he did. Won't that be grand?"

"But Garia, surely you don't mean to marry because of what Mr. Ruan can do for us?"

Garia flinched at this bald question. "Not only that," she said quickly. "I will be happy in my own right. Charles Ruan is the only man I could ever marry." That was true enough, she thought glumly. "May I trust you to make everything right with Egan and Bennet? I know you have great influence with them — they look up to you, as well they should."

Jeremy looked doubtful, but he assured her that he would do everything in his power to alleviate any concerns his brothers might harbour. In an unusual show of affection, he kissed Garia's cheek and said, "I'll wish you happy now, even though it is a bit premature. Tomorrow you'll be lost in a maze of good wishes, and I want mine to be the first!"

He left her then, and she leaned her still-throbbing head against the chair-back. She was sure she had made the right choice. Many happy marriages had been founded on friendship and mutual respect, and she had no real wish for a grand passion, whatever she may have thought at sixteen. She would do better to emulate her practical, unromantic sister, who had wed to please the family, and ever since had been content with her husband and their vast and ever-increasing brood. Anyway, Garia told herself, her marriage wouldn't be one of convenience only. Charles Ruan was fond of her, and she liked him very much. From the moment she agreed to become his wife, all of her loyalty and affection would belong to him. But what, she asked herself, would be Lord Lindal's reaction to the news of the betrothal? And why must she care about it so terribly much?

Early the following morning Garia received yet another missive from her suitor, this one couched in such terms as to make her decision seem perfectly reasonable and even more desirable. He wrote that he had lately enquired at the boys' school in Kilkenny; it had places for all three of her stepbrothers. He looked forwards to calling upon her in the afternoon to discuss not only the possibility of enrolling them after the New Year, but also (heavily underscored) other business of a personal nature.

Garia placed the letter on the drawing room mantel and joined her family in the library. She imparted to her brothers the news that they might all be going to school soon. The younger boys exchanged unhappy glances, but

Jeremy, sensitive to the fact that his sister might wish to be alone with her aunt, bore them away.

"Garia, your decision to send the boys away seems rather hasty," Judith Laverty pointed out gently. "And though I agree that Bennet would benefit from school discipline, I thought you preferred to keep Egan at home. And however will you contrive to pay the fees?"

"That will be Mr. Ruan's responsibility. I hope you will wish me happy, Aunt. I intend to be, you know."

Glancing at Garia's calm, determined face, Judith could not doubt her words, but neither could she believe her to be perfectly easy in her mind. Garia looked as if she had slept ill, and a hint of sorrow lurked in the smoky blue eyes. Judith remained silent; she would wish Garia happy at the proper time, when the engagement was a settled thing. The gentleman hadn't yet made an offer, after all.

Too preoccupied with her own thoughts to notice her aunt's lack of enthusiasm, Garia stared out the window and wondered at what hour Mr. Ruan would call. For too long she had neglected to visit the McEvoy cottage to soothe Molly's fears about the plague that had befallen her geese. And somehow she must prevent the smouldering feud between Molly and Bridgie O'Patrick from erupting into the full conflagration of out-and-out war. If her first attempt at peacemaking proved unsuccessful, she wouldn't hesitate to ask Father Rourke to compose a sermon on neighbourliness for next Sunday's mass. It was an effective measure and one she preferred not to resort to lest it lost its efficacy.

A half hour later she set out in the gig, hoping the fresh air would blow her megrims away. When she pulled up before the McEvoy's stone cottage, she was greeted by excited children, geese, ducks, and Molly herself.

"It's sorry I am to see you here, Miss Garia, if you've come on account o' the geese," said Mrs. McEvoy, wiping her floury hands on the shawl that was seldom, if ever, removed from her broad shoulders. "Sure, and I ought to have sent word to the big house, but it slipped my mind entirely. Pat, get away from the car and horse and let the lady step down!"

Garia had come laden with bounty, and while she dispensed seed cakes to the McEvoy children, she asked Molly if the geese had recovered from their affliction.

"Aye, but 'twill be a long day afore Stew McEvoy recovers from the affliction I put on his head!" the Irishwoman declared. "For wasn't it his own fault that half our flock was ill taken?"

Relieved to learn that Bridgie O'Patrick was no longer regarded as the malefactor, Garia waited patiently for further explanation.

After a few choice denunciations on the stupidity of husbands, Molly began her tale in atypically succinct fashion. "'Twas the potheen, Miss."

"What about it, Molly?" All of Garia's tenants produced the highly intoxicating liquid rendered from steeping barley in water and distilling the mixture over a peat fire. The substance that resulted was clear as morning dew and unbelievably potent.

"Well," Molly said, shaking her head dolefully, "Stew McEvoy had poured the drink into empty bottles, which he hid in the thatch above the roof, and somehow them bottles came to be broken. The potheen spilled all down into the water trough below, which was empty at the time through the fault o' that lazy Pat, who forgot to fill it. Sure, and the stuff looks just like water — how were the poor creatures to know? Flat on the ground they fell, them geese, one after another. And I at my wit's end, thinkin' they was cursed — or poisoned!"

"Oh, dear. And did they die?" Garia asked, her voice quivering with ill-concealed mirth.

"Only for a whileen, Miss. We put the bodies in the shed and within four-and-twenty hours they had risen and was screechin' for their corn. 'Twas a miracle we thought, and were just afore goin' to the church to give thanks to St. Francis when we noticed Pat and Baby Mary wobblin' about the yard as if drunk they were. Which was no more than the truth, and how we discovered 'twas potheen in the trough."

With commendable control and a solemnity that she was far from feeling, Garia murmured that she was happy to hear that Bridgie O'Patrick was acquitted of the charge of cursing the geese.

"Oh, as to that, it's entirely certain I am that she caused the bottles to break in the first place!" was Molly's blighting answer. "Now 'tis my Stew who wants to wring her neck, but there's no sayin' what curse she'd put on us did he try it."

After listening to an impassioned condemnation of the red-headed O'Patrick witch, Garia beat a hasty retreat. She chuckled to herself all the way back to Dromana House.

Upon her return, she was desperate for diversion, lest the doubts that had kept her wakeful all night come crowding back. But McCurdie informed her that her aunt was busy in the poultry yard, and as usual, the boys were off on some spree. Deciding to prepare for the impending ordeal, she changed into a fresh gown, one that made her eyes appear darker in contrast to its light cerulean hue. She sat down in the drawing room with a volume of poetry on her lap, and as the hour that would seal her fate approached, she began to feel an unwelcome sense of doom. She tried to concentrate on the verses, but the ticking of the clock, the footsteps of the servants. and the gentle rush of wind outdoors all conspired to prevent it.

Briefly she considered the fact that when next she met Lord Lindal it would be as an engaged woman. As the memory of his green eyes, his crop of black hair, and the faint traces of dissipation in his countenance obtruded, she felt as if she might weep. If only she were a different being, someone of his world, or if he were of hers, then the hopes she did not dare to admit to herself would not be so futile. But then he wouldn't be himself, with all the qualities that had won her anew — compassion, good humour, generosity. But he also had a roving eye, she reminded herself sadly, and was something of a libertine as well. She had always known it, even before she had known him, and knew she was to be twice pitied for falling under his spell.

On the day after the de Lacys' party, Torin often thought of Miss Ivory, and the awkwardness that had attended their last meeting. From the moment of their introduction at the Cloncavan Assembly, he had been conscious of her charm, and in subsequent encounters, she had further captivated him. He was reminding himself of this when his butler informed him that an unexpected visitor sought an audience. "Master Bennet Howard awaits your lordship's leisure."

Torin looked up from his breakfast. "It can hardly be noon yet. An early hour for making calls by our London standards, eh, Cobbe? Never mind, you may send him to me."

"Very well, my lord. But I feel it incumbent upon me to warn your lordship that Master Bennet is not unaccompanied. He has brought his dog."

"I am sufficiently warned."

One of his lordship's visitors bounded into the room, wagging his tail; the other entered dispiritedly and sat down at the table uninvited. Although Torin invited Bennet to partake of any of the excellent dishes laid out on the sideboard, the child shook his head forlornly and said he wasn't hungry. He fixed his large eyes on his host's face and heaved a great sigh.

After a few minutes of this intense scrutiny, Torin remarked pleasantly, "I, too, shall lose my appetite if you persist in staring me out of countenance. What brings you to the Castle at an hour when I would have supposed you to be learning lessons or chasing after sheep with Nonny?"

Bennet shook his head. "No lessons today."

Remembering Garia's stiffness the other night and her colourless manner, Torin asked quickly, "Your sister's not unwell?"

"Nay, sir. It's *me*. That is, I'm not unwell, precisely, but I'm in a desperate case. That's what I've come to tell you. I thought perhaps you could help me — help us all — for it's important!"

Torin put down his fork. "What is the matter? Nonny hasn't been feasting on the neighbours' hens or disturbing the peace in any way, I trust?"

"No, nothing like that. It's worse. Garia is about to become engaged to Mr. Ruan, and I think she's going to *marry* him, too." Bennet stated this in a rush, and seeing Lord Lindal's black brows draw together, he said, "You don't like it either — I knew you wouldn't. I told Egan so, but he just said I was imagining things again. Oh, sir, can you not stop her? She's only doing it for us — for me 'n Egan and Jeremy!"

Torin's expression relaxed just a bit, but still he frowned. "She told you that?"

"Not me, but Jeremy. After I went to bed, and Garia came home from the party, I — " The boy paused, then continued manfully, with high colour, "I went downstairs and listened at the keyhole while they were talking in the library."

"Shameless! But how can you know that Miss Ivory's engagement is imminent? The full tale, if you please!"

Bennet faced his interrogator squarely, almost defiantly. "I read the note Mr. Ruan sent her this morning. Garia left it in the drawing room. On the mantel."

Torin raised a brow. "On the *mantel?*" he repeated.

"I climbed up on a chair," the child admitted. He waited for the Earl's censure of this tactic, but apparently none was forthcoming, so he continued. "Mr. Ruan is calling on her today for the—the-purpose-of-discussing-business-of-a-personal-nature!" he quoted all in one breath. "So from that I guessed he meant to speak the hard word!"

"The hard word?"

"Ask her to marry him — Nurse calls it speaking the hard word. And Garia will say yes, because last night she told Jeremy that if she weds Mr. Ruan, he can legally guardian us. I think it's on account of his being a lawyer. But though she thinks things will go better for us if she marries him, they'll just be worse. 'Cause Mr. Ruan don't like little boys too much."

"Doesn't he? How very obtuse of him, to be sure!"

"He has found a school in Kilkenny, and means to send all of us there, even Egan. Garia says it'll be wonderful, even though she'll miss us, but my brothers and I think it a monstrous plan. Jeremy believes Mr. Ruan wants us out of the way after he marries our sister. Why should he? Garia is always saying she wishes she could keep us with her forever!"

"One can't help but wonder why she would!" But Torin's smile faded quickly. "I'm afraid you credit me with greater powers than I possess, Bennet. It is very much your sister's affair, and I have no right to interfere in what does not concern me."

If the lady chose to engage herself to the attorney, whatever her motives, it really was none of his concern. Or was it, he wondered. Suppose she had come to a standstill and was in dire need of money? Perhaps she believed Charles Ruan was her only ally, the only person who was willing to take on the responsibility of her three stepbrothers. She might accept him out of necessity; Torin did not doubt her devotion to the boys ran to such lengths. If she was about to sacrifice herself to matrimony, it would explain her constraint last evening, and it indicated that she was reluctant to enter into marriage with the lawyer.

But she deserved a choice, didn't she, some other alternative?

And on the heels of that thought, Torin admitted to himself that he couldn't let the lovely Irish lady become Mrs. Ruan — for a number of reasons, the most important being that she deserved a higher station in life. She would make an excellent Countess, for instance. And, he told himself, in a sense he was even obligated to set right that wrong he had done her years ago. Marriage to Miss Ivory might be a drastic step — perhaps it was taking chivalry too far — but he decided then and there that it would suit him right down to the ground.

The marriage contract, safely locked away in his desk, was his trump card, if he chose to use it. And despite what he had just told Bennet, he did indeed have the power to keep Miss Ivory from accepting Mr. Ruan's proposal. That document was legally binding, as the lawyer would realise as soon as it was brought to his notice.

Bennet, seeing his lordship's sudden triumphant smile cried, "I *knew* you would help me! What shall you do, sir? Challenge him to a duel?"

Torin threw back his head and laughed. He reached out a hand and did further damage to the child's tousled hair. "No, you bloodthirsty little ape, I shan't challenge Mr. Ruan to a duel. His respectable offer of marriage is hardly provocation enough for so desperate a measure as that! Now then, I must hurry to Dromana and speak to your sister before Ruan arrives." He strode over to the tall window overlooking the river, where he thought long and hard for several minutes. When at last he turned back to Bennet, he said with an air of authority, "Never a word of this to anyone, my lad! Have I your promise on that head, in exchange for mine to take care of things to your satisfaction?"

"Oh, yes!" Bennet assured him breathlessly.

"Excellent! Now, run along to the stables and bid Con O'Patrick to harness Trinket and Tory to the curricle — tell him to bring it round at once. And I'm sorry, but I must leave you here, else your sister might suspect your part in this scheme."

Bennet ran from the room with the Earl hard on his heels.

9

Then with burning speech and soul, I looked at her and told her that to wed a churl like that was for her the shame of shames.
— Egan O'Rahilly

Mr. Charles Ruan's neat chaise drew up before Dromana House at half past twelve. McCurdie admitted him and took his hat and stick with a polished bow. The elderly retainer's manner had been less than gracious on the occasion of Mr. Ruan's previous visit, but he was obsequious to the extreme as he ushered the gentleman into the drawing room. For as all the servants were aware, on some not too distant day Mr. Ruan would become their master, and thus demanded respect.

Garia greeted the soberly dressed lawyer with a strained smile and bid him be seated. "I hope you had a pleasant drive," she remarked. "The weather is perfect for one." He had not been in the house more than a few minutes, and already she was reduced to platitudes.

"My dear Garia, you can have no notion how endless the miles between the city and Dromana seemed to me today!" Mr. Ruan told her.

With tolerable composure she replied, "But you must often wish we were not so far removed from town, sir. Speaking for myself, it is a comfortable distance."

"You had my note this morning?" he asked, and she nodded. "What do you think of the Kilkenny scheme? I have the headmaster's word that he can take all of your stepbrothers after Christmas."

"That is good news indeed." She hesitated, then said, "But I've been thinking this morning that the school at Waterford might answer just as well. For Jeremy and Bennet, that is, for I've never considered sending Egan away."

He shook his head. "You spoil that boy."

"No more than the others," Garia responded, twisting her fingers in her lap. "And I don't think I would like sending any of them so far."

He continued glibly, "Oh, the school in Kilkenny is far superior to the one in Waterford! But we need not decide the matter just now. Are your brothers at home?"

"Egan is always up at the Castle nowadays, and I believe Jeremy has ridden over to the Manahans'. Bennet has his dog to play with." Garia described Nonny and his gargantuan appetite, then spun out the tale of Molly McEvoy's geese. She was determined to discuss anything, everything, except the reason he had come, and why this should be so, she didn't like to think.

"On my way here this morning, I stopped to speak with Mr. Doyle," the gentleman said, leaning slightly forwards. "He tells me one of your best ewes was lost to a colic. What do you mean to do about it?"

Hot resentment surged through Garia's veins and flared in her eyes, for she disliked his officious air; it was not yet within his rights to take on the business of running her estate. "I shall purchase another, I suppose. Although I have not yet had the opportunity to discuss the matter with Mr. Doyle," she said repressively. "I will abide by his advice, which has always been excellent."

Charles Ruan shrugged. "On that point we differ. I have found him stubbornly reluctant to instigate necessary improvements. Garia, you really must consider enclosing your land to make it more profitable. For too long you have chosen to ignore the fact that you could make better use of your arable land."

"No," she said curtly. "That is, I cannot — no, I *will* not do that. And you will find me just as stubborn as Mr. Doyle in opposing enclosure. It would be ruinous if I chose to break the existing leases and evict my tenants, most of whom have lived here for centuries. They are just as much my responsibility as my brothers. They, too, were left in my care." She saw her answer had displeased him, but she didn't care. "How *can* you suggest I cast them off? You, who once lived on the land, whose father held on to his small freehold until his dying day. You should be ashamed!" Her bosom heaved with indignation.

"Garia, this is not a matter of sentiment, but one of business," he said, dragging his fingers impatiently through his auburn locks. "Your precious tenants are a lazy, drunken lot, always behind on their rents. You owe them nothing."

Before she could contradict him, which she had every intention of doing, McCurdie announced that Lord Lindal had just arrived and was desirous of speaking with her at once. The butler beamed, for the Earl, already a prime favourite with the Dromana staff, had greased his fist handsomely upon being told that Miss Garia would not wish to be disturbed.

"Very well, you may show him in," Garia said, with no thought for Mr. Ruan's possible objections. This was the second time the Earl had intruded upon her and Mr. Ruan at a sensitive moment, and again she could not be sorry. And when his lordship subsequently stepped into the room, tall and elegant and heartbreakingly handsome, the power of his presence was like a brutal blow. It was the ultimate proof of how foolish and futile had been the hasty decision she had made after parting from him last night. How had she ever thought she could marry Charles Ruan, she wondered, when her senses scattered at the sight of another man. It would be wrong to marry under false pretenses; it would be disastrous.

The Earl greeted the obviously disgruntled lawyer with every appearance of pleasure, saying, "Ah, Mr. Ruan, how fortunate that you are here! An attorney is exactly what I require. Miss Ivory, I'm glad to find you well — no indisposition precipitated your early departure from the de Lacys' fête, I hope."

"No," she choked, having forgotten that her reply was far from the truth.

Charles Ruan stepped forward and said stiffly, "My lord, I will be happy to call at the Castle on my way back to Waterford. But I'm afraid this is not the proper time to discuss whatever business you have in mind. Miss Ivory and I are engaged — in a discussion of private matters," he amended.

"You don't understand, Mr. Ruan — although to be fair, there is no way you could. But you may take my word for it that any matter that concerns Miss Ivory also concerns me." Torin turned to Garia. "Madam, I hesitate to inform you before a third party, but — really, this is too embarrassing! It is all your fault for receiving another gentleman before me."

Mr. Ruan exploded, "What right have you to censure the lady?"

"The right of a husband-to-be," Torin declared.

The lawyer confronted the lady, whose expression was utterly blank. "Is this true, Garia? Why did you say nothing, and let me — "

"I know nothing," she whispered, staring at the Earl. Had he taken leave of his senses? But he shook his head at her as if warning her to hold her tongue, and she bent to a will even stronger than her own desire to know more.

Torin pulled a sheaf of papers from his coat pocket and handed them to Mr. Ruan. "Read these over, sir, and then tell me whether or not I may claim Miss Ivory as my bride." He went to Garia and placed a gentle hand upon her shoulder. "My dear lady, those are the very documents which sealed our betrothal ten years ago. While Mr. Ruan acquaints himself with their contents, let me assure you that they are binding. You didn't know it, but you are, in fact, engaged to marry me."

"It can't be true!"

He lowered his voice to say, "The truth of your situation is this — you are in no position to accept any other gentleman's proposals." His hand on her tightened. "You aren't going to faint, are you?"

"No — oh, no," she murmured, "I never faint. Are you quite sure of this, my lord? And how did you know that Mr. Ruan was going to — that he would — "

"I guessed it when I heard that his carriage had been seen in the neighbourhood. His intentions are no secret, you know." He released her and turned back to Mr. Ruan. "Well, sir? Are you convinced of the proof of my claim?"

Charles Ruan was rapidly scanning each page. Looking up, he answered grimly, "There seems to be little doubt of your obligation to Miss Ivory, but I would need to make a more careful study before saying more."

Garia tugged at Torin's sleeve. "But you don't intend to — you don't want to — "

" — Marry you?" he finished for her. "Why else would I have come to Dromana this morning, if not to inform you that we are promised to one another? I do hope you aren't disappointed," he added apologetically.

The hilarity of the situation in which she found herself suddenly struck Garia, and she sank into a chair, laughing softly. "This is preposterous! Here, Mr. Ruan, let me have a look at those documents." She glanced at them briefly, then looked up at the Earl. "How long have you known about these, my lord?"

"A fortnight or so. I was waiting until the proper moment to tell you the happy news," he said, smiling down at her.

Garia tried desperately to subdue the thrill she experienced every time he looked at her that way. She felt not unlike she had on the hunting field, galloping beside him, wholly caught up in the excitement. "I can see that I require legal counsel," she said shakily. "Mr. Ruan, what am I to do?"

The lawyer shrugged. "At this point, I would say there is little you can do, unless it is to persuade Lord Lindal to release you from this contract." He looked at the Earl expectantly.

"I regret, sir, that I have no intention of releasing Miss Ivory." Torin went to the door and turned back to say, "I will seek out Miss Laverty and bid her good-morning — no, it's already afternoon, isn't it? By the time I return, Mr. Ruan, I hope that you will have convinced Miss Ivory not to oppose me. I don't believe that she would enjoy being dragged through the law courts on a breach-of-promise suit."

"Well!" said Mr. Ruan when the Earl was gone. "I shall obtain a copy of those papers and have them read by an expert. If he is

151

indeed in earnest, I'll not permit him to force you into marriage."

"I don't believe he has any power to do so, Mr. Ruan, nor do I think that he really wishes to marry me. This is only some jest, and in the end it will no doubt come to nothing, as it did before. I do appreciate your calling on me today, but I think you had better go. It is rather an awkward position for me, you know." The ghost of a smile was in her eyes as she held out her hand in farewell.

Mr. Ruan gripped it tightly. "Yes, I'll go." He added in a savage undertone, "I never suspected Lord Lindal might be my rival, but he'll not succeed in undercutting me! Garia, you must tell me, if he had not interrupted us, what would have been your answer today?"

She pulled her hand away. "We mustn't speak of that now. You, who so scrupulously waited until my period of mourning ended before resuming your courtship, must understand why I cannot answer your question. For the time being I must regard myself as promised to Lord Lindal."

"I shouldn't have asked, I know, but I only need look at your face to know what I have lost this day. Believe me, I am regretting his lordship's intrusion as much as you are!"

Mr. Ruan left her with the assurance that

he would pursue all means of releasing her from the contract.

When he was gone she couldn't help but feel a little guilty, as though she were in some way at fault for leading him on, even though she'd had no knowledge of the documents strewn across the settee. The moment the Earl had walked into the room with those fateful papers, Garia had stepped into a dream, and she had no wish to wake from it. He had known of her intention to wed Mr. Ruan and had hurriedly come forward to prevent it by claiming her as his own. Only for the present, perhaps, for it was probable that she would be rudely pulled out of this dream as she had from the similar one of ten years before, but she didn't care. She was sorry about Mr. Ruan, but her present happiness was greater than her distress on his account.

"You have sent him away?" Torin asked when he returned. "Most commendable. He was very much in the way. Are you *terribly* angry with me?"

She lifted her chin and replied candidly, "I ought to be! Do you know that if you'd arrived but a moment later, I'd be engaged to Mr. Ruan now?"

"Impossible — you were already promised to me, only didn't know it." He walked over to her, and after gazing down at her for a silent moment, he reached out to cup her face in his hands. "Would you really have accepted him, my dear? Oh, I admit he's a respectable fellow, well enough in his way, but not the man for you."

"How can you know that?" she retorted, even as her limbs melted at his touch.

"The answer to that is because you are mine, given to me by your father a decade ago." He bent his head to hers and placed a warm, brief kiss upon her rosy lips. "There, now our betrothal is sealed." He placed his forefinger upon her brow and asked, "What have I said or done to cause that crease?"

"It is just that I scarcely know you, and this is all so strange and sudden," she explained.

"You've no other objections?"

"It seems to me that it matters little if I do or don't," she sighed, turning away. "You will drag me into the law courts if I refuse you, Lord Lindal."

"Your fear of legal recourse is a pitiful reason for accepting me as your husband. By the by, I cannot bear hearing you call me Lord Lindal. My Christian name is Torin, and from now on you must use it."

Garia refused to meet his eyes. "Oh, I could not, indeed, I don't know you well enough!"

"Of course you do. Recollect that I have

once partnered you in the dance and we have ridden to the hounds together! Never before have I been so well acquainted with any lady, I assure you."

She thought of the dozens of mistresses he must have had and wondered that he could say such a thing, even in jest. He must be quizzing her, enjoying himself at her expense, and her pride would not permit that. With a flash of anger she asked, "Are you mocking me?"

"Of course I'm not. Garia — and I hope you don't object if I choose to call you so — tell me if you accept this betrothal."

He hadn't really asked her to marry him, she warned herself, only to accept the fact of their engagement. It was ridiculous to believe that he would honour the old contract, that it would be fulfilled at the altar of St. Anne's Church in Cloncavan. But to fight his claim — and her own desire — would be useless, so she inclined her head. "Very well — Torin. I accept it."

"And I swear you shan't regret it, Garia," he murmured, pulling her close. Her slim, straight figure seemed very fragile to him, but he was aware of the strength of her resistance as she stood stiff and unyielding in the circle of his arms. He released her with infinite regret. "Forgive me," he said in a low voice. "I am rushing fences and making you acutely uncomfortable in the process. I will refrain from such displays if they are distasteful to you."

Garia bit her lip uncertainly. "I'm sorry. I mean, I'm sure I shall grow accustomed, in time. My lord, will you grant me a favour?" she asked in a rush.

"A dozen, if you wish."

"Might this engagement remain a secret? I had rather it had not become known in a general way, lest — lest you change your mind. You did once before, you know," she pointed out, and her face was grave.

Torin shook his head. "I am *not* going to change my mind, Garia. I deserted you once before, most cruelly, and will never do so again. I give you my word on it."

One final, persistent hope, that he might care for her, shriveled and died. At least one of her questions had been answered. He intended to marry her out of pity, as reparation for his past actions, and his kisses were prompted by duty, nothing more. What did it really matter, she asked herself despondently, when she had been prepared to accept Mr. Ruan without loving him, primarily for the sake of the boys. How much simpler it would be to wed this man, so virile and compelling, whom she did love. He would probably make her miserable — in fact, he had already accomplished that. But it might not be so bad, for they had some interests in common, such as hunting and farming; many marriages were built upon far less. And he was a kind man, a generous one, whatever else his reputation argued.

With more resignation than enthusiasm she said, "Then our betrothal may be as public as you wish, my lord."

Torin could hardly bear to look at her woebegone face, and her answer failed to satisfy him. "Are you afraid to refuse me because I told you — quite falsely, I swear it — that I would hound you through the courts?" he asked. "I only said it in jest, to frighten Ruan. Never you."

"I am not afraid," she maintained, "and I accept the betrothal willingly. When must we be married?"

"That shall be your decision. For myself. I would not be opposed to a long engagement. Perhaps by next spring you will feel you know me well enough to marry me."

Her smile was slightly askew as she replied, "Perhaps."

Torin told himself he would do better to tear up the contracts on the spot, for Thomas had been right when he'd said the knowledge of them would hurt her. But selfishly, he could not. "I need not send a notice to the Dublin or London papers just yet," he went on, "but I would like to announce our betrothal to the neighbourhood. And you will want to let your relatives know."

"My sister Rosamund will be quite shocked," Garia realised. "I hadn't yet informed her of your return to Cloncavan. There will be some awkwardness here, I suppose, for our engagement will revive the old tales of how you jilted me before."

"Country gossip is seldom malicious, only interested," he reminded her. "I will confer with your aunt, whose experience as a London hostess will prove invaluable. She might give a small dinner party at which we may inform our friends of our plans," Torin suggested. "I gave her a hint of my intentions earlier, and she will be longing to know all that has transpired. I will leave you now, and we can continue this conversation later."

Garia lifted her face, expecting that he would kiss her once more, but instead he pressed her hand and said goodbye. As she watched him go, she wondered just when he'd made up his mind to reveal the existence of the betrothal contract. Had it been after the hunt, or last night, after she had treated him so ill, and with so little cause?

If only she'd known what was in Lord Lindal's mind, she would never have encouraged Charles Ruan to the extent that she had. And remembering her near-quarrel with that gentleman, she wished she had asked Lord Lindal whether he, too, would want to enclose the lands of Dromana and bundle her brothers off to school as soon as they were wed.

Miss Laverty accepted her niece's news in good part and with only a modicum of surprise, and said she had suspected something of the kind. "To be sure, his lordship had the audacity to admit to me that he'd come for the express purpose of seeing that Mr. Ruan's business didn't prosper. Did you ever hear of such a thing? And to think that you've been legally bound to him all this while! Well, I'm glad I waited to wish you happy, my love, for had I done so this morning, I'd have been premature indeed."

Garia accepted her aunt's felicitations in a subdued fashion, then asked, "Are you truly glad of this, Aunt Judith?"

"Most truly. I fancy you'll go on a great deal better as Lady Lindal than you'd have done as Mrs. Ruan."

"Why, Aunt, it is not like you to be so concerned about titles or wealth!" Garia cried.

"I'm not," was the older lady's tart reply. "I was thinking of the gentleman, not of his high estate. I like Lord Lindal, and it's plain as a pikestaff he likes you. What's more, he'll accept the boys, and a blind man could see that they worship him. That consideration must have weighed with you when you agreed to marry him."

This, oddly enough, was one aspect of the match that had not previously occurred to Garia. "Certainly he has been very good to them," she acknowledged. "Oh, I do hope they'll be pleased."

And they were. Jeremy was astonished to learn that Garia was to marry their neighbour rather than the attorney, but he asked no questions about her sudden change of heart. Egan was overjoyed to hear that one day he would live at the Castle, no longer separated from the glories of its library and picture gallery by the distance of two miles. And Bennet stared at his stepsister with his mouth open, quite as though her words were incomprehensible to him. When he finally understood that the threat of Mr. Ruan had been utterly vanquished by his conspirator's masterly tactics, he looked down at Nonny and said blissfully, "I knew the new Earl was a capital fellow!"

By bedtime the entire household was aware that Miss Garia had received one gentleman privately in the drawing room, only to emerge from it engaged to another one, and he the

Earl of Lindal. From housemaid to groom to stableboy the news travelled, until by noontime the next day nearly every family in the district had heard a version of the story. The local gentry approved the match, for the consensus had long been that Berengaria Ivory could do better for herself than a mere attorney from Waterford. The ladies who began planning suitable entertainments for the Earl and his betrothed were only a little disappointed that their own daughters had failed to attract his notice. He might be a nobleman, but there was no denying he had a shocking reputation. As Mrs. de Lacy told Lady Neale, their young friend was quite old enough to know her own mind, and she was certainly not accepting a pig in a poke. Such a pity, though, that Sir Andrew and the old Lord weren't alive to see their dreams of an alliance come to fruition at last.

10

I would walk the dew beside you, or the bitter desert, in hopes I might have your affection, or part of your love.
— Irish Folk Poem

By the time Miss Ivory's engagement to Lord Lindal was announced at a select dinner party given by the lady's aunt, it was already common knowledge. As they raised their glasses in toast and offered felicitations, the guests agreed among themselves that the couple had conducted the affair most circumspectly. The Earl's attentions to his betrothed were within the bounds of propriety, and she received them with a becoming and well-bred detachment. But the behaviour of the newly engaged pair disappointed the younger people of the neighbourhood, who would have preferred that the lovers act as such; to them, the entire business lacked the requisite aura of romance.

Garia herself was inclined towards the latter opinion. She would never cease to lament her failure to respond to his lordship's initial embrace and kiss, and she had relived that moment during many a wakeful night. Her rejection of his advances had even set the tone for their subsequent encounters, for although he was scrupulously polite and unfailingly cheerful, he had never again attempted familiarities of that kind. She discovered, too late, that she'd inadvertently erected a barrier against him, and so far he had made no attempt to break it down. It wasn't for lack of opportunity, either, for they saw one another regularly. And on those rare days when he failed to visit her, he sent a gift of game or a selection of fruit from the Castle hothouses, accompanied by a note in his own hand.

But at least he was doing her the courtesy of feigning courtship, she told herself, even though it was taking place after the betrothal instead of before it.

As the days passed, she often wondered what her fate would be after the marriage ceremony transformed her into the Countess of Lindal, that mythic, as yet nonexistent creature. She would not change, but her circumstances would, for she would then belong to her husband in every possible way. And strangely, the physical aspect of that belonging troubled her far less than its other ramifications. For instance, his lordship's every wish and whim would regulate her life — that in itself was an alarming prospect for a young woman accustomed to independence. But Torin had given her no real reason to suspect he might be a tyrannical spouse. Quite the opposite, really, for he consulted her wishes on even the most trivial points.

He seemed to enjoy driving her about the countryside in his swift curricle, and one afternoon when they were thus occupied, he asked whether she would like to accompany him on a duty visit to Bessborough, near the village of Piltown. "I am obligated to call there once more, and I've heard the Ponsonbys will not be in residence for much longer. Do you know them?"

"I met Lord and Lady Bessborough a few years ago, during their last visit to their Irish estate," Garia replied. "But I didn't know you were one of their set."

"Hardly that. Still, they are my near neighbours in Cavendish Square as well as here in Ireland. Her ladyship takes a great interest in political affairs, so one meets all the most interesting people at the Bessboroughs' London house. Shall we drive on?"

Garia glanced down at her burgundy pelisse, which, however new, was not a very fashionable garment. "Oh, dear," she sighed. "I'm not likely to make a good impression as I am now."

"Am I to interpret that as no?" Torin asked.

But Garia, who was gazing at the trees and whitewashed cottages flashing by as they bowled along the lane, had not heard his question. She was telling herself that sooner or later she would have to make her first foray into the world of lords and ladies, one in which she must take her place someday. Marriage would thrust her into elevated society, and for a lady who had lived retired for so long it was an unwelcome prospect. Her previous acquaintance with titled people had been during the season of her presentation in Dublin, a brief and not especially happy period.

She stole a glance at the gentleman seated beside her, whose thoughtful green eyes were fixed on the road ahead. She had voluntarily, if unthinkingly, taken on the responsibility of living up to all that he personified. Never one to back down from something she viewed as a challenge, she brought her inner debate to an abrupt conclusion. Lifting her chin, she said that she would be happy to visit Bessborough.

Upon their arrival, a servant showed Garia and Torin to an elegant salon. Three persons, two ladies and a gentleman, were playing cards at a table drawn up to the fireplace. Lady Bessborough, a handsome woman of middle age, graciously welcomed her visitors and introduced Garia to her daughter and son-in-law. They had all heard of Lord Lindal's engagement to Miss Ivory, and after touching on that subject briefly, her ladyship enticed her noble guest into a discussion of Irish politics.

Left to her own devices, Garia glanced about the room, taking in the ceiling, decorated with ornate rococo plasterwork, and the chimney-piece supported by caryatids. Her attention was quickly claimed by the Countess's daughter, a nervous, hollow-eyed creature. Despite the chill of the salon, this young woman was clad in a diaphanous white muslin gown that enhanced her ethereal appearance. She possessed a childish quality that was attractive, though it rather startled Garia, who judged Lady Caroline to be something near her own age.

"William, go and talk to Lord Lindal and my mother," the young woman commanded her attractive, dark-haired husband. When he wandered off, she tossed her little cropped head and said with a worldly air, "You cannot learn to manage a gentleman too soon, so do not put it off until you are wed. William would do anything I ask — indeed, he is kinder to me than I deserve." Her face fell for a moment, then she changed the subject. "Didn't I meet you a fortnight ago, at Lismore Castle, Miss Ivory?"

"I have never been there," Garia answered.

"But Lord Lindal was at the ball, I'm quite sure of it."

"Yes, I believe he was."

"My cousin Hart — the Duke of Devonshire — was *furious* when I told him how disappointed I was with his castle! On the outside it looks most promising, and the moment I saw it I expected to find dungeons and gloomy Gothic apartments haunted by ghosts." Lady Caroline fetched a sigh and continued sadly, "But inside it resembles nothing so much as a Cit's villa at Highgate, with neat parlours fitted up in the modern style. I couldn't find a single suit of armour. I vow, it quite broke my heart."

Garia smiled. "Your ladyship will think me a paltry creature, but I must say I hope Cloncavan Castle is *not* haunted."

"To live with a ghost day in, day out, might be rather an inconvenience," Lady Caroline conceded. "Is Lord Lindal's castle damp? Lismore is, though Hart persists in denying it. I can't *tell* you how glad I was to get away from there." She gave a reminiscent shudder, then embarked upon a lengthy monologue describing the ball her cousin had given and comparing it to those she had attended during the London season.

Half an hour later, as Torin guided his grey

horses back to Dromana, he asked Garia how she had gotten on with Lady Caroline.

"She's an odd young woman," Garia stated, "but nice enough for all that. Only, she is so fey and fanciful that I cannot think her well matched with that solemn, sober young man."

"She is partly responsible for her husband's sobriety," Torin told her, "for back in the days when he was a carefree younger son he was quite a gay blade. His brother Peniston's demise altered his prospects significantly, and that's why the Ponsonbys permitted him to wed Caro. Did she happen to mention why she has accompanied her parents to Ireland?" Garia shook her head, so he explained the lady's penchant for Lord Byron. "Her supposed *affaire* with him was the talk of London all spring and summer. The family thought it best to remove her from his orbit for fear the impassioned couple would run off together. Though I suspect there was little chance of it — Lady Caro's histrionics were too excessive even for the poet's taste. The scandal has brought William's career in Parliament to a virtual standstill, but he has stood by his wayward wife, despite the fact his family, the Melbournes, have been at him night and day to separate from her."

"Goodness," said Garia, "I'm glad I didn't know all that before I met her. And to think

I sat discussing damp castles with a poet's inamorata!"

"I'm not sure she qualifies as such any longer," Torin said wryly. "Was she complaining of Lismore again? I had an earful from her on the subject at the young Duke's ball. I don't envy young Devonshire the task of improving that pile he has inherited."

"In Lady Caroline's opinion, the romance of an Irish castle depends wholly upon its possessing damp walls, and an adequate supply of ghosts," Garia told him, laughing.

"Indeed? Well, she would be sadly disappointed in Cloncavan if that is so. Unlike Lismore, it has been lived in continuously. Happily, my ancestors were a forwards-thinking lot, and as a result, it is tolerably comfortable for a place of its size. I hope you will find it so. And I promise that you won't be troubled by damp, nor by any restless spirits. Except, of course, my own."

When they reached Dromana, Garia invited him to come inside for tea. After the butler had delivered a heavily laden tray to the drawing room and departed, Torin informed her that the Cloncavan hounds would be running on the morrow. "Do you plan to join the chase?" he asked.

"I wish I might," she replied as she tipped the teapot towards his cup, "but Egan has his drawing lesson in Waterford. I'm very sorry."

"You needn't apologise for it. Naturally Egan has the prior claim." Torin sipped his tea, then asked if she would have time to undertake a commission for him during her visit to the city.

"I will be most happy to oblige you, my lord," she assured him. "What would you have me do?"

"Take yourself to the finest modiste in all Waterford and order some new gowns."

Garia stared at him, for to her it seemed an outrageous and unreasonable request. "But why should I? Does my appearance offend you in some way?"

"Of course it doesn't. I merely supposed you might wish to dress in the latest modes."

"But I don't at all," she protested.

He gazed at her incredulously. "Surely you know that shopping is supposed to be a woman's greatest joy."

"For many women it may be so, but I've had other things upon which to spend my time and money — three of them!" she retaliated with some heat.

"Berengaria Ivory, you are the most unnatural female it has been my pleasure to meet. Whatever will I do with you when we go to London?"

"I'm sure I don't know." She peered up

at him and asked, "*Are* we to go to London?"

"Eventually. I've a seat in the House of Lords, as Lady Bessborough never tires of reminding me, and I own several lesser properties in England, you know." Torin noted her stricken expression and said blandly, "But if you prefer to remain in Ireland during the Parliamentary sessions, I will not press you to accompany me. That is something we can discuss later."

"Yes, of course," she murmured, wondering what his preference might be and too afraid to ask. The visit to Bessborough had been unsettling enough, for it had provided her with a close view of a society marriage.

Her insecurities came crashing down upon her as she realised why he had raised the subject of her dress. "Did I compare unfavourably to the fashionable Lady Caro Lamb, countrified creature that I am?" she asked. "I warned you that my appearance would do you little credit."

"You do me great credit," he contradicted.

But she couldn't help thinking of his acquaintance with other, better-dressed females. No doubt he had paid for plenty of finery and jewels in his time, she fumed, and before she could stop herself she said, "If you meant to imply that you would frank a shopping expedition for me, as though I were one of your lightskirts — " She flushed and bit her lip in frustration. She had made a vow never to speak of his past. Nor did she dare let him suspect that she would notice, or care, if he chose to consort with other females after she became his wife.

"You foolish girl, I meant nothing of the kind," he told her. "Naturally I supposed you must have enough money of your own to buy new gowns. Don't you?"

Reluctantly she confessed that she did, but added swiftly, "But I have set it aside for my brothers. I've no intention of wasting my savings on fripperies for myself. Anyway, I had some new gowns made up quite recently."

"In Carrick," he said with a disparaging shrug. "If you attend Lady Neale's dress ball in that same blue gown I've seen you wear on at least three occasions, it is entirely your affair. But as you are some sort the guest of honour, I thought you'd wish to dress in the latest mode."

This criticism was past bearing. Stung to the core, she rose jerkily from the sofa and declared, "Lady Neale's dress ball is the height of pretension, and you are just as bad as she! If you dislike the way I dress, or anything else about me, you are free to terminate our — our arrangement at any time." She would have stormed out of the room, but he had put himself between her and the door.

"What, and be thought a worse jilt than before? Never!"

"You are laughing at me!"

"Neither a moment ago, nor now. Don't ruffle your feathers, my little dove. It wasn't of myself I was thinking — and your blue gown is very pretty. Sit down, Garia — no, not over there, but here beside me." He drew her back to the sofa and took her hand in his. "Don't worry about keeping your money for the boys. I will buy the moon for them if that is your desire, though I can't imagine what they'd do with it. Listen to me, now — don't turn your head away. Go to Waterford and order a pretty gown or two, or ten, or twenty. I ask you to because I think it will do you good, and not because I dislike the way you dress. Perhaps I cannot command you, but as you have seen, I will make your life a misery if you refuse."

"You would do it, too. You are capable of anything." She was smiling now, albeit unwillingly, and she shook her head at him as though he were Bennet discovered in a prank. Her angry outburst a few minutes ago seemed to have created a breach in the wall of reserve she had built between herself and him, and she wasn't sorry for it.

"That's better!" he approved. Taking her

hand, he said slyly, "And, Miss Ivory, permit me to say that I long for the day when your dressmaker's bills will become my responsibility."

"*Must* you say such things?" she asked impatiently, pulling her hand away.

"Shocked, are you?" He grinned mercilessly as he said, "And yet, Miss Prim, several times now you've betrayed a most unseemly and unmaidenly knowledge of the ways of gentlemen and their — lightskirts, I believe, was your epithet? I can see that the sooner your stepbrothers are under my wing, the better. They must be sadly depraved after their years in your household. I only hope my sober and virtuous presence in their lives will prove beneficial."

"How ridiculous you are," she said, choking back a laugh.

"And how stubborn *you* are! Do you realise that you haven't called me Torin once today? Did you think I haven't noticed that you are at pains to avoid calling me anything at all?"

He leaned closer, and she read the blatant invitation in his eyes. Though she had longed to see it and ached to respond to it, she bounded up from the sofa like a bird flushed from a wood. "Oh, do go away — *Torin!*" she said, with awful emphasis on his name. "For I am no lady of leisure like the Countess of Bessborough and her ilk, with nothing to do but entertain callers all day, and I really must ride over my west field to see how the winter wheat progresses."

Rising, he said easily, "Very well then, I'll be off. But before I go, I should tell you that I've bidden Thomas to begin planning a picnic, to be held on the Castle grounds. When you are in Waterford, be sure to purchase something splendid to wear for the occasion!"

He left her on that teasing note, and as soon as he was out of sight, Garia ran to the window. Peeking past the curtain, she watched until the curricle and pair rounded the rutted drive and vanished from sight.

Should she have invited him to ride with her, she wondered. Had she made yet another mistake? It was a dangerous game she played, and a trying one, for she must always be on her guard with him, constantly fearful that some glance or expression might give away the secret of how deep her feelings ran. Meeting his eyes was a sore trial; sitting beside him an exquisite torture. In time she might grow accustomed to his teasing and tormenting ways, but she had begun to doubt that familiarity would ever still her racing pulses. She accepted that her future as his wife might be a difficult one — possibly even a lonely one, if he should abandon her for half the year to reside in London. But how he could make her laugh, and what a joy that was!

Letting the curtain fall, she reflected that she had never laughed with Charles Ruan as she did with Torin. And for some curious reason, it made all the difference in the world.

The next day Garia visited numerous Waterford shops. She gave herself up to an orgy of spending and quite surprised herself by revelling in it. She purchased bonnets, gloves, shawls, and ribbons at the milliner's, then ordered a colourful array of morning dresses, evening dresses, and a perfectly divine ballgown. In but a few hours she managed to spend nearly half of the sum she had saved so carefully and for so many months, but the remainder would be spent on her brothers, although not in a way they would thank her for. She had made up her mind to engage a private tutor for them. Torin had suggested it, assuring her that she needn't send her brothers away unless it was her ambition for them to attend Eton, the only school worth considering.

Egan's drawing master, Mr. Howell, resided near the River Suir in a neat row house. Over the years Garia had formed the habit of taking tea with the gentleman's wife, and that was her intention when she directed Padraig to drive the parcel-laden carriage back to Lombard Street.

But as she exited the vehicle, she noticed a familiar figure approaching the Howell house. "Mr. Ruan — I didn't expect to see you!" she cried, and walked up to him, forgetting altogether that this meeting might be an awkward one.

"It was impossible for me to keep away, knowing well that this was the day of your stepbrother's drawing lesson," the lawyer replied. "It is a pleasant day for walking in the park — will you join me?"

Garia hesitated, uncomfortably aware of old Padraig's interested presence. "I still have some errands to accomplish — presents for the boys, and my aunt . . ." She trailed off uncertainly, for he showed no sign of accepting her muddled excuses.

"It is important that I speak with you," he persisted.

So she capitulated and tried to convince herself there could be no harm in it. She soothed her overactive conscience with the reflection that Charles Ruan was her attorney, after all, and in the past they had frequently strolled together in the park and on the streets of Waterford. Lord Lindal wouldn't object, and besides, it was unlikely that he would ever hear of it.

"What have you decided about sending the lads to the Kilkenny school?" Charles Ruan asked as they walked along the pavement.

"I've decided to provide them with private instruction instead. The Earl feels that they would benefit from a tutor, and I think he may be right. I never considered it before, thinking the expense would be too great, but I find I can very well afford it. At least, until — " and she paused.

"Until your marriage to the Earl," the gentleman concluded dolefully. "Are you so determined to wed him, Garia? I've seen no notice in the papers, and thus was encouraged to hope that you had reconsidered, or that Lindal had relented and set you free."

"Nothing has changed," she told him gently.

"But if I could find an inconsistency in the contract, what then? I have taken the liberty of consulting someone who is more learned in these matters than I, and he says I need not despair of freeing you from this iniquitous betrothal."

She had not the courage or the cruelty to tell him nothing could alter her decision to marry the Earl. Nor could she confess exactly why that should be. So she said, "It was my father's ambition that I wed Lord Lindal, and I have given my pledge to do so. I will stand by it."

"Have you forgotten that your father also permitted me to pay my addresses to you?"

She paused on the path and turned to face him. "That is true, but Papa was a man of his word, and as such he would expect me to uphold his earlier promise to Lord Lindal."

"Of course you are right," he conceded, so unhappily that it wrung her heart.

She placed her hand on his sleeve and said, "I hope you know I would never have encouraged you had I known I was honour-bound to Lord Lindal. And though I can understand how you might wish it otherwise, I hope we can remain friends."

Mr. Ruan smiled at her. "You will always have my friendship, Garia, of that you may be sure. But I do not know that I can meet his lordship with complaisance, for I almost hate him for returning to Ireland and interfering in our lives. Tell me, when is the marriage to take place?"

"The Earl has mentioned a spring wedding, so I suppose it will not be till after Lent."

"Then I may hope, indeed, for much can happen in so many months!"

This cheerful comment was troubling to Garia, and it echoed in her mind even after he parted from her.

She pondered his share of the conversation

on the road home, until she and Egan and those of her purchases that were not to be sent on by carrier reached Dromana. As her parcels were removed from the carriage, she suddenly realised that she had failed to buy any gifts for the members of her family, and when Judith Laverty eagerly opened and inspected each enticing box, she mentally castigated herself for being a monster of selfishness. In an attempt to remedy her unfortunate oversight, she presented her aunt with a handsome figured shawl. As for the boys, well, she told herself, she would just have to make it up to them in some other way.

She didn't mention her encounter with Mr. Ruan, not even when she and Judith sat sewing by the fire after her brothers had gone upstairs to bed. If she'd been less concerned by the lawyer's persistent belief that her engagement to the Earl would be short-lived, she might well have discussed it. But she'd always been reluctant to burden her aunt with her problems, especially those that had no solution.

She suspected that eventually the lawyer would forget he had ever wanted to wed her. Men, she had concluded, were incapable of forming a lasting passion, regardless of what her early novel-reading had told her. If she could believe there was a chance, however slight, that Lord Lindal might requite her increasingly strong feelings for him, she would throw caution to the winds, sink her pride, and do everything in her power to make him love her. But she was older and wiser than she had been at sixteen, and she doubted that his lordship would be best pleased to discover his well-bred bride possessed an undeniably wanton streak. It was more important to her to retain his respect, for in its way it was as valuable as love, and where Torin Montrose was concerned, far more durable.

But these matters she chose to keep to herself, and to Judith she confided only that she had rather enjoyed her day of pure indulgence. Privately she had decided she would never be as comfortable in the new riding habit or in any of the other of her new gowns as she had been in her old ones. But as the future Countess of Lindal, she accepted that it was her duty to present a creditable appearance, as well as to exhibit a proper degree of decorum. On the heels of this reflexion she fell to wondering whether his lordship would prefer her in the low-cut white satin ballgown or the flowing rose silk. And then she began to plan her toilette for Lady Neale's dress ball, mentally selecting and discarding accessories with the same interest she had once shown in deciding which fields to plant in barley and which in rye.

11

The dark-haired girl who holds my thoughts entirely yet keeps me from her arms and what I desire.
— Turlough O'Carolan

Not many days after her visit to Waterford, Garia was trapped in the upper regions of her house, acting as mediator in a battle royal between Nurse and Mrs. Aglish. It was time for the housekeeper's twice-yearly cleaning, and its effects upon the household were dramatic. The maids wore harried expressions as they scurried about with pails and brushes, occasionally colliding with each other in the hallways. Nan, the former nurserymaid, was Nurse's creature; she followed her senior's orders from force of habit, even when they conflicted with those of the housekeeper. Cora sided with the autocratic Mrs. Aglish and was likely to forget — or ignore — any order issued by Nurse. Affairs between the aged combatants and their younger partisans were at a sorry pass when Garia threw herself into the breach. She drew a line of demarcation, giving Nurse and Nan territorial rights for the upper floors of Dromana, encompassing all garrets, servants' rooms, and bedchambers. Mrs. Aglish and Cora were given responsibility for cleaning the ground floor: the drawing room, dining room, kitchen, and servants' hall. Various others, the scullery maids and McCurdie, were divided equally between the two generals, like so many troops.

After laying down the law, Garia hurried to kitchen to warn Cook — a martial female in her own right — of Mrs. Aglish's imminent assault. Despite the fact that this was a biannual occurrence, the tactless housekeeper was likely to ruffle the cook's sensibilities, in which case the family would starve.

She found the rotund artist of the kitchen in the process of making a crust for a game pie and shuddered at the necessity of interrupting so delicate an operation. But Cook was in a benevolent, if condescending, mood. "Well," she said haughtily, "I trust that after nigh on thirty years of running this kitchen, I also keep it tidy enough to suit Mrs. Aglish's notions!"

A relieved Garia was on the point of beating a hasty retreat, when Bennet's pup pranced into the room. With a wag of his tail and a playful yap, he indicated that he stood in need of sustenance. Cook dropped her toplofty manner at once and went to the cupboard, from whence she brought forth a bowl of giblets, which she placed before the fawning animal.

"There, poor beast, and were ye after starvin' for it?" she asked fondly as Nonny gulped down these delicacies.

Garia knew all too well that Nonny was a bone of contention between Cook and Mrs. Aglish, and she cast about in her mind for a way to warn the former to keep the dog out of the latter's way. "Cook, you must be aware by now that Mrs. Aglish is not fond of dogs," she began, feeling her way carefully.

The woman turned an innocent face upon her mistress. "Aye, and no more am I, but this one is not any dog, Miss Garia. He's direct descended from Ailbe."

"I see," Garia said vaguely. "The wolf dog of legend."

"Why, Ailbe was after bein' the most valued dog in Ireland, for didn't the King of Ulster and the Connaught ruler offer six thousands of milking cows and a horse-drawn chariot to the King of Leinster in exchange for the animal? And didn't the men do battle among themselves that they might win the poor beast, with Ailbe the Hound a-battlin' alongside the Ulstermen, fit to destroy them men o' Connaught? Why, the fierce creature took hold the axle-shaft of the Connaught prince's chariot in a jaw-grip so tight — " Cook illustrated by clenching her fist — "he was still holdin' on to it after they sliced the poor dog's head off with a sword!" She cut the air viciously with the carving knife she held in the other hand, her expression as fierce as any warrior's. "Aye, and that place is *still* called Mag-Ailbe for the grand, strong animal."

Garia looked down at Nonny. He was growing more massive with each succeeding day, and she could well believe him to be the descendent of the warlike Ailbe of Irish lore. But she gave him a warm pat for all that and said, "He's a very dear dog, but I must beg you to help me keep him out of Mrs. Aglish's way during the next few days."

" 'Tis likely he'll be roamin' the country with Master Bennet, Miss Garia, and ye need have no worry. But I'll feed him out o' doors if that's your wish."

Garia had to be satisfied with this gracious offer. After complimenting Cook on the beauty of the piecrust, she slipped out the back door, intent upon a refreshing walk through the kitchen garden. Most of the flowers were long past their glory, but herbs and late vegetables still made it a green and attractive retreat from household cares. Looking back towards the house, she made a mental note to send for some men to affix the wooden shutters to the windows, for the weather had turned noticeably cooler during the past week. And though winters at Dromana were mild, the shutters always went up during Mrs. Aglish's autumn reign of terror.

Garia reflected that it was pleasant to spend the day at home for a change. She had begun to weary of paying calls, receiving visitors, and attending the neighbourhood parties. The announcement of her engagement to the Earl had prefaced an unprecedented wealth of social activity in the environs of Cloncavan: whist parties, turtle dinners, and Assemblies were the order of the day. Mrs. Manahan's attempt at a musical party had, up until now, been the highlight of these entertainments, but Garia suspected that Lady Neale's forthcoming dress ball would eclipse all that had come before it. For herself, she looked forward to the Earl's picnic far more than she did the ball.

And she smiled as she remembered his most recent visit. Torin, riding his high-bred chestnut, had led a curious procession that had consisted of two sheep, driven by Con O'Patrick, Bennet, and Nonny bringing up the rear. The addition to Garia's flock was welcome, although his lordship's demand for payment had been most unorthodox. "A kiss for each ewe!" he had cried, his eyes so bright and merry that she hadn't been able to refuse. In full view of his groom, her brother, the dog — and the sheep — he had bussed her soundly on each cheek.

Now, two days later, the memory of it still had the power to make her blush. And despite her tendency to be overcautious, she permitted herself to hope that the incident was proof that she need not entirely despair of winning her lord's affection.

The day of the picnic was unseasonably warm for October. Garia spent half the morning trying to decide what to wear, and finally settled upon a sea green muslin gown with Mameluke sleeves. Because the weather permitted it, she wore no other wrap but a Norwich shawl across her shoulders. Judith Laverty persuaded her to wear an unadorned gypsy hat, saying that nothing became Garia more than its simplicity. Then both ladies turned their attention to the boys.

"What on earth shall we dress them in?" Judith sighed.

"Let them wear whatever they please. If we send them off to the Castle dressed as though for church, it would mean the ruination of their Sunday suits," said the practical sister.

The Dromana party found Cloncavan Castle looking its best that day: the lawns had lately been scythed and the hedges trimmed by the army of gardeners whose business it was to keep the Earl's residence looking tidy. Mrs. Tobin, his housekeeper, greeted the ladies in the front hall as she had always done during the old Earl's day and showed them to the small antechamber set aside as a retiring room.

The picnic was to be held on the riverbank, and everyone agreed that this was a delightful spot for an *al fresco* affair. Miss Laverty joined the dowagers who had seated themselves beneath a tree to enjoy tea, whist, and gossip. The gentlemen of the party strolled the lawns, talking of horses and politics as they made their way towards the stable block to inspect the Earl's livestock. The children of the neighbourhood cavorted upon the grassy slope like lambs at play, chasing one another and tossing balls back and forth. Several young ladies and gentlemen wandered off together to explore the grounds under the watchful guardianship of the Manahans' governess, who had accompanied her charges as chaperone. And Jeremy Howard's contemporaries, those youths who were too old for childish games and too young for flirting, took the boats and punts that were to be found at the boathouse and the small dock, and amassed a flotilla upon the quiet river.

Torin, seeing that his guests were comfortable and suitably entertained, went in search of Garia. He found her chatting with Frances Ashgrove and Caroline de Lacy. With a nod and a smile for her companions, he said, "I hope these ladies will not take it amiss if I lure you away."

Frances laughed. "Rather, we should thank you, my lord! Garia demonstrates a most unseemly reluctance to discuss her trousseau and has no notion how her wedding dress will look. We are well rid of so dismal a creature."

Garia was uncomfortably aware of her betrothed's quizzical eyes upon her. "You mustn't tease me, Frances," she said. "The wedding is so many months away, and there is an abundance of time to decide such things." She placed her fingers on Torin's outstretched arm and allowed him to lead her away.

As soon as they were out of earshot he said, "Come into the garden with me. You look lovely today, and I want my flowers to see you!"

The once-colourful display of roses was somewhat muted, but some of the varieties were holding their own against the chilly autumn nights. As Torin and Garia strolled between the bushes, he matched his stride to hers. "Are you enjoying yourself?" he asked.

"Most certainly, as is everyone here. It is a delightful party, don't you think?"

"Indeed, for your pleasure ensures my own," he told her gallantly. "I wanted this day to be perfect for your sake, and I only regret that my duties as host do not permit me to stay by your side the whole afternoon."

She laughed softly. "Perhaps it's just as well. Doting behaviour on your part would be duly noted by our good neighbours — and discussed at length!"

"True. And I do intend to be a pattern-card of respectability. But not just to keep the quizzy ones from gossiping, Garia. I do so out of consideration for you, and your feelings."

He plucked a half-blown rose and presented it to her with a half-bow. Watching as she buried her nose in the pink petals, he wondered if she would dislike it very much if he took her into his arms here, in the secluded garden. For so long she had held herself aloof, almost as if she feared him, although certainly she had sufficient cause to do so. And whenever he became impatient with her shy, shrinking manner, he reminded himself that he had ten years of prejudice to overcome. He intended to do it, or die trying, but it would take time — and patience.

Unconsciously speaking his thoughts aloud, he said softly, "I *shall* earn your esteem, Garia, on that I am determined."

Garia lifted her face from the fragrant bloom and eyed him doubtfully. "But you have it already."

"I wonder," he said, under his breath so she should not hear. He'd harboured an unpleasant suspicion of late, and perhaps this was time to voice it. Suddenly he asked, "Did you enjoy your conversation with the estimable Mr. Ruan during your visit to Waterford the other day?" Her startled expression prompted him to say, more harshly than he intended, "How did I know? But I had the news from Con O'Patrick, who had it from Padraig, your coachman. They are drinking partners at the Swan, you know."

Garia, furious at what she deemed his effrontery in listening to servants' gossip, flashed back, "And are you using my own groom to do your spying?"

"Not at all, though I admit I don't scruple to heed the various tales Con picks up at the Swan. It behooves every landlord to be well-informed, don't you think? But you haven't answered my question about Mr. Ruan," he reminded her. The only answer he received was a view of her slim, straight back when she turned away from him.

For Garia could no longer bear to meet his angry stare nor to read the accusation in his dark face, for the lines were deeper, more pronounced than she had ever seen them, proof of his displeasure. He was a proud man, that she knew, but she'd never suspected he might be jealous, and with so little cause. Now she wished she had mentioned the fact of her brief conversation with the attorney, if not its substance.

Torin took a step towards her. "*Did* you go to Waterford with the intention of meeting Ruan there?"

She whirled around to face him. "No! It was not an assignation, if that's what you're asking. You are unjust, my lord, for I met Mr. Ruan by chance, and we parted after a brief conversation and a very short walk in the park."

Torin said, more gently, "Forgive me, Garia, for accusing you of clandestine behaviour. But when I heard that you had met Ruan and knew you had not mentioned it to me, I was greatly disturbed."

"Do you think me so stupid a creature as to risk offending you, after you have been so kind to me, so good to the boys?"

"No, I don't think you stupid." He took one of her hands in a firm clasp. "You may be honest with me. Tell me, are you regretting our engagement? Had you rather marry Charles Ruan?"

Garia's voice was suspended by threatening tears, and all she could do was shake her head.

"My poor girl, I never meant to make you cry!"

"I'm *not* a poor girl, and you haven't," she choked, blinking at a furious rate. "It is only that I've made you angry, and unwittingly at that. Mr. Ruan is my friend, as he has ever been, and even if I were free, I would not marry him. You mustn't doubt my loyalty, Torin, for it is all yours," she concluded simply, and she prayed he would believe her. His love she might never know, but his trust she could not bear to lose.

Torin continued to look down at the slight member he held, which was sheathed in a lemon-coloured kid glove. He traced the seams with his forefinger, then lifted the hand to his lips. In a subdued voice he said, "Then I must take care to deserve that loyalty."

"But your actions could never alter my allegiance," Garia hastened to assure him. "I understand what you require in a wife, and I promise never to embarrass you by — by hanging upon your sleeve, or with jealous outbursts."

"Of the kind *I* have just made?" he said wryly. "Unfortunately for you, I am not so generous. In fact, I suspect I'll become a jealous, even a demanding husband. During these months before our marriage, I shall hope for a great deal more than unswerving loyalty from you, Berengaria Ivory." With an odd twist to his mouth, he added, "Whether I shall get it remains to be seen."

Garia's eyes widened with shock as the import of this remark became clear.

Her outraged expression made Torin laugh aloud. "I don't mean what you are evidently thinking, you peagoose! It is an easy thing to read your mind by watching your face — you should guard it more carefully. I do wish you will stop looking at me as though I were about to ravish you here, amongst my roses. This missishness is not like you, nor is it becoming. Do I truly seem so wicked?"

"No." She smiled weakly, in relief. "I suppose not."

"Well, that's a beginning," he remarked obscurely. "Now, come along, my dove. I've left my guests to themselves quite long enough. My reputation being what it is, our absence may be remarked, and you would not like that."

They rejoined the company on the riverbank, and soon everyone sat down at the long tables to partake of the excellent feast prepared by the Earl's French chef. Cobbe, every inch the stiff English butler, saw to the proper placement of the food, and numerous liveried footmen waited on the guests, pouring wine and bearing trays. Ham, dressed fowls, salad, cakes — even ices — were laid upon the board for all to sample. The children were delighted with the China oranges and sweetmeats, but they didn't linger long at the table and were soon off again, running and laughing and shouting.

Garia took her place on Torin's right, as the guest of honour. She was seated across the table from Thomas Montrose and Miss Ashgrove, who conversed together for the duration of the meal, much to the dismay of Ralph de Lacy, on the young lady's other side. For the first time Garia realised how well her friend and Torin's cousin complemented one another; Thomas was so steady and Frances so lively. Both were the children of clergymen, both were clever and well read.

But making matches was the pastime of matrons and dowagers, and Garia, betrothed for a mere fortnight, was appalled by her own temerity. And she knew only too well that Frances had a habit of being pleased with any male she chanced upon. More than once she had laughingly confessed that she was hopelessly fickle. Perhaps she was no more interested in Lord Lindal's cousin than she was in the adoring Ralph de Lacy. Nevertheless, it occurred to Garia that her friend was more than usually flirtatious whenever she was in Thomas's company, and that could signify something.

Of the gentleman's feelings there could be little doubt. His eyes followed the Rector's daughter when she deserted him at last, going off with young Ralph to look at the fishpond. Garia thought it more than likely that Mr. Montrose, her own good friend and former suitor, was already deeply in love with Frances. Had she been so caught up in her own affairs that she had failed to note this interesting development?

After the tables were cleared, the elders settled down to whist while the younger members of the party resumed their games and their flirtations. Bennet Howard managed to untie one of the rowboats and take it onto the river by himself. Nonny, heartbroken at being left behind on the bank, plunged into the water and swam out to meet his young master, thereby delighting the nursery set. When the excitement subsided, Lord Lindal took Miss Ivory and Egan out in one of the boats, entertaining both of his passengers with suitably expurgated tales of his travels in Italy.

By the time the party broke up, it was nearly nightfall. The Dromana party were the last to depart, due to the disappearance of the river-soaked Nonny. Jeremy eventually found him on the cherry walk, where the noble dog had managed to tree a kitchen cat. Nonny, exhilarated by this victory over his spitting adversary, was not at all distressed when he was refused a place in the family carriage. He trotted contentedly behind it all the way to Dromana House, where he fell asleep on the hearth rug, exhausted from the adventures of the day.

12

My love came near
up to my side
shoulder to shoulder
and mouth on mouth.
— Irish Folk Poem

The next day was the complete antithesis of the one that had preceded it. Blowing wind and falling rain kept everyone at Dromana indoors, where they soon wearied of dodging Mrs. Aglish and the housemaids still busy scouring the house from attic to basement. The housekeeper complained about the weather, saying gloomily that proper cleaning was impossible without proper light. How else were those stupid girls to see the dust and dirt, she asked Garia, as though it were her fault the sun failed to shine. Fortunately the question was rhetorical, and Mrs. Aglish soon bustled away to make sure "that clumsy Cora" was taking proper care of the crystal drops on the dining-room chandelier and sconces.

Judith Laverty wisely took refuge in the library, which had been cleaned while the family had been at Cloncavan the previous day, and the two older boys followed her. Egan settled in the window seat to wrestle with a bit of verse that had come to him in the night, and Jeremy bent his head over a back number of a gentlemen's quarterly. Bennet escaped to the stables to help Erris polish the harnesses.

Garia retreated to the drawing room, as yet undisturbed by Mrs. Aglish and her chief minion, to read a letter from her sister. It contained no news of the impending confinement — Lady Kelsey's fifth — but overflowed with felicitations on Garia's engagement. A full page of the letter was devoted to a description of the beautiful wares on display at a Dublin silk mercer's establishment. Would dearest Garia like to come to town to have her wedding dress and bridal clothes made? Such important work, Rosamund declared, could not be trusted to provincial dressmakers. Garia could well imagine the haughty toss of her sister's elegant head as she had penned that slighting remark. Evidently Rosamund and Lord Lindal were of like minds, she thought, folding up the letter, for his lordship had been similarly disparaging about the skills of the local seamstresses.

That gentleman soon turned up on her doorstep, and quite unexpectedly. Although she was happy to receive him, as he handed his dripping greatcoat to her butler, she asked, "Why have you come out in this horrid weather, my lord?"

"I fancy my coachman wonders the same thing," Torin said, tugging at his gloves.

Garia ushered him into the drawing room and closed the door in McCurdie's face. "You needn't have gone to the trouble of visiting me on a day like this, you know."

"Oh? I thought otherwise, since I am leaving for Dublin tomorrow."

Her face fell from gladness at his arrival to sorrow at his words. "Important business?"

"Not to me, but I go nonetheless. A distant cousin of mine has died, and Thomas, who is more nearly related to her than I, must attend the funeral and help settle the estate. And I hope his unstinting devotion to an unpleasant old lady does not go unrewarded. He won't admit it to me, but I believe he has hopes of being remembered in her will. In any case, he has asked me to go with him, and I agreed. I know so few of my Dublin kin, although I'm quite sure they know all about me. Do not look so distressed, my dear! I shall strive to keep Thomas out of bad company during our sojourn in the Irish capital!"

"It will be the other way round, more like," she retorted.

"Your lack of faith cuts me to the quick,

Garia. I'll be a model of respectability whilst out of your sight — I will even outdo my ascetic cousin!"

She laughed, but it was a strangely mirthless sound; she had just realised how sorely she would miss him. "How long will you be away?" Her words sounded forlorn even to her own ears, and she hated herself for her transparency.

"So you *are* sorry to see me go," Torin observed. "I rather doubted you would be after our conversation in the rose garden yesterday. I'll be gone for a few days, no more, and expect to return in good time for Lady Neale's ball. Does that please you?"

"Well, I own it would be horrid of you to miss it when I have gone to the great trouble and expense of ordering a new ballgown," she replied with a saucy smile.

"*Touché!*" he cried, acknowledging her hit.

She began to thank him on behalf of her family for entertaining them so well at the picnic, but broke off suddenly. "You haven't heard a word I've said!" she cried, as she became aware that he was not attending.

"Forgive me. I was thinking how lovely you look today."

"Confess, you are disappointed to find me in one of my old gowns! But I never thought you'd come this afternoon, and besides, we're in the midst of housecleaning. These days I live in expectation of being called upon to perform some menial task or other."

"I'm not disappointed at all. Now what were you saying a moment ago, when I was so distracted by your pretty eyes."

She coloured at the compliment. "I suggested that you call upon my sister during your stay in Dublin, since she resides only a few miles from the city. Not that I would presume to *dictate* to you, my lord!"

He grinned. "I wish you could bring yourself to try—I daresay I'd benefit from it immensely. But you are behindhand, for I had already formed the intention of visiting Lady Kelsey. It is important for me to enlarge my study of the domestic life, you know, as I am to become a husband myself one of these days."

Garia laughed softly. "My sister's household will be more daunting than encouraging. She has four children and expects a fifth quite soon — literally at any moment! But as a rule, Blanchlands is so well ordered that Dromana seems a madhouse by comparison. Rosamund says I allow my servants too much license, the boys too much freedom, and that I have little talent for managing a household!"

"If your sister is so critical of you, I begin to fear she and I will deal badly together."

"Oh, she can't help being elder-sisterish,

and she only disapproves of my methods, not of me," Garia declared. "Our dispositions are quite different. But at present I am very much in her good graces. Now that I'm to be married, she fancies me redeemed!"

"Redeemed because you are wedding a libertine Earl, a gazetted here-and-thereian who has jilted you, and that when you were only a child? A strange creature, your Rosamund!" Torin said quizzically.

"But she says if your reputation doesn't weigh with me, then it is none of her concern," Garia replied. "Rosamund was mad to have me married, you see, and she had quite given me up as a lost cause. As far as she was concerned, I was on the shelf — though perfectly content to stay there, I might add. But now you've taken me down and dusted me off, and my grateful sister will probably fall at your feet."

"Were you so very contented with the single state? It was my distinct impression that you were on the verge of accepting Mr. Ruan not so many weeks ago."

Garia shifted uncomfortably in her chair. "It is hardly a matter of concern now."

"What makes you think that? Come now, my dove, you do owe me an explanation of why you favoured Ruan's suit. I can't believe it was affection, because if you had loved him you would never have agreed to marry me, no matter what evil consequences I threatened you with."

She crossed to the fireplace and fidgeted with one of the porcelain figures on the mantel. "I liked him well enough. And he cared for me."

"You'd have wed him for the sake of your brothers, and with no thought for yourself," he said, but with no hint of censure.

"Yes," she confessed, shamefaced, "at one time I thought I *could* do that. But it never came to the sticking point, so I shall never know if I'd have had the courage. It wasn't a mercenary decision," she hastened to point out, "for his fortune never appealed to me so much as the fact of his being a lawyer. I thought he would know how to prevent my stepmother from taking the boys from me, should she ever return."

"That is understandable," Torin said. "And did you accept me for similar reasons?"

Whatever it lost her, Garia couldn't let him think her so coldblooded. "No!" she cried, facing him again. "Jeremy and Egan and Bennet might not have existed at all, for I didn't even think of them till afterwards." And then sinking her pride at last, she admitted, "I wanted to marry you before I ever knew I *had* to."

Torin hastily covered the short distance that separated them. "Garia, what are you saying?"

Garia put up her hand as though to ward off the question, but he seized it and gripped it firmly, to stay her. She experienced that familiar, skipping heartbeat and such a constricted feeling in her chest that she thought she might faint, for his green eyes blazed with what, inexperienced as she was, she recognized as desire. He then took shameless advantage of her immobility and drew her into his embrace. Garia could do nothing but yield her face, then her lips, and she prayed he would never stop kissing her. For in his arms she could almost believe that he loved her, that this was not some fleeting passion that once assuaged would be a bygone thing.

His lips grew more insistent, and at last she began to struggle, only to feel his hold on her tighten. "Please," she gasped, and realised, to her dismay, that she wanted him to continue, not desist.

"Stop wriggling," he said calmly. "Do you know, I used to be afraid my attentions would be repulsive to you, but no longer. You aren't as indifferent as you'd like me to think, Miss Ivory. No, don't look away, I want to see your eyes. So very pretty they are, even when you are a little frightened." He bent his head and kissed her again.

When she was able, she murmured in confusion, "You really are detestable."

He laughed, his heart lighter by a hundred-weight. "Oh, you've demonstrated just how detestable you think me! No, my girl, you cannot kiss me back in that brazen way and then deny you meant anything by it."

He would have continued to torment her had his sharp ears not caught the sound of footsteps in the hallway. He released Garia at once and prudently put several paces between himself and his betrothed. And not a moment too soon, for Mrs. Aglish stormed into the room, followed by Cora, who carried dusting rags and brushes.

"A good day to your lordship's honour!" the housekeeper greeted him, nodding in his direction. But so intent was she on the task ahead that she failed to note that his lordship's cravat was somewhat askew, and her mistress's hair in a tangle. "Now, Cora, first there's the mantel to be polished, and mind you don't destroy them urns, nor the gold clock neither, for they were precious to the first Lady Ivory. And where's Mr. McCurdie? Drat the man, he's nivver where he's needed!" This complaint was addressed to her mistress. "Sure, and he's supposed to take the pictures down from the walls for proper cleaning!"

"I'll — I'll tell him he's wanted," Garia faltered, trapped between vexation and a desire to laugh out loud. She beckoned to Torin, and he followed her out of the room. They saw the butler making his stealthy way down the hall, intent upon escape, but Garia forestalled him and delivered the housekeeper's summons.

With a sigh, she turned to Torin and explained, "Mrs. Aglish has made our lives a misery these two days past."

"And poor McCurdie has been pressed into service, I see. Will the same fate befall me if I linger?" he asked, smiling at her. "I think I'll take my chances, for I confess I'm reluctant to end our conversation — and just when we were so close to achieving an understanding," he murmured provocatively. "Is there some place where we can be assured of privacy?"

"They will be laying the covers in the dining room by now, and the library is occupied."

"And that infernal rain continues outdoors — no hope there. In that case, let us seek out your family so I may bid them farewell, and then I must be on my way."

This was duly accomplished, and Garia retrieved his hat and gloves and saw him to the front door.

As he shrugged into his greatcoat, he said, "Tell young Bennet I'm sorry I missed him. And Nonny too, of course."

She smiled. "I will."

He reached out his hand and gently brushed

a stray curl from her forehead. "My lovemaking has left you somewhat dishevelled," he observed. "How I hate to leave you, but there's no help for it. Damn this Dublin scheme — I've half a mind to let Thomas go alone!"

"Oh, you mustn't!"

"Well, I could — very easily, I assure you! Yet it might be better to go, and then perhaps you'll miss me." After placing a gentle kiss on the top of her head, he hurried down the front steps. With a final wave, he disappeared into the waiting carriage, which was nearly obscured by the heavy downpour.

The tenderness of his parting kiss had touched Garia, even more deeply than the passion of his earlier ones. Could it be that he had begun to care for her, she wondered, hurrying to her bedchamber to shut herself away from curious eyes. One glance into her looking glass showed that she was quite mussed — what must Aunt Judith have thought? Probably she had drawn a perfectly correct conclusion, but Garia was past caring.

She went to the window and gazed unseeingly at the swaying treetops, so savagely lashed by the wind and rain. Looking back to the conversation in the rose garden yesterday, she reviewed Torin's every word, each nuance of expression. How stupid of her to have held herself aloof then, and before — it was no wonder he had often asked her if she regretted their engagement. And though she had not given him any reason to suppose she was pining for Mr. Ruan, to him it must have seemed so, especially when she neglected to inform him of her recent encounter with the lawyer.

Her heart swelled at the thought that she might yet win the love of one who had grown so dear to her, so completely necessary to her well-being. Oh, let it be true, she prayed, even though she knew he had dallied with some of the most beautiful women in the world — that Torin's mistresses had been anything but lovely was impossible to imagine. She had no remarkable degree of beauty, nor was she well versed in the arts of flirtation that seemed to beguile gentlemen of his sort. She had never lacked for suitors, but that she could appeal to a man of strong passions and wide experience — it was something she had never expected. And she refused to be troubled by the fact that she might not be her Torin's first love; she was more determined that she should be his last.

Her buoyant, hopeful mood continued for the rest of that day and into the evening. Not even a sharp after-dinner quarrel between Bennet and Egan could depress her spirits. And when Jeremy angered both parties with his lofty condemnation of their childishness, she allowed her aunt to intervene. By the time McCurdie carried in the tea tray, peace was restored: Bennet apologised to Egan for threatening to throw a book at him, and Egan reluctantly agreed that Bennet was the better player at spillikins.

There was no more rain the next day, although the weather continued gloomy and grey and the trees still dripped with rain. When her brothers left the house, Garia was thankful. She knew they would return hopelessly muddied, but a day in the fresh air would do them a world of good and keep them out of the way of the housemaids.

She spent the morning sorting through her now-burgeoning wardrobe to find clothes that might be given to Mrs. Ashgrove for the poor. Winter was fast approaching, and many would be seeking relief. When she had accumulated a promising pile of discards, she tied them in a bundle and informed her aunt of her intention to carry them to the Rectory.

She discovered that Miss Ashgrove and her mother were already entertaining a visitor: Mr. Dickinson, the Earl's librarian. He excused his presence to Garia by informing her that his employer had entreated him to take a holiday, and bade her tell Egan that he needn't come to the Castle that afternoon.

"He'll be sorry to hear it," Garia said truthfully. "Did Lord Lindal depart this morning?"

"He and Mr. Montrose were gone before most of the household were awake, Miss Ivory."

"They will have a very muddy journey," Mrs. Ashgrove remarked.

Garia's arrival precipitated the gentleman's departure, and when he was gone Mrs. Ashgrove went into another part of the house with the bundle of cast-off clothes. As soon as the two young women were left alone, Garia asked Frances if Mr. Dickinson was a regular caller.

The Rector's daughter tossed her brown head restively. "And if he is? Now that you are engaged, what interest can you possibly have in a single gentleman?"

"None whatsoever," Garia said, laughing. "He is entirely your own. But tell me, is Mr. Montrose destined to suffer a disappointment? And what about Ralph de Lacy?"

Her friend gave a diffident shrug. "Ralph is very much a boy still, and I have made up my mind that a grown man is more to my liking. You are my model in all things — advise me, my dear. For you have made an admirable choice for yourself!"

"Don't be so silly, Frances! I can no more

advise you than I would ask your advice."

"Cruel, too cruel," Frances sighed, dropping into a chair. "As you may have noted, sharp creature that you are, Thomas Montrose has been very attentive of late, most particularly at the Castle day before yesterday. I do think he's the nicest, ablest, finest gentleman I have come across — this week! Likely I'll change my mind about him as soon as some other promising suitor approaches me. You know my fatal flaw — I am too fickle to attach myself to just one fellow."

"So you always say." But Frances had proclaimed her instability so often and so loudly that Garia couldn't help but wonder if it might be a convenient pose.

"And anyway," Frances continued, "Mr. Montrose has neither fortune nor position, whatever his more commendable attributes." Then she changed the subject with an abruptness that answered all of Garia's unasked questions.

As the carriage bore her home, she pondered her friend's artful disclaimers. It was true, then, she thought, Frances had a decided partiality for Thomas Montrose. What a pity that he was only a poor relation, with no prospects other than an old lady's legacy, which was hardly likely to improve his station in life. But perhaps Torin might do something for him; Garia intended to raise this possibility as soon as he returned.

He was hardly gone, yet she had begun to experience a curious sense of deprivation. In response to it she was inclined to hoard the little, inconsequential occurrences of her day to relate to him, as well as the greater matters that suddenly were so important that she confide. There would be no more secrets between them; she had sensed that yesterday and was glad of it. As she had done for many hours now, she drew the memory of their tender parting about her like a warm, protective cloak.

But her serenity was shattered and her confident smile vanquished by McCurdie's face when he opened the front door to her a little while later. The butler was so alarmingly pale that she wondered if perhaps he'd actually seen one of the many Irish ghosts in which he steadfastly believed. She was about to ask him this when she was seized by a sudden premonition, and her own colour receded.

"One of my brothers is hurt," she gasped, as one trembling hand flew to her breast.

"Nay, nay, the little lads are not even come home yet." But nonetheless, McCurdie continued to wag his snowy head dolefully.

"Not my aunt? Tell me quickly, what is the matter?"

"You'll not be believing it, but 'tis a fact.

Lady Ivory herself is here at Dromana, for not an hour ago she drove up in a chaise. She's come back, Miss, and oh, what troubles have befallen poor us!"

13

How highly and mightily she proceeds
at large in her colours and silken cloak.
— Brian Merriman

Garia's worst nightmare had come true, and she felt her limbs turn to stone and her heart to lead. "Where is Lady Ivory now?" she asked, hardly recognising the thin, quavering voice as her own.

"Upstairs, in the sitting room," the butler answered quietly, as though he half expected that the lady in question could hear him through the floorboards. "Being that she was tired from the journey. What are we to do, Miss Garia? She's not mistress here, and every servant, man or woman, is knowing it. Do you want that we'll take orders from herself?"

Garia considered carefully before making her reply. The servants would be only one of a myriad of problems Josepha's return presented. Best to get used to what there is no changing, she told herself bitterly. "Yes, McCurdie, you and the others must obey Lady Ivory's requests as you would those of any other guest at Dromana." She spoke up so Mrs. Aglish, who had emerged from the back of the house and stood listening with folded arms, might hear and heed her. "My aunt and I will remain in charge of the household, and if you encounter any problems among the staff, I know I can count upon you to tell one of us."

"Aye, that you can, Miss Garia," the housekeeper said. "And I hope you're not after bein' angry with me for giving Lady Ivory her old room. 'Twas all I could do, for all she has no right to it no more!"

"She is my father's widow, and will be treated with the respect she is due," Garia said with unwonted severity. And then she wished she could think of something to say that would drive the apprehension from their eyes and faces.

As she went up the stairs she tried to convince herself there was no point in worrying until she had spoken with Josepha, but it was a futile effort. She could divine only one motive behind this visit, if visit it was: her stepmother wanted money. And Garia mourned the vast savings she'd squandered so thoughtlessly in Waterford, for it might have been enough to placate Josepha. Now only a paltry sum was left, just enough to pay a tutor's salary and perhaps buy some new hangings for the drawing room.

She went to her room and removed her bonnet and pelisse, all the while wondering how best to inform her stepbrothers of their mother's unexpected arrival. Garia had always taken great care that they should hear nothing ill of the woman who had brought them into the world, but a child possessed the intuition of any young animal. It would be no secret to the Howards that their only parent was no favourite within or without the walls of Dromana House. They never mentioned her nor seemed to regret her desertion of them three years ago, but Garia did not doubt they still felt the pain of it. Not that Josepha had been especially attentive; during her brief tenure as mistress of Dromana, she had been more absent than not.

A soft knock on the door prefaced Judith Laverty's entrance, and at the sight of Garia's stricken face, she held out her arms. Her gentle, sensible words acted as a soothing balm upon her niece's sore heart when she said, "There now, you mustn't be imagining the worse, my love. She'll soon grow bored here at Dromana, as she has ever done, and will be off again before the cat has time to lick her ear." She stroked Garia's dark, curling hair, and continued, "If you but meet your stepmother in a friendly fashion, she'll realise you aren't afraid of her — and then she can be no threat to you."

"But I *am* afraid of her," Garia whispered.

"You must strive to forget that. And I shall hide my own feelings as best I can, of that you may be sure."

"Have you seen her yet?" When Judith shook her head, Garia summoned up a faint smile. "Much as I hate to admit it, I am curious to see what the years have done to Josepha. Perhaps India has made her sallow. If she has lost some of her beauty, then perhaps she will no longer have the power to terrify me so." Then she heard the tramping footsteps that indicated the return of her stepbrothers, first on the staircase, then along the corridors, and said, "Home already — oh, whatever shall I say to them?"

"You will know. Go to them, my dear," Judith advised her, "for it is best they hear the news from you."

Garia gave her aunt a grateful hug, then hurried down the hall to the nursery. She found the three boys seated on one bed, poring over a large and dusty book. Three tousled heads and one grey furry one looked up at her entrance.

"Garia!" Bennet cried enthusiastically, jumping up and running to meet her. "You should have been with us! Nonny found *wolf* tracks in the damp earth by the stream — at least, they looked like wolf tracks, but Jeremy says it must have been quite a large dog instead. What do you think?"

Garia smiled down at him. "You know as well as anyone that the last wolf in Ireland was killed a century ago. "It must have been a dog."

"Or a fox," Egan offered solemnly. "We are looking in this book to find out how large they can be."

With a sigh, Jeremy said, "Bennet and Egan must have frightened away every fish in the water with their antics. I had no sport at all, not even after they ran off in search of their 'wolf.' "

Garia pulled up a chair and sat down in it. Without preamble she announced, "Your mother has come back to Dromana." Then she paused, uncertain of whether or not this bald statement of fact required further embellishment. She noted their diverse reactions: Jeremy frowned, Egan looked bemused, and Bennet seemed about to burst into tears.

Egan was the first to find his voice. "When will we see her?"

"Soon — before dinner. She is resting now. Why, Bennet, you mustn't cry! Come here and tell me what is the matter."

The child was too large to climb into her

lap as he had formerly done, but he looked as though he would derive great comfort from it. Instead he clutched at her skirt fearfully and asked through his tears, "Will she take us away to India? I don't want to go with her."

"And who says you will have to?" Garia hadn't believed she could sound so calm and unconcerned.

Jeremy said slowly, "But you must suspect that, too, don't you, Garia? Has she any right to take us?"

Garia had noticed that none of them had yet referred to Josepha as "Mama." "Well, she is your only living parent. But I haven't spoken with her yet, so I don't know why she has come." She tightened her arm around Bennet, who sniffed audibly. "Bear up, dearest. She is your very own mother, and she'll be so happy to see you after all this time. You must show her what a little man you have become." She climbed to her feet, still smiling, and said, "Now all of you, go wash your faces and comb your hair, for it is nearly time to dress for dinner. I shall see you downstairs in an hour."

Jeremy muttered something unintelligible and when Garia asked him to repeat it, he threw back his head defiantly. "She will never be our mother! I won't call her so — not *ever!*"

He was in general so even-tempered that his volatile outburst startled Garia. He'd grown so this last year, she realised, and his brown eyes were on a level with her own. She swallowed past the lump in her throat and said firmly, "Your refusal will make things very awkward, Jeremy, besides being quite rude and a poor example to your brothers. I thought better of you."

On this disapproving note she left the room, having successfully conquered her desire to weep with Bennet and throw her arms around each one of them. But it would not do for her to communicate her own fears, or that in trying to comfort them she had only succeeded in depressing her own spirits even further, which she had not believed possible. And however much she sympathised with Jeremy, she could not permit him to denigrate his mother in front of the younger boys. As the oldest, he remembered Josepha much better than Bennet or Egan, and it was not surprising that he should be bitter. But she was determined he should be civil.

As soon as she changed her gown, Garia went downstairs, steeling herself to meet the beautiful, petulant face she remembered so well.

Her stepmother was in the drawing room,

standing by the window, and when she turned around Garia was startled to find her so changed — and yet so very much the same. Her expression was not petulant; rather, it was grave, even guarded. And although her beauty was still evident, she could no longer pass for twenty as she had done when Garia had last seen her, for this woman looked at least thirty, and was four years beyond that age. A tracery of faint lines hovered at the corners of the sapphire eyes and the generous mouth, but Josepha's voluptuous figure, with its improbably tiny waist, was still intact. The rich mass of auburn hair was arranged in an elaborate coiffure, and the lavender gown had been fashioned in a style that Garia assumed to be the very latest, and probably French.

Lady Ivory was the first to speak. "Permit me to extend my condolences," she said in the low, husky voice that was so unusual, and one of her greatest charms. "When I received your lawyer's letter, I could well imagine how Sir Andrew's death must have pained you."

"It was your loss as well," Garia replied without thinking that the remark might be inappropriate. To her own ears it sounded as though she were baiting her stepmother.

Josepha lifted one shoulder in a languid, characteristic gesture. "I *am* sorry, but I cannot dissemble and pretend my life is blighted.

Nor would you wish me to. Where are my sons?"

This was directness indeed, and Garia met it staunchly. "They'll be down any moment. I told them you are here."

"I've brought them presents. You do not object?"

"It is hardly my place to object. You are their mother, after all."

Josepha's eyes glittered like the sapphires they so nearly resembled. "Don't you worry that I'll be a bad influence on children of tender years, Garia?"

Thinking it prudent to ignore the question, Garia asked her stepmother when she had learned of Sir Andrew's death.

"In the spring. Mr. Ruan's letter found me just before I left India."

"Left?" Garia echoed. "But where have you been living since then?"

"In Paris."

Josepha's full lips parted in one of the smiles she used to such effect, and Garia winced as she saw a reflection of Bennet in his mother's face. "What in heaven's name were you doing there in wartime?" she asked. "Did you travel there with your — that is, did you go there alone?"

"I did. Does that surprise you? If so, you will be quite shocked to hear that I have no protector at present. And alas, the *affaire* that enticed me from this land three years ago did not outlast the voyage to Calcutta. My gentleman friend was no official in the East India Company — he turned out to be a mere clerk. I did make other friends in the East, however, although I won't bore you with a recitation of my adventures." Josepha sat down, taking great care with the arrangement of her silken skirts. "Yes, I've been in Paris. And because I pretended to be Irish, I was perfectly safe. And not at all lonely, you may be sure."

Garia also sat down. Eyeing her stepmother warily, she asked, "What exactly do you mean by coming back to Ireland, Josepha? I thought you had done with us here."

"Perhaps I have returned to claim Dromana House, and my late husband's estate."

Garia's head swam for a moment, but she made a swift recovery. "If so, your errand is wasted. Papa left the entire property to me, and Rosamund inherited his private fortune — what was left of it," she said pointedly.

"I am familiar with the terms of Sir Andrew's will, Garia, for Mr. Ruan's letters to me have been quite specific." And the young woman's amazement was such that Josepha frowned. "But you must know that he has been corresponding with me for several months."

"No, I did not know!" Could it be true?

Garia wondered. Knowing her stepmother as she did, she had to doubt it.

"In fact," Josepha went on, "I spent most of yesterday in Waterford, closeted with him." Her mouth curved slyly. "Quite a good-looking fellow, and *so* devoted to your interests."

"He must have told you the will cannot be overset."

"Can it not? I'm afraid he has failed to convince me of that, and I am determined that a judge should rule on the final disposition of your father's estate. To speak quite plainly, I am contemplating legal action. Yes, I mean to involve myself in the national pastime, for I seem to recall that suing is a veritable passion with you Irish."

"A lawsuit!" Garia cried. "You must be mad! You've no grounds, no money. And just *think* of the scandal!" She drew a deep, calming breath, then said, "If you are in need of funds, I might arrange for a settlement of some sort. Not a very large sum, perhaps, but — "

"Blackmail, Garia? Thank you, but I should prefer Dromana. The estate is not a large one, I know, nor especially profitable, but it would provide me with income enough to take up residence in England again. And I rather like the idea of having a country retreat for my old age." Josepha's lovely face was inscrutable, almost sphinxlike, as she said, "Your Mr.

225

Ruan and I came to a compromise of sorts yesterday, so I shall leave it to him to explain everything to you. Ah, here are my children." And she rose as Miss Laverty and the three boys entered the room.

The young Howards greeted their mother with more politeness than enthusiasm, as if she were a stranger, and an unwelcome one at that. Garia saw Jeremy's look of fierce distaste when Josepha commented on how her older sons favoured their late father. And watching as her stepmother knelt down to speak to Bennet, she wondered if Josepha was thinking about the young man who had sired him before going off to the wars and his death on that battlefield in Spain.

A stiff, stilted conversation ensued, but Garia was only half aware of the lackluster reunion taking place as she glanced down at her own clenched fists. A lawsuit! But, she reminded herself, she had many friends and allies, and Josepha had none.

She could not bring herself to give up her seat at the head of the dining room table, although by right it belonged to Lady Ivory. Nor did Judith relinquish her customary place opposite Garia. The three ladies managed to speak to one another with a semblance of civility during dinner, but the boys were uncommunicative and merely picked at their food.

But the mealtime passed without incident until Josepha made an unfortunate remark on her sons' excellent behaviour at table, which incited Bennet's wrath.

He glared at her across the table, his eyes flashing blue fire. "We are *not* well-behaved," he said in a tone that clearly indicated his displeasure at being so described. "And if you hadn't run away, you would know it!"

"Bennet, that is quite enough," Judith Laverty said, frowning at him.

But he would not be repressed. "She might be my mama, but if she tries to take us to India I shall set Nonny after her!" He threw down his napkin and ran out of the room.

Garia's face was red with shame as she apologised for the child's bad manners, but she was relieved to see that Josepha appeared to be more amused than angry. Yet when Jeremy followed his little brother, leaving his plate virtually untouched, his mother pressed her lips together as if in pain. It was not long before she excused herself and withdrew to her upstairs sitting room.

Garia and her aunt made their way to the library, where a crackling fire awaited them. For a while they discussed the most trivial of matters in order to avoid the glaring difficulties facing them, but finally Garia revealed her stepmother's plan to lay claim to Dromana. "And

227

if it turns out that Charles Ruan has indeed known of her whereabouts all this time, I shall be most annoyed with him. How *could* he settle for a compromise? He is said to be so ruthless in the protection of his clients that I can't believe it's true."

"I think she is only trying to frighten you," Judith stated. "But at least she hasn't come to take the boys, Garia. You can be thankful for that."

"I wouldn't let her have them!" Modulating her tone, Garia said more quietly, "I dislike having to shelter her while she is conspiring against me. And I hate it that you are trapped here, caught in the midst of all these troubles. I know very well that you refused to visit Dromana when Josepha was its mistress."

"She was *never* that," Judith said tartly. "And do you really think I would abandon you just because that hussy is living under this roof once more?"

Garia shook her head sadly. "You've just proved my suspicion that it's duty alone that constrains you. If you remain with me, it will give me more pain than consolation. You really should go away for a time, Aunt Judith."

"And where do you propose to send me? All the way to London?"

"Rosamund's baby is due any day."

"True," Judith conceded.

"You might stay with her until Josepha has gone. Dublin is not so very far, two days' journey at the most."

"Well, it's true I must begin to plan my future, because I will have to shift for myself very soon. I don't doubt for a moment that Lord Lindal will be pressing for an early marriage. By the time he left the house yesterday you looked as if you'd been dragged backwards through a bush! I was appalled." But Judith's sentimental expression belied her words.

Garia smiled for the first time since McCurdie had informed her of her stepmother's arrival. "Yes," she said softly, as a wave of happiness washed over her, "perhaps he will want to move the date of our wedding forwards. And if you doubt his ability to deal with Josepha and her schemes, then you are mistaken!" Although she had said this to convince her aunt, Garia knew that this was perfectly true.

Yes, Judith agreed, the Earl of Lindal was more than capable of battling on Garia's behalf, should it prove necessary. Rising from her chair she said, "Very well, then, I'll begin my letter to Rosamund tonight and offer to stay at Blanchlands during her confinement." She didn't say it, but silently she prayed the Earl of Lindal would return soon and provide her niece with a similar refuge from the shameless Josepha.

14

Suffer agitation calmly.
— Irish Poem

When Garia entered the dining room the next morning, she found her stepmother seated alone at the table, dining in solitary state, and knew the unpleasant events of the previous day had been no dream. Josepha airily explained that when she had sat down to break her fast, the room's occupants had scattered like leaves in a high wind, and Garia, who wished she might respond in a similar fashion, could not in good conscience abandon her. Her own position as mistress of Dromana was endangered by the other woman's presence, but it would not be strengthened by treating her unwelcome houseguest rudely. She performed the honours of the table, ringing for a fresh pot of coffee and seeing to it that Josepha's egg was cooked to her satisfaction. But she could think of nothing to say.

Her stepmother had no such problem. "Your aunt tells me you are to be married," she said, bending her russet head over her plate. "The Earl of Lindal! At first I thought she meant that disagreeable old man, but I understand that he is dead and Melbury has stepped into his shoes. Such a conquest, my dear — I am all over envy of your good fortune." She sipped her coffee, and setting down her cup, she continued, "But I admit to some confusion. Yesterday I received the impression from Mr. Ruan that *he* expects to marry you!"

Garia met her stepmother's curious eyes and replied calmly, "You must have misunderstood him. Although Mr. Ruan did secure Papa's permission to pay his addresses, in the end nothing came of it."

"A handsome enough fellow, and probably well-off, like most lawyers, but I agree he's nothing when set against an Earl's coronet — even if only an Irish Earl," said Josepha consideringly. "You will follow both English and Scottish Countesses in the order of precedence, you know, but there's the Castle, of course."

It was on the tip of Garia's tongue to retort that it was the man, not the coronet or the Castle she was marrying, but she deemed it bad policy to quarrel with her stepmother and therefore said nothing. Josepha continued to carry the burden of conversation, asking for news of the neighbours, whom she described as a set of provincial poppets, and listened with apparent interest to the tidbits of local gossip that Garia recounted.

During all of that day and into the next, Garia was conscious of the strained relations between Josepha and her sons. She confessed to her aunt that she was astonished by her stepmother's patience with them; Josepha seemed to know that by courting the boys' trust and affection too actively, she would only estrange them further. To which Judith Laverty replied that most likely the cold piece didn't care a bit for the boys, or whether they liked her or not. But Garia would not allow this to be true; she believed that beneath the unconcerned exterior, Josepha was hurt and bewildered by her sons' persistent avoidance.

One day Garia received two letters in the post, an almost unprecedented occurrence. One was a brief, businesslike epistle from Charles Ruan, informing her that he would be in the neighbourhood that afternoon and telling her to expect him. The other, far more welcome, was from the Earl of Lindal.

The funeral was over, the reading of the will had been tedious, he reported, but Thomas Montrose had his legacy, and a substantial one at that. Torin wrote that he had visited Lord and Lady Kelsey at Blanchlands, and Rosamund was pressing him to move the marriage date forwards. Garia's cheeks turned pink with pleasure as she read that Torin concurred most heartily with Lady Kelsey's determination that the ceremony should take place well before Lent, and he added that her ladyship was the most sensible female he had ever met, with the possible exception of her sister. The letter was written in an affectionate vein, and reading it, Garia could almost imagine he was speaking to her. She read it through several times, lingering on each word, before folding it up at last and tucking it into her workbasket to be retrieved and read again. There was more than the news of Torin's eagerness to marry to cheer her: it was entirely possible that Thomas Montrose might marry Frances Ashgrove, now that he had some money of his own.

According to the letter, Torin intended to leave Dublin as soon as he had interviewed and engaged a tutor for the Howard boys. Garia immediately decided to grant her brothers a holiday from their lessons until their tutor arrived, for she felt strongly that they ought to try to know their mother better during her visit. And since the Earl wrote that he still planned to return to Cloncavan in time for Lady Neale's dress ball, Garia sought out Judith to tell her she could leave Dromana with an easy conscience.

★ ★ ★

That afternoon Charles Ruan arrived at
Dromana, and in a far more cheerful frame
of mind than he had been during his brief
colloquy with Garia at Waterford. Certainly,
she told herself, he was in better spirits than
she felt her present situation warranted. But
his warm, friendly greeting encouraged her
to hope that he did not despair of losing the
battle with Josepha. As soon as they were closeted together in the library, she took him
to task for his secret correspondence with her
stepmother, and also for concealing Josepha's
recent whereabouts.

"Why did you never tell me she had left
India for Paris?" she wanted to know.

"Out of consideration for your feelings," he
replied gently. "Would you really have been
better off, knowing that only two channels of
water separated Lady Ivory from you and your
home?"

Garia winced to hear him refer to her stepmother by her proper title; neither she nor
Judith Laverty could ever bring themselves
to use it, whether speaking directly to Josepha
or while discussing her between themselves.
"I suppose not," she acknowledged. "It makes
no difference now, for I am anxious to get
to the heart of this business at once. You must
know I am gravely concerned about my step-

mother's stated purpose in coming here."

The lawyer gave a curt nod and, going to the desk, opened his black tin document box and removed several sheets of paper that Garia recognised as her father's last will and testament. A year ago she had sat in this very room on a cold and rainy day and listened to the lawyer read it aloud. "Dromana House and the estate were left to you outright, Garia," he began, "and the authenticity of Sir Andrew's will cannot be called into question. But he neglected to provide his widow with any jointure, and thus she feels she has some grounds for suing. As I see it, your problem lies not in her claim to your property, but in her threat to take you to court over the matter."

"But how *can* she," Garia protested, "when I owe her nothing? It seems to me she gave up any right to a jointure, or any other kind of support when she deserted my father. If she is in dire need, I'm willing to settle a small sum upon her. But outside of that I refuse to jeopardise my own rights by agreeing to any sort of compromise!"

"Only consider for a moment before you refuse. A lawsuit is a disagreeable thing, I know it well. And it's particularly true here in Ireland. It could drag on for years, for generations, as so many do. Bribery is not, I regret to say, uncommon. Whether or not Lady Ivory has any right to the property seems to me to be immaterial at this state. And, as the mother of the Howards, she has some bargaining power with you, does she not?"

Said Garia with considerable heat, "Even so, she cannot force me to give up my home!"

Mr. Ruan glanced down at the papers. "Dromana will not be yours for much longer, however, for you are to be wed. Under the marriage laws, all of a woman's property belongs to her husband."

Garia was silent.

"Lord Lindal is away at present, I believe?"

She nodded. "He had business in Dublin, but today I received a letter from him, and I expect him to return within a very few days."

Mr. Ruan said gravely, "I can understand how uneasy you must be as a result of his absence, for I'm sure you cannot be unaware that the city offers many diversions for a gentleman of his lordship's tastes."

"What are you implying?" she asked him coolly.

The lawyer's thin lips twisted in a sad smile. "Poor Garia, you cannot always live in a dream world, like little Egan. You must prepare yourself for the likelihood that marriage to you will not curtail the Earl's visits to Dublin — even to London."

With quiet dignity she answered, "I am not entering into marriage blindly, but neither do I expect to suffer from it. I have come to know Lord Lindal quite well, far better than I did a few weeks ago."

"Can it be that he has cajoled and flattered you into thinking yourself in love with him? That would be cruelty indeed, for though you'll recover from the delusion in time, it may not be until after it is too late to save yourself from this marriage. Can't you see, Garia? He is past thirty, no longer a young man, and he wants an heir. You are a convenience to him, nothing more. He regards you as a conformable wife, as good for his purposes as any other female. Better, in fact, because you were already betrothed to him and have thereby saved him the trouble of seeking out someone he would have to court in the approved manner! Oh, I have heard the tales, the gossip about him all these years, just as you have. And I cannot believe anything but that he has come to Ireland to play at lord of the manor until he grows bored of it. And will you be content to remain in Ireland and breed his heir, while he junkets across the globe pursuing his amours?"

Garia, appalled by this speech, cried out, "Don't — oh, you are wrong, very wrong!" That he should dare to rip open her newly happy heart with his insinuations about Torin — it was too cruel. But, she remembered suddenly, not so long ago Torin himself had suggested he might leave her behind when he journeyed to London. Had she been wrong these few days, counting upon his fidelity simply because he had kissed her goodbye so sweetly?

Charles Ruan saw how her face fell. "I am sorry if my words have pained you," he said unhappily. "I never meant to raise the subject of your marriage today, though it is something I can never entirely forget. I will never cease to regret your choice, for reasons that can be no secret to you."

"You mustn't continue to hope for something that can never be," she told him as kindly as possible. "Even if I were free, I don't believe I could marry you, sir, for I'm not sure we should suit. And I hope you will cease to think of me in — in such a way, for you know I have given my pledge to another man. No matter what manner of man he may be," she added, more to herself than to him.

He looked at her regretfully for a moment, then said, "My deep regard for you is something I shall never be ashamed of. And I hope you will not take it amiss if it prompts me to offer a warning."

"I'd rather you didn't," she said quickly, but he failed to heed her.

"Your stepmother is an appealing woman, I'm sure you must be aware of it. And Lord Lindal's history points to his being a very susceptible gentleman. If you have indeed set your heart upon this marriage, you would do well to prevent a meeting between them. And I urge you to do all in your power to be rid of Lady Ivory as quickly as possible, whatever it costs you in the way of money — or other things."

His insinuation was most unwelcome, and Garia preferred to ignore it. But her voice was slightly unsteady as she pointed out, "We have rather strayed from the purpose of your visit, Mr. Ruan."

He returned to the desk to pick up one of the documents strewn across its gleaming surface. "I have here a letter of intent from Lady Ivory, stating that she will relinquish any and all claim to Dromana House and the surrounding property if you comply with her request for a settlement of five hundred pounds per annum, and the full guardianship of her minor sons. She will take up residence in London and will not intrude upon your life in any way in the future."

Garia stared at him, struck mute by his words, and it took her some time to accept the truth of her dilemma. Josepha could not have asked her to make a more difficult choice, and she could neither accept nor could she refuse the terms. In her panic she told herself that her love for her brothers must surely outweigh any other consideration. But to give up Dromana, home to the Ivorys for the last century, the only thing of material value she had in all the world — that was equally impossible. And the five hundred pounds a year, why that was half her present annual income!

Her first thought, that Torin might be her salvation, did not long survive. How could she involve him in this tangle with her stepmother, she asked herself, for as Charles Ruan had said, Josepha was quite beautiful. But even more significant, she was greedy. Suppose she decided to cast out lures to the Earl? Even Garia's father, a sober, sensible man, had succumbed to her wiles, and Torin had a reputation for dalliance. What if he should respond by flirting with Josepha, or worse? Garia didn't believe he would set her stepmother up as his mistress under her very nose, but if he did make Josepha the object of his gallantry on even the most harmless level, it would be hard to bear. She'd had no real proof of his constancy as yet and knew not how well it would stand any sort of test. In addition to losing Dromana or her boys, she might well lose a husband.

She did not reveal this concern, however, and summoning up her voice at last, she replied, "I quite understand my stepmother's terms, and I will weigh them carefully. How long have I got before I must make a decision?"

Said Mr. Ruan, "That depends upon how soon you wish to be rid of Lady Ivory. I would advise against a delay." He rolled up the papers, tied them together, then deposited the roll in his document box. "But remember this, Garia. You mustn't confront her, or discuss any of this with her unless I am present. Do you understand?" She nodded, and he went on, "As soon as you've made up your mind what to do, send me a message and I'll return to draw up the necessary papers."

Garia held out her hand to him in farewell, but she withdrew it suddenly, self-consciously, when Josepha appeared in the doorway.

"Ah, Mr. Ruan," Lady Ivory greeted the attorney, "and how does your business with my stepdaughter prosper?"

"Your ladyship will discover that in good time," he said repressively before turning back to his hostess. "You needn't ring for your butler, Garia. I know my way out."

When he was gone, Josepha said apologetically, "I didn't know he was here, and I never meant to intrude at an inopportune moment."

"You didn't. Is there something you want?" Garia regarded the other woman with stony eyes.

"Have you any laudanum?" Garia shook her head, and Josepha heaved a small sigh. "Then perhaps you might tell me where I can procure some. Alas, I am cursed by sleeplessness — a souvenir of my India days, I'm afraid. But I daren't buy the drug locally — people talk so, you know."

"There's a chemist's shop in Carrick," Garia informed her and, as an afterthought, asked what about India had been so disturbing.

"The hot nights," Josepha replied. "As a result, I am still unable to fall asleep with perfect ease. Most annoying, you'll agree."

Garia bit back a tart retort about guilty consciences and excused herself, for she could no longer support being in the same room with the woman who was bent upon ruining her. She paused uncertainly in the dark hallway and pressed her hands together to keep them from trembling. Give up Dromana or give up the boys: no, she must not think of that now, or she would fall into hysterics. Then, remembering she'd promised to help Judith pack for the journey to Dublin, she went upstairs. She would not burden her aunt with her newest woe, on that she was resolved; nevertheless, her face and manner were clear indications that something was amiss.

"I'm not sure I ought to rush away like this," Judith told her doubtfully. "I feel like a deserter on the eve of a major battle."

"You are merely being fanciful," she replied in bracing tones. "Dear Aunt, you'll never be comfortable living under the same roof as Josepha, I know it well, and there's no saying how long she will remain. Torin — Lord Lindal — will return as soon as he has hired a tutor for the boys, so you need not think they'll suffer from your departure, nor will I. So you may go to my sister Rosamund with a clear conscience. The two of you must put your heads together about the wedding preparations, for I'm sure I don't know where to begin!" She hoped her assumption of confidence had fooled her aunt, but a telltale pucker of concern decorated her brow.

Judith noted it, but was unable to resist her niece's imploring eyes and thus gave the only possible answer. "Very well, my dear. If you are so determined, I shall leave for Blanchlands tomorrow. But you must promise that if something goes wrong, or you have any need of me, you will send word."

"Oh, I will," Garia agreed, knowing she would never do so, whatever happened. For the battle she faced was one she must wage alone.

15

My arms shall encircle you
While I relate my sad tale.
— Irish Song

When Judith Laverty abruptly left Dromana for Dublin, the young Howards immediately laid the blame for this development on their mother. Jeremy grew more silent and withdrawn every day, and whenever he was in Josepha's company he regarded her with suspicious, shadowed eyes. Bennet announced flatly to Garia that he and the faithful Nonny preferred to eat their dinner in the nursery rather than in the dining room. And Egan, who only half heard the ensuing argument, was perfectly aware of it. Although he behaved more or less as usual, he watched his family closely, and as soon as faces were transformed by strain — or rage — he reverted to the dreamy abstraction in which he normally took refuge from the world.

Upon her aunt's departure Garia resumed the rigorous duties of running the household. She wondered if she should make an effort to speak with each child individually, but could think of nothing comforting that would not raise false hopes. It saddened her, seeing that the three lively, hearty boys had turned into brooding, ill-tempered versions of themselves. She knew they were afraid of being taken away from her, but now that this danger was a very real one, she doubted she could soothe their fears; her own were too great. Her unease was exacerbated by the upper servants, who tiptoed around the house as if fearful of putting a foot wrong. In that mysterious way of their class, everyone from McCurdie down to the lowliest scullery maid was aware that Lady Ivory coveted Dromana House. Their loyalty belonged to their Miss Garia, but they took great pains not to offend the enemy.

Josepha's sudden but welcome decision to take her meals alone, in the privacy of her upstairs sitting room, relieved her stepdaughter's mind considerably, and mealtimes lost some of the strain that had characterised them of late. One morning at breakfast Garia took advantage of her absence to deliver a brief homily to the children on the twin evils of treating guests rudely and unchivalrous action towards one's own blood relations. It was wrong, she told them severely, to reveal their animosity to one who had done them no harm.

Bennet was the first to reply to this charge, and his bright blue eyes were wide with astonishment as he said, "But, Garia, don't you dislike her, too? She is *bad* — she ran away from us!"

"Even if she should be a monster, she is still your mother. Have you stopped to consider her feelings, which must be hurt by your unkindness? To say nothing of the fact that I must appear a poor teacher and guardian to all of you, for your behaviour reflects as badly upon me as it does on yourselves."

"Garia's right," Egan piped up unexpectedly, startling his table companions, Garia included, for he seldom entered into family discussions or offered an opinion of his own. "Our mother came back to Dromana, didn't she? I don't think she's so very bad. And anyway, Ben, it isn't a bit fair to Garia to put her in an uncomfortable position."

"Little idiot, our mother didn't come to Dromana because of *us*," Jeremy interjected bitterly. "She came to make trouble, and I won't have anything to do with her." He pushed his chair back from the table angrily and charged out of the room.

"Never mind your brother," Garia told Bennet and Egan, her eyes on the window. As she watched the wiry youth stride across the lawn towards the stables, she hoped he would find a release for his ill-humour in a vigorous gallop. Looking down at the younger boys, she went on, "But I know I can rely upon the two of you to make your mother comfortable here at Dromana for however long she may remain."

Delighted at the prospect of outdoing Jeremy in Garia's esteem, and eager to please her as he had not, Egan and Bennet agreed to visit their mother's sitting room without delay. They recalled that she'd often mentioned an intriguing collection of elephants carved from ebony that she had brought with her from India. Moreover, Bennet remembered that he hadn't sufficiently thanked his parent for the handsome toy soldiers she had bestowed upon him.

At last the long-anticipated day of Lady Neale's ball dawned, but Garia had not yet received word of Lord Lindal's return. She was doubtful of the propriety of attending an evening party alone, with no escort and without suitable chaperonage, for Lady Neale was a high stickler. And naturally no invitation had arrived for Josepha, who would be most unwelcome at that or any other local assembly. As the morning gave way to afternoon, Garia began to resign herself to the prospect of staying at home that evening.

She made up her mind to follow Jeremy's

example and go for a long cross-country ride after writing to Lady Neale, for she had scarcely strayed beyond the confines of the house since her stepmother's arrival. It was no wonder she was looking so pale and drawn, she thought, critically surveying her reflection in the looking glass that hung above the drawing-room mantel. These days sleep eluded her, all food seemed tasteless and unsatisfying, and inwardly she railed against Josepha for causing the disquiet that had been so detrimental to her looks. Fear and concern had gnawed at her ever since Josepha crossed the threshold of Dromana House, and there seemed to be no end to the problems her presence created. And because Charles Ruan's cautionary words about Torin's possible activities in Dublin had fallen upon fertile ground, she couldn't help but wonder if his lordship's tardiness was indicative of his inconstancy. Had some bewitching beauty crossed his path, she wondered in agony. And as she reached for some writing paper so she could pen her regrets to Lady Neale, she wished her imagination weren't quite so vivid.

She had just sat down at her desk when the insistent pounding of the door-knocker caused her spirits to plummet even further. She was in no mood to receive anyone, but it was already too late to warn McCurdie; she could hear voices in the hall. But a moment later, when she looked up to see her visitor's tall, impressive figure on the threshold, she uttered a jubilant cry.

"Oh, Torin, you are returned at last!" She supposed the state of her heart was writ clearly on her face, but in that moment she didn't care and held out her hands in a mute invitation.

He responded to it immediately, enfolding her in a crushing embrace. He kissed her repeatedly, and when at last he raised his head to look down at her, he said, "You must have missed me indeed!"

"Oh, *so* much," she breathed, clinging to him. His nearness, the comfort of his arms was most welcome, and she rested her cheek on his white shirtfront while he stroked her curls. Then she looked up to say, "I'm very glad you are here."

Torin bent his head to hers to print another kiss upon her upturned lips, but paused as he read the trouble in her face. "But what's this? You are not the same blooming creature who bid me farewell a week ago. Is something amiss?"

His arrival, just when she had given up hoping, had momentarily chased Garia's troubles away, but his question brought them crowding back again. She extricated herself from his arms, and tried to marshall her scattered wits.

"What *is* the matter, Garia?" he asked again. "None of the boys is ill, I hope."

"No," she said, turning away. "They are well enough in body, if not in spirit. Josepha has returned, you see, as I always feared she might."

"Returned?" he repeated. "Are you saying that Lady Ivory is here, in this house now?"

Crossing to the settee, Garia replied, "She is indeed, and may well intrude at any moment, for that is her habit."

Torin followed her, frowning. "How long has she been here?"

"Since the very day you left for Dublin. Oh, Torin, it is *dreadful,* much worse than I ever imagined it could be! She has laid claim to Dromana and threatens me with a lawsuit and means to take the boys away — oh, it is too terrible to contemplate! The children dislike her. Bennet has been quite rude, and as for Jeremy — I never thought to see him behave so badly. The servants wander about the house looking so fearful, and my aunt has gone to Rosamund. Each day seems more difficult and uncomfortable than the last, and you cannot guess how worried I am."

He sat down beside her, saying, "I can't imagine Miss Laverty would abandon you at such a trying time, however much Lady Kelsey might depend upon her in coming weeks."

"I knew it was for the best; Aunt Judith can't abide my stepmother. She went reluctantly all the same, but when I reminded her that you'd soon return, she agreed to go to Dublin." Garia smiled faintly. "But her departure leaves me oddly circumstanced, with no other female companion but Josepha. Which is as good as saying none at all."

"You must be run distracted, poor little dove. So much so that it sent you flying into my arms!"

"It was most undignified of me to fling myself at you that way," Garia admitted, "but I had just been thinking you might not return today after all, and when I saw you standing there — I was so thankful," she said simply.

His reply was to kiss her again, long and thoroughly. But Torin was conscious of restraint on her side, of the kind he had hoped never to encounter again. This troubled him, and it pained him, too, when she rose and walked over to the window and away from him. "I have been counting the moments till I could be with you again," he told her with a warm smile she could not see, for her back was towards him.

"Oh?" she said softly, and when she looked over her shoulder, he saw that her eyes were shadowed with doubt.

"My dear, what more can I do to prove it to you? I have already offered you my name and my title," he said.

But was his heart also a part of that offer, she wondered as he joined her at the window. How much of it could she realistically hope to possess? She had expected his return to banish the fresher of her troubles only to be disappointed, for it had served to remind her of several stale ones. *Could* she win his love, she asked herself, or should she give it up as a hopeless ambition? And although he made a move to draw her into the circle of his arms once more, she pushed him gently away. "There is no time for that, Torin. If Josepha learns you are here she will descend upon us, and I would have you gone before she does." She could not explain her reluctance for him to meet her stepmother, so she said evasively, "From now on, it may be difficult to achieve privacy, even under my own roof."

He looked down at her curiously. "This is a brief reunion indeed. But I shall swallow my sorrow and cheer myself with the reflexion that I'll see you at Lady Neale's ball tonight."

Garia shook her head and told him, "I'm afraid I mustn't go, for I've no chaperone now that Aunt Judith has gone. Josepha is not invited — and she's cross as briars about it, you may be sure."

"Send a message to the Rectory pleading some problem with your carriage, or anything else that comes to mind," he suggested, retrieving his hat. "Your friends will know the real reason, but that won't matter. At least you'll have adequate chaperonage, though why you should want it is beyond my ken. And," he added with a twinkle, "if you go with the Ashgroves, I may thus assure Thomas that his own inamorata will be present. He has much to tell Miss Frances — but I mustn't betray his confidence."

Pressing her hands together, Garia said thankfully, "Oh, I hoped it was so." And she felt a kind of envy for Frances and Thomas, whose happiness was now assured in a way she feared hers would never be.

That evening Garia, determined to present an appearance worthy of her future lord, dressed with especial care. She thought of asking her stepmother to assist at her toilette, for her taste was excellent, and after her recent sojourn in Paris her knowledge of the niceties of current style would be far greater than Garia's. However, she couldn't quite bring herself to take this drastic step, and so relied upon her own instincts. These served her well enough, and even her own doubtful eyes told her she looked well in her ballgown of pearl-coloured satin, embroidered all over with gold thread. She wore the pearl necklet and ear-drops that had belonged to her mother, and carried a gold-spangled fan.

When Cora had dressed her hair to her satisfaction, she made her way along the narrow passage toward the staircase and met her stepmother coming up. "*Trés distinguée*," Josepha murmured appreciatively. As she reached out to make a slight adjustment to the gauze stole around her stepdaughter's shoulders, there was more than a hint of regret in the droop of her full mouth.

Garia had to pity her. To be treated as an outcast by everyone in the neighbourhood must always have been extremely unpleasant, and she was suddenly angry with her hostess for not including Sir Andrew's widow in the invitation. "Oh, Josepha, Lady Neale really *ought* to have sent you a card!"

The other woman shrugged. "She would rather shave her head, I think. Pray don't worry on my account, Garia, for I anticipate a pleasant evening *en famille*. Egan has asked to see the watercolours I did in India, and Bennet actually prevailed upon Nonny to offer me his paw. I hope for even better things to-night." The brilliant smile faded and Josepha said huskily, "I am grateful for whatever it was that you said to my younger sons, for it has wrought a remarkable change. If only Jeremy would — well, poor lad, I cannot blame him for despising me, yet I wish it were otherwise."

Garia clasped Josepha's hand more warmly than she had ever thought possible. "He will relent, Josepha, I am sure of it. With Jeremy, everything takes time. The wonder of him is that he glides through life so smoothly and without the least difficulty, and when he does encounter an obstacle, he's somewhat daunted by it at first."

Lady Ivory gave a self-deprecating chuckle. "I imagine that I'm proving a fearsome obstacle! There, I see the carriage lamps coming along the drive — you had best hurry down, Garia. But wait a moment — I have something for you." She darted into her chamber and returned a moment later with an evening cloak draped over her arm. It was blue velvet trimmed with white cord and tassels, a most regal garment. "Here, you must wear this," she said, wrapping it around Garia. "Now you are complete to a shade and your Earl of Lindal will fall at your feet!"

Touched by this act of generosity, Garia stammered her thanks, but Josepha motioned her towards the door.

Sir John Neale's residence was a Palladian

villa situated some five miles beyond Cloncavan village. His lady's social pretensions were legendary in the neighbourhood, and tonight she had gone so far as to affix flambeaux over the front door. When Garia and the Ashgroves entered the house, they found a row of well-fashioned youths decked out in footmen's livery lined up in the hall, but their ruddy complexions and the firmly muscled limbs revealed by their hose gave away the truth of their everyday occupation, that of farm labourer. Frances whispered to Garia that she wouldn't put it past Lady Neale to offer her guests pink champagne, the *ne plus ultra* of fashionable beverages.

Her ladyship was an elegant, imperious woman, supremely conscious of being the daughter of a Baron. Her three handsome daughters stood beside her at the top of the stairs to greet the new arrivals, and affable Sir John welcomed the Ashgrove party, complimenting the young ladies on their looks and wishing them a surfeit of dancing partners.

Arm in arm, Frances and Garia traversed the highly polished ballroom floor in search of friends. "Look, it's Cecilia Manahan over there," Frances pointed out. "Poor dear, her mama ought to take care to dress her better. That colour doesn't become her at all — it makes her look sadly green-faced, don't you think?"

"I suppose so," Garia said absently, searching for a particular black head. She spied it on the other side of the room and smiled in relief. Torin stood with his cousin, who had every appearance of a gentleman facing an unnerving ordeal. As well he might, she thought, for staid Thomas was about to make a marriage proposal that might actually be accepted. "There's your admirer, Frances," she told her friend.

"Where? Oh, you mean Mr. Montrose," the young woman said. "I didn't realise he and the Earl had returned from Dublin." She sighed, then went on, "Well, for your sake, my dear, I am glad." She began to ply her fan agitatedly as the two gentlemen approached. "You know, Garia, you are like all engaged persons, hoping everyone else will follow the same dull path to matrimony that you have chosen. Only see, Caroline de Lacy and her brother Ralph are beckoning to me. I had better go to them." And without another word, she hurried away with a rustle of silken skirts.

Thomas Montrose was clearly disconcerted by this rebuff, and his hurt eyes followed the Rector's daughter. Garia advised him gently, "Go after her, sir, for I truly believe she hopes you will."

As his cousin wandered off, Torin murmured, "How curious is woman. I'd have said Miss Ashgrove just meant to deliver a snub to poor Thomas. Just as I assume you intended this afternoon when you dismissed me so abruptly. Or was I similarly mistaken?"

Garia glanced up at him worriedly. "I'm sorry if I gave you that impression, my lord."

"Did you have another lover secreted away?" he teased. "I can think of no other reason for your hurrying me out of the house so swiftly."

Garia choked on a laugh. "Don't be ridiculous!"

"Ah, now *there* is the girl I was hoping to see tonight. And I've never seen you in better looks." She looked magnificent in her finery, Torin realised, every inch the countess she would one day be. He had always been conscious of her beauty, but it had never affected him so strongly. Despite the fact that she had reverted to her former restraint in his presence, he hoped to rekindle the spark of passion he had struck the day he had left for Dublin. The fine creature standing before him in her white satin, she whom he had once spurned, had come to embody all of his hopes for happiness. And somehow he must convince her of it, he told himself as his eyes lingered on the low décolletage adorned with garlands of gilt leaves.

"Stop ogling me, you wretch!"

He laughed and took her arm. "You are more familiar with this house than I — is there some place that we may be alone? It will be a little while yet before the dancing begins."

"There is a conservatory," Garia informed him, blushing at her own boldness.

As the couple strolled beneath Lady Neale's prized palm trees, Garia raised the subject of her brothers' tutor. "I hope they will like him," she sighed.

"I think it likely. I was fortunate to find a very learned and pleasant young gentleman," Torin told her. "He won't arrive until later this week, but I've already ordered my old schoolroom to be made ready. No, don't shake your pretty head at me, for I have made up my mind that the boys will come to the Castle each day for their lessons, and after we are married — by the by, when *are* we to be married?"

"Next spring," Garia replied demurely, eyes downcast.

He stopped short and turned her towards him. "Nonsense! I mean to be riveted to you long before the bluebells appear, and I'd prefer a date not much after the New Year."

"But that's two months from now!" she cried despairingly.

"Yes — much too long a wait," he jested.

"Yes — much too long a wait," he jested. "very well, let us be wed at Christmas. Do you have any strenuous objections, Miss Ivory?"

"Well, not very strenuous," she admitted. "But — but what about Josepha? I don't see how I can plan my wedding with her threats hanging over my head." She added reflectively, "Yet, my case may not be so desperate as I led you to believe earlier today. My stepmother did seem to be making friendly overtures this evening, for the first time, and I can't help but wonder if she might not be reasoned with. Mr. Ruan warned me against being taken in, or discussing anything with her, but — "

"Ruan? What has *he* to say about anything?" Torin did not quite succeed in hiding his displeasure, for the lawyer's name had stirred up the temper that churned beneath the smooth surface of his amiability.

"He called the other day to advise me," Garia explained.

"I think perhaps I ought to call upon him myself," he said. "You are my future wife, and I'm not sure I like his meddling in matters that do not concern him."

"But he is still my attorney," she reminded him. "*And* my friend."

He caught the faint note of warning, and because he did not wish to provoke a quarrel, he let go of the subject of Mr. Ruan. "Then let me speak to your stepmother," he suggested. "If she's as mercenary as you have often said, she might be persuaded to leave the boys in your care in exchange for a large settlement, which I can easily afford."

Garia's brow creased. "I don't know," she faltered.

Torin touched her forehead with his finger. "She cannot be such a dragon, Garia. All will be well, I promise you, and now let us speak of happier things. Will you be riding with the Cloncavan pack on the morrow?"

"It is the first word I've had of the meeting. I'm glad of it — I need the diversion, and so does Jeremy, for he is much troubled by Josepha's presence. All of the children are afraid of being taken from me, I think, but with Jeremy there is something else as well, but he won't speak of it."

"Probably he remembers those years before Josepha Howard brought her fledglings to Ireland — I fancy the memories aren't pleasant ones for him. Certainly he's of an age to remember his own father, and no doubt he also remembers his mother's string of admirers. He may even doubt his own paternity, Garia."

"But he and Egan are undoubtedly Mr. Howard's true sons. They are alike in many ways and different from Bennet. It's so obvious to me that I never suspected he might question it. How clever you are, Torin."

"Merely wise in the ways of boys of that age, my love. Jeremy is growing out of his boyhood and entering into a period where he will experience self-doubt and extremes of mood. Had Josepha not reentered his life, something else would have turned him broody."

"I daresay you are right." She tugged at his sleeve and said, "I think we must return to the ballroom — the fiddlers have begun tuning their instruments."

Torin cocked his head and caught the faint strains of music. "I wish I might open the dancing with you, my dove, but alas, it is my duty to partner the eldest Miss Neale. But before we go I must take care of something I have neglected too long. Give me your left hand." She obeyed, and he slipped a ring onto her fourth finger.

Rose-cut diamonds caught the light and sent it winking back at her, and Garia gasped aloud.

"Much of the time in Dublin was spent at the jewellers' shops," he said, "trying to determine what you would like best. Rosamund approved my taste, but if it's in any way unsatisfactory — "

"But it is lovely, Torin!" she breathed, still staring down at the sparkling stones. "I hardly know what to say."

"You need say nothing. But might I suggest another suitable form for expressing your gratitude, my dear?" And he drew her into an alcove shaded by waving palm fronds and softly scented with orange blossom.

16

Oh, my girl, I can see 'tis in trouble you are.
— Irish Song

Jeremy Howard paced impatiently back and forth in the downstairs hall, eager to be on his way to Cloncavan Castle and the hunt. But his stepsister, usually so punctual, had not even appeared at breakfast. Already he had been waiting for her for a quarter of an hour, and his brothers, after following him out of the dining room, joined in speculating on what could be the cause of Garia's delay.

At last she emerged from the library, clad in her new riding habit of blue cloth. The boys drew a unified breath of admiration, but paying no heed to this tribute, she apologised for her tardiness. "Forgive me, Jeremy, but I had to speak with Erris, who had a message for me. And I'm afraid I will have to alter my plans for this morning, for old Cleary, papa's valet, lies ill at his cottage and I must go to him. I'll drive myself in the gig so as not to tire Brutus, and afterwards I can join the hunt."

Jeremy's face fell. "It would be a shame if you didn't meet us, for we'll be after the foxes at Smallridge. And the scent today should be running breast-high at the least."

Bennet tugged at Garia's long skirt. "May Egan and I ride out on our ponies to watch the hunt? Mama says we must ask you."

She looked up to see Josepha standing in the doorway of the dining room, clad in a splendid saffron-coloured gown that shimmered with her every motion. "No, Bennet," Garia replied, shaking her head, "I'm afraid that won't be possible. You can't go to Smallridge alone, and I've already sent Erris to the village to have one of the farm horses shod. Why can't you keep your mama company today, instead of dashing about the countryside?"

Josepha said, in a tone of commiseration, "Poor Garia—so many supplicants! And I must add my voice to the chorus. Might I have the use of your carriage today? There's a bit of shopping I should like to do in Carrick."

Garia could hardly refuse so innocent a request from one she had been careful to treat as a guest. "Certainly, I've no objection, but with Erris gone, and Padraig — " She hesitated, then said inventively, "And Padraig indisposed, the new groom will have to drive you." The new groom, a former stablehand, had received his recent promotion following Padraig's adamant refusal to drive Lady Ivory. The ancient coachman had informed his young mistress that loyal as he was to the family, he would give up his post before he would wait upon "that woman."

A loud crash sounded from the dining room, startling all five persons in the hall, who hurried to see what tragedy had occurred. They found Nonny ecstatically gulping meat from the carpet, for somehow he had succeeded in knocking one of the plates from the table to the floor.

"Nonny, you shameless creature!" Garia cried furiously, lashing out with her riding whip in an attempt to frighten the young dog. As soon as she chased him out of the room, she turned to Bennet and said severely, "How many times have I warned you never to leave Nonny unattended when there is food about? If that plate had been broken, I'd have handed him over to Mrs. Aglish for retribution — no, I would have wrung his neck myself! Put your dog outdoors at once and go to your room!"

"But Garia — "

"Enough! I am not at leisure to carry on a debate with you."

As she swept out of the room she heard Egan say softly, "But Nonny *wasn't* unattended — Mama was still in the dining room when we left it. How were we to know she would come into the hall?"

The truth of this was undeniable, but Garia was in no mood to belabour the point. Turning around she said firmly, "Nonny is not your mother's responsibility, nor is she well enough acquainted with all of his idiosyncracies to be on her guard. I haven't time to argue this matter — we'll sort it out when I return." It was the barest concession on her part that she might have been over-hasty in laying the blame on Bennet.

She set out in the pony-drawn gig for the tiny cottage where her elderly pensioner resided with his widowed daughter. A recent cold had left Mr. Cleary bedridden and bored, and he was most eager to learn all the news from the Big House. Garia, feeling a trifle guilty for not having visited him sooner, told him about the boys' latest antics and described Nonny's various misdeeds. And she permitted the old man to reminisce at length about the halcyon days at Dromana when the first Lady Ivory had been mistress there. It was so pleasant to be reminded of that long-ago time before Josepha had entered her life that Garia ceased to chafe at being kept from the hunt for so long.

Eventually she rose from the chair by the

bedside, and with a promise to send a bottle of claret to the sufferer, she bid him farewell. But at that moment Father Rourke arrived, and Garia was further detained. The priest thanked her effusively for giving her servants leave to attend confession, and he gave her a thorough report on who had and had not attended the Mass on the Feast of All Saints. By the time she drove back to Dromana, there was a biting chill in the air, and it was well past the hour at which she expected to join the hunt. To her great disappointment, she found Mr. Ruan's neat chaise standing at her front door, and she feared yet another delay. As she guided the pony to the stableyard, she considered creeping into Brutus's stall, saddling him herself, and riding off before anyone realised she had returned. But she was forced to abandon this reckless plan; she supposed the lawyer had come to discuss Josepha's threats and perhaps to offer some solution.

As soon as she entered the house, McCurdie came rushing forwards. "Oh, Miss," he whispered hoarsely, "'tis bad tidings I have!" His manner was very much as it had been the day of Josepha's return, and she held her breath in fearful expectation, waiting for the blow to fall. "'Tis the little lads — Master Egan and Master Bennet are gone."

Garia wavered on her feet and clutched at

his arm, only to discover that the butler was trembling all over. And she realised what must be the truth before he spoke the words.

"Herself has took them away, Miss — right after you left the house this mornin' and before Mrs. Aglish and myself realised what she was about! Master Jeremy was off to the hunt already, else he'd be stole as much as they."

"Mr. Ruan — I saw his carriage. Where is he?"

"In the bookroom, Miss."

Garia went blindly towards the library, her brain a senseless whirl of frantic self-condemnation. She ought to have known better than to put Josepha in charge of the boys — what an arrant piece of stupidity! And it had been sheer folly, giving her stepmother leave to use the carriage.

Charles Ruan came forward to meet her, shaking his head. "My dear Garia, I am so very sorry this has happened. How pale you are," he said, leading her to the sofa. "You must take a glass of wine."

"No, no," she protested, "It is imperative that I keep a clear head. And I don't know what I *can* do, now that the worst has happened!"

"There, now, it is not a hopeless case. First I think you should read the note Lady Ivory left behind."

Garia took the single sheet of paper he held out to her, but it gave her no answer to the multitude of questions chasing round and round in her mind. It was a brief statement of fact, written in her stepmother's spidery hand, and Garia read it aloud, in a faint voice. "*I have taken Egan and Bennet. I had no other choice.*" She looked up at the lawyer and said in despair, "I was mad to trust her, even for the space of a morning."

Josepha must have intended to make off with her sons all along, Garia told herself, and had simply been awaiting the perfect opportunity. No doubt she had been trying to instill a sense of false security last night, with the kind words and generous loan of the velvet cloak. Fool, fool, Garia's conscience shouted, you have only yourself to blame for being taken in, for Josepha's past proved that she was capable of every kind of treachery. She was clever and conniving, and cared for no one but herself.

"Fate has conspired against me," Garia said, "for Padraig, whom I could trust, wasn't driving the carriage, nor was Erris. Josepha could easily have bribed the new groom, for he's very young and his family quite poor. She might even be halfway to some port by this time!"

"I doubt that, Garia," Mr. Ruan said soothingly. "Remember, she also wants Dromana, so she would not stray too far from it. In Waterford she and the boys would be recognised, but in Kilkenny — or Dublin — she could hide herself. What luck that I had business with Sir John Neale today! I can only be glad that chance brought me to your door at such a moment, when I may be of assistance to you. My horses are quite fresh, and I believe them capable of overtaking Lady Ivory."

"Go after her? You would do that?"

"Both of us will go, for you'll want to assure yourself that the little lads are well. My chaise is well sprung, and even though our pace would be quick, you would be comfortable. What say you?"

It was strange, she thought, that his urgency did not calm her raging fears; rather, he had managed to unsettle her all the more, something she hadn't believed possible. Instinct warned her to find the Earl of Lindal at once and lay the matter before him. But that was impossible, for he was somewhere on the hunting field, and by now could be as many as ten miles off. Any attempt to locate him would take up precious time, perhaps several hours.

"Yes, let us go at once," she said, rising hastily. "But I must leave some message for Jeremy."

"I'll do it for you, while you go upstairs

to fetch a wrap, for it is growing bitter cold. But we must be quick, and you haven't time to change."

Garia rushed up the narrow staircase, so blinded by her tears that she stumbled on the risers. But this was not the moment to give way to grief, so she kept it at bay. As she groped in her wardrobe for her warmest cloak, she prayed her stepmother had been possessed of equal foresight where the children were concerned and had provided them with mittens and a carriage rug. Egan was so prone to colds and fevers but Josepha would not know that. Garia picked up an enormous muff of black fur, for her own hands were chilled through her gloves, and she hurried back down the stairs.

Mr. Ruan was waiting outside, and he helped her into the chaise. Once inside, Garia leaned back against the seat and listened as he conferred with his coachman. Their breaths left tiny puffs of vapour in the frigid air, and she pulled her wrap closer around her to ward off the incipient cold.

Moments later, the carriage was bowling past the Rectory and through the village. "Are we going to Carrick first?" Garia asked the gentleman. "She may indeed have gone there to hire some other conveyance, and we might discover her destination."

"Oh, there can be little doubt she is bound for Dublin," Mr. Ruan declared confidently. "I have every hope of catching up to her at Kilkenny, which is the natural place to break a journey to the capital."

"But in a town that size we have almost no hope of finding her! And how shall we ever make up the time? She has been on the road for two hours at least."

"She has no idea she is being followed, because she expected you to join the hunt," he pointed out. "Moreover, we are taking a swifter route than the one from Carrick to Kilkenny. We'll cross the bridge to Fiddown, and then join the Waterford- Kilkenny Road."

Garia ventured no reply, but clasped and unclasped her hands nervously inside her muff. Her fingers closed around the stub of a pencil, and again hot tears stung her eyes. During matins last Sunday Bennet and Egan had been drawing in their hymnals, the naughty children, and she had snatched their pencil away. Such a scold she had given them — they would not soon forget it. Nor could she cease to regret it, and her misery increased when she remembered how cross she had been with Bennet that very morning. She wished she could take back those harsh, angry words. And if only she had not been in such a hurry to visit Cleary, she thought miserably. She should have taken them with her, for then this tragedy would have been averted.

She stared out the window, and as the chaise lurched along the lane, each rut and bump jangled her nerves. Jeremy, poor lad, what bitter news he would receive when he returned from the hunt. There would be no one to offer consolation save for the frantic and incoherent servants. And Torin might not learn of the boys' disappearance for several hours. How much better she would feel if he were sitting beside her now, accompanying her on this desperate chase.

Mr. Ruan broke the oppressive silence by saying, "I feel entirely responsible — I could have discouraged you from housing that vile woman. That she should dare to cause you one moment's distress!"

Looking at him, Garia replied, "You must not be imagining that you are in any way at fault. Josepha is very cunning — I think anyone might have been taken in by her. And she *is* my father's widow — I had no choice but to let her stay at Dromana."

She turned her head and continued to gaze at the landscape. There was not a sign of civilisation to be seen, only a vast expanse of waste and bogland and very few cultivated fields. She wondered that her escort should have chosen this out-of-the-way route, or that he should think it a quicker one. From what she remembered of the road from Fiddown, it connected with the Waterford-Kilkenny Road beyond Mullinavat, and only after a long and arduous journey along narrow, winding roads like the one they were on. Most travellers from Cloncavan went by way of Carrick-on-Suir. On their present route, if a horse went lame or any accident occurred to the wheels of the chaise, they would be at the mercy of whatever poor farmer they chanced upon. The road was primarily used by smugglers and other persons who had little wish to be traced.

And this reflexion made Garia's heart skip a beat, for it suddenly occurred to her that Mr. Ruan might not be taking her to Kilkenny. Although he was most definitely carrying her farther and farther from Dromana, and for reasons that might have nothing at all to do with the children, or Josepha.

17

Possessions,
not people, is all you value.
— Irish Poem

Garia tried to damp the fever of panic that threatened to consume her, but it was a futile attempt, and her voice was unsteady as she said, "Mr. Ruan, I wish you would tell your coachman to stop at once. I want to turn back." He looked over at her curiously, but because his eyes failed to quite meet hers, it was confirmation of her unwelcome suspicion. "It's just as I thought, then," she whispered. "We *aren't* following my stepmother to Kilkenny."

A guilty flush spread across the lawyer's face. "No," he confessed. "But I can explain. When you understand why — "

"I don't care about any explanation," she interrupted. "I only want to find Bennet and Egan."

"They are in no danger, I swear it," he hastened to assure her. "It is probable that they are still at Carrick with Lady Ivory. I merely took advantage of her absence, for she has not taken the children. Forgive me for causing you such worry, and for practising this small deception, but I had to get you under my protection and it seemed the best way."

"But it is not your *place* to protect me!" she protested. "You must take me back to Dromana at once, Mr. Ruan!"

"Not yet," was his firm, unyielding reply. He reached for her hand and when she shrank from him, he added more gently, "You needn't be afraid. We will talk, and you will see that I've taken the right — the only possible action under the circumstances. We'll be stopping at a public house just this side of the river, fast by the bridge. I shall bespeak a private parlour for ourselves, and I shall lay everything before you while we take some refreshment."

Garia saw that he would not be dissuaded from this course, and it was all she could do to keep from screaming her frustration. Why did he refuse to turn back? And how many miles lay between them and Dromana House, she wondered, wishing she had paid more attention to the landmarks they'd passed along the way.

The pace slowed, and the chaise pulled up in the muddy yard of the Rock and Anchor, a small tavern perched on the bank of the

River Suir. After they alighted, the gap-toothed publican showed them into a filthy front parlour and grudgingly asked their desires. Mr. Ruan requested a pot of tea and some bread and cheese, while Garia, most disheartened by her dismal, dirty surroundings, sat down at the small table. In a short time the food was quickly and unceremoniously deposited on it, and the landlord took himself off.

"You had best eat something," Mr. Ruan told Garia, pushing the plate towards her. "I have no way of knowing when we will dine."

"But aren't you going to take me home?"

"No," he said quietly, "not immediately."

"But when? My family will be so worried, and goodness knows what sort of mischief Josepha will get up to in my absence," she added.

"Lady Ivory will not trouble you for much longer, Garia, of that you may be sure." He reached across the table and put his hand on her arm. "My dear, by the time we go back to Dromana, we shall be man and wife." As she stared back at him mutely, he continued, "I am determined to make you Mrs. Ruan before Lord Lindal returns from Dublin. And when he does, I will take great pleasure in informing him that his damned betrothal contract is of use only for lighting a fire!"

Garia felt the colour drain from her face, for there was no doubt in her mind that he was perfectly serious. "But I don't want to marry you," she said, "and the Earl has already returned. Last night he gave me this." She held out her shaking hand to show him the diamond betrothal ring.

"But today *I* will give you a wedding ring!" he told her brightly. With great deliberation and the satisfied smile of a man playing his trump card, the lawyer removed a small gold band from his breast pocket, then a paper, which he brandished at her. "I procured this special licence before Lord Lindal ever came to Ireland. For even though I hadn't yet stated my intentions to you then, I nevertheless regarded you as my promised wife. And I still do."

Garia shook her head at him and said, "I don't understand why. Have I ever given you any reason to suppose I regret my engagement?"

He further startled her by saying, "Indeed you have, though you may not realise it. Garia, you are too fine and good for a man like Lindal, who does not have your best interests at heart. He will uproot you from the home you love, from Dromana, where you belong. You'll be thrust into the society he prefers — have you ever asked yourself how you'll fare in the company of his aristocratic London friends? They will regard you as an Irishwoman, an alien." His voice took on a bitter quality when he said, "I have lived amongst the English, as you have not, and have experienced their strong prejudice against our race."

"But I have thought about these things," she answered, "and they matter not at all. Nothing will persuade me to marry you, not ever. You've made a grave mistake, Mr. Ruan, if you thought that by playing upon my insecurities you might move me to accept your proposal." She abandoned her chair so swiftly that it nearly toppled over, and standing before him, her fists clenched at her side, she said, "I can't believe that you, my friend, would try to *force* me to the altar."

He smiled faintly and replied, "I was not contemplating anything so dramatic — or drastic. I think, Garia, that you'd best resign yourself to the fact that by tomorrow you must become my bride or be ruined by your refusal."

Garia opened her mouth to call for the landlord, then closed it, for she knew no support lay in that quarter. Charles Ruan had money enough to bribe the man, and she had none. And unfortunately, abductions were not only common, they were enthusiastically endorsed by the peasantry, who inevitably championed the abductor. That had been proved three decades ago during the lamentable affair involving the Kennedy sisters, so famous in the south of Ireland that it had achieved the status of legend.

Anne and Catherine Kennedy of County Kilkenny, coheiresses to their late father's modest but highly exaggerated fortune, had been courted by a Mr. Byrne and a Mr. Strange. This pair of enterprising young bucks had followed the established custom of organising a party of their friends to help them kidnap the girls. The terrified sisters were forced to take part in a marriage ceremony, but afterwards had staunchly refused to accept the young men as their husbands. For a full five weeks their heartless captors dragged them from town to town, county to county, showing them off to the interested populace, until the poor girls had finally been rescued and restored to their widowed mother.

"Abduction is a capital offense in Ireland," she stated in the hope that this reminder would move her misguided swain. "Mr. Byrne and Mr. Strange were hanged for it, you know."

"My dear Garia," he said, rising from the table, "your situation is hardly comparable to that of the Kennedy girls. You were not carried off at gunpoint by a party of ruffians. As you may recall, you entered my chaise willingly, and without a word of protest."

"Only because you deceived me!"

He shrugged. "Even if you tried to lay a charge against me, our prior attachment would assure me of the jurors' sympathy."

"But Lord Lindal — "

"He is definitely not a man to embroil himself in a sordid trial, for of all things scandal is most distasteful to persons of his order. I hate to destroy your illusions about masculine chivalry, but to be quite frank, not even the Earl would champion a female with so tarnished a reputation as yours will be when your disappearance becomes known."

As he approached her she cried angrily, "Do not dare to touch me!"

He shrugged, then walked over to the door. He looked back to say, "I trust that after a period of reflexion, you'll agree that we should seek out a priest without delay."

When Garia heard the unmistakable sound of a key turning in the lock, she began to tremble all over, a reaction to the fear and fury she experienced from such treatment. She was as helpless as a rabbit in a snare, and oh, what a fine trap had been set for her!

Charles Ruan had laid his plans with great care — possibly in collusion with Josepha, Garia told herself bitterly, for there was no denying he had arrived on the scene in a very timely fashion, and at a moment when she had been too distraught to think clearly. He had shown her that note, which on the face of it had not been especially incriminating. And his suggestion that she go upstairs to get a wrap had not been a kindness; it had been a ruse to get her out of the room. What message had he left for Jeremy, or had he failed to write one at all? He'd been very quick to bundle her into the waiting chaise, with those fresh horses so conveniently between the shafts, and had given her no opportunity to consider some other, more effective measure.

As she paced the confines of the small parlour, the dreadful fate of the Kennedy sisters was foremost in her mind. After all of their many sufferings at the hands of that ruthless party of gentlemen, who had inflicted threats and even physical violence, Anne and Catherine had undergone the indignity of a trial. And they, the innocent parties, had been reviled for what the public deemed their heartless refusal to save their lawful husbands from the gallows. Thereafter, whenever they appeared in Waterford or Kilkenny, they were hissed and hooted by the crowd. Eventually both girls had married other men, but neither had been happy; all in all, their lives had been destroyed by a tragedy in which they had been the victims.

It was this aspect of the thirty-two-year-old scandal that most concerned Garia. Mr. Ruan might not have laid a finger on her — yet — but she was as good as ruined already. He had been right when he'd said no one would take her side; too many people were aware of his long courtship of her, and her reception of it. And if the tale of the long-forgotten betrothal contract ever came to light, it would paint Torin in the colours of an encroaching villain. An English one at that, for he had lived abroad too long to be accepted as a true Irishman. And Garia was too well acquainted with her countrymen to suppose they would side with a nobleman against a commoner, particularly one like Charles Ruan, who had vastly improved his station in life through hard work.

But Garia was even more disturbed when it occurred to her that Torin might well believe she'd been planning to run away with the lawyer all along. He had already demonstrated some suspicion of her relations with Mr. Ruan as a result of her concealing the truth of their meeting in Waterford. And just last night she had angered him by mentioning that she had turned to her friend and former suitor for advice. Torin might even regard her apparent defection as some sort of revenge for the slight he had inflicted upon her a decade ago when he jilted her.

She ceased her increasingly frantic perambulations and walked over to the single casement window. It was coated with grime so thick that the latch was permanently stuck. Any attempt to break it would be next to useless, for the glass panes were small and thick and closely leaded together.

Then she remembered that she did have one instrument of salvation at her disposal and retrieved her muff. Reaching inside, she closed her fingers around the pencil stub. She knew it was a gamble, but if she wrote a plea for help, properly phrased to appeal to the landlord or one of the servants, it might elicit some sort of response.

The bill for the food was tucked beneath the chipped teapot, and she dislodged it. Turning it over to the blank side, she printed plainly: *"A lady in distress desires that some word of her circumstances be sent to Cloncavan Castle, parish of St. Anne."* Then she crossed through the last two words and beneath them wrote "St. Brendan." The proprietor of the Rose and Crown would be a Catholic, and there was a greater likelihood that he would have heard of the Roman church at Cloncavan.

The sound of the key in the lock warned her of Mr. Ruan's return, and she hastily replaced the bill beneath the teapot, making sure the side with the itemized charges was facing upwards. She tried to appear unconcerned as he entered the room.

He carried a full wineglass, which he held out to her, saying, "I think you'll find that this will compose you as that tea will never do."

Fighting the urge to dash the contents in his face, Garia accepted it, for she stood in desperate need of courage and cared not that it had been poured from a bottle. As she sipped, she eyed the gentleman warily over the rim of the glass and saw that he was similarly watchful and appeared to be on edge.

When she had drained the wineglass of most of its contents, she set it down on the table and said quietly, "Mr. Ruan, a little while ago you were all concern for me and my prospects of happiness with the Earl, but somehow it did not ring true. I know you dislike him, but I can't believe vengeance is your only motive for doing this heinous thing. And if you truly cared for me, you would never have placed my reputation in so much danger. I possess no fortune, nothing of any value to tempt you. Why, then, have you taken this step?"

"Nothing of value, Garia? But surely you haven't forgotten Dromana." He spoke the name slowly, gently, as if it belonged to a woman he loved.

Her head jerked upwards and she stared at him in astonishment. "But you've a fortune of your own, and a fine residence in town. Why should you care about a shabby, run-down house and land that is as unproductive as mine?"

He smiled at her and shook his head. "But after I've made enclosures, and as soon as I evict the more useless of your tenants, it will be an extremely profitable estate."

"You presume too much," Garia warned him, her eyes flashing. "Neither I nor my inheritance will ever be yours!"

Taking a step towards her, he said, "Then you delude yourself. Why, I believe your own father meant for me to succeed him as master of Dromana, and so I shall. If I hadn't prevailed upon him to leave the estate to you, you would not be its mistress. The property would have been sold and after the settlement of all debts any money left over would have been divided three ways, amongst you, your sister, and your stepmother."

"But I don't understand," Garia said, perplexed. "Are you saying Papa meant to make some provision for Josepha?"

"By law a widow is entitled to one-third of her deceased husband's property," Mr. Ruan explained. "Yet I knew Lady Ivory had not the means to fight her exclusion from Sir Andrew's will. During his last illness, I persuaded him that she deserved no bequest. And because I pointed out that Lord Kelsey had made ample settlements upon your sister, in the end he agreed that you alone should inherit Dromana."

This intent, steely-eyed Charles Ruan was a stranger to Garia, and she whispered hoarsely, "All this time I've been afraid of Josepha, but it is you who are the enemy." She had been manipulated, conspired against, trapped — and by a man she had trusted implicitly, someone she had called friend and looked to for advice, never guessing it could be so wholly self-interested. "You've been scheming to get Dromana all this time, and I never guessed it."

His voice was hard and toneless, his face devoid of all expression when he said, "I am not ashamed of what I've done to achieve my rightful position. As a boy I saw my parents — of pure Irish blood and the true Irish church — struggle and starve and die. My father would not accept work nor would he take charity from others, and from him I learned the dangers of misplaced pride. I submitted to the indignity of being sent away to a charity school, and tried to seem grateful when a parish subscription saw me through university. I laboured hard at my studies, and harder still at my profession when I returned to Ireland." The lawyer's face twisted as he said, "I swallowed my pride each time your father and Sir John Neale and the late Earl patronised me, putting a little business my way like a bone tossed to a clever dog. I even gave up the religion of my forefathers, that I might become a property owner one day. So do not put your fine nose in the air and tell me you had rather not wed me, Garia Ivory. I've done everything in my power to make myself a gentleman and worthy of a gentleman's daughter."

"You can't call yourself a gentleman," Garia shot back when he paused for breath, and her voice shook with loathing. "And don't flatter yourself that you're a man of the people, for if you truly cared for the sufferings of others, you'd not be so eager to make enclosures and force good Irishmen from their land!"

"I don't expect you to approve of my methods, but in time — "

"An eternity would not be time enough to erase my contempt of you." But her words were not as forceful as she had intended them to be, because she suddenly felt drained of all emotion. She fought to hold her head upright, but it required a great effort. "I feel so ill," she murmured, groping for a chair.

And then her befogged mind seized upon the cause of her lassitude, and she looked up at the lawyer accusingly. "The wine — you've drugged the wine." Her legs gave way, but he was at her side, his arm around her waist, and she was too weak to push him away.

"Just a little laudanum, Garia, that is all, to calm you. To help you sleep for a little while."

Her eyelids fell, shutting him out, and she remembered something Josepha had said about laudanum — and India. "The nights are so hot," she repeated over and over, parrot-like, as he wrapped her cloak around her. She didn't struggle when he led her out of the room and along a corridor. He lifted her in his arms and carried her down several steps, and then the ground beneath his feet gave way; he struggled to keep his balance.

She was slipping out of consciousness by the time he laid her down upon some sort of bed. Her cheek brushed rough canvas, and she was vaguely aware of a rocking motion, almost as though she were on the sea. Or in the rowboat with Torin, as they had been on the day of the Cloncavan picnic. If only she could open her eyes, so she might see the river-walk, and the green lawn and the Castle again — but even that simple act was beyond her, so she gave in to sleep.

18

O'er mountain, moor and marsh, by greenwood, lough and hollow, I tracked her distant footsteps with a throbbing heart.
— Egan O'Rahilly

After a long and arduous morning in the saddle, the Earl of Lindal returned to Cloncavan Castle with his cousin Thomas and Jeremy Howard, whom he had invited to dine. Throughout the meal the boy and Mr. Montrose aired their disparate theories on the proper feeding of foxhounds. Torin contributed little to this debate, and from time to time glanced thoughtfully at the mantel clock. He'd been disappointed by Garia's failure to join the hunt, but had set her absence down to nothing more momentous than an unfortunate domestic crisis at Dromana House. Jeremy had explained about his sister's duty visit to some old pensioner, but the hands of the clock stood well past noon, and angel that she was, it was highly unlikely that Garia had been seated at the bedside of an ailing servant this long while.

His lordship's speculation about Miss Ivory's whereabouts and present activity was interrupted when the stately Cobbe entered the dining room to announce that Lady Ivory had called. Torin, noting the angry thrust of Jeremy's jaw, told his butler to show her ladyship into the blue salon. "Tell her I'll be with her directly," he said, laying down his fork.

"Must you receive her?" Jeremy asked, when the butler left to carry out his master's order.

Torin smiled as he rose from the table. "Don't look so distressed, young cub. I expect your sister has sent her here with some message."

Jeremy's brow cleared. "I suppose so." He renewed his attack upon his bread and butter and returned to the argument with Thomas, his mind apparently at rest.

But at heart Torin was not so hopeful as his words had indicated, for he had instantly suspected Garia's plaguey stepmother of coming to make trouble. He paused on the threshold of the salon and inspected his visitor, who was seated in a delicate chair on the far side of the room.

It had been some eight years since he had last seen the former Mrs. Howard, and he was amazed to discover that time had not damaged her bounteous good looks. The auburn hair was still rich and lustrous, the eyes were the same brilliant blue, and her complexion was as flawless as ever. But whatever her history had been since their last meeting, it had left its marks, and her enchanting visage was somehow the more interesting for it. She was near his own age, he supposed, but could still pass for a younger woman. He had been entirely immune to her opulent beauty years ago, and now he found her even more resistible. Her face and figure moved him not at all, for his heart and mind carried the image of a certain dark-haired lady, slender and graceful as an aspen, whose sweet face was dearer to him than any other he had ever seen or would see.

Josepha, aware of his scrutiny, had risen. "How long has it been since we met?" she asked in the striking voice he remembered so well. "You were Viscount Melbury in those days, and never one of my admirers, for which Garia must be profoundly thankful. I hope you told her so."

Her frankness amused him. "I did."

"Is she here?"

"No, Lady Ivory, she is not. Garia failed to meet the hunt this morning." Only then did it occur to him that the lady, who looked capable of sustaining anything, was quite pale and evidently distressed by this reply.

"Oh, I was so *sure* she must be here — I was hoping!" Her enormous eyes searched his face. "Jeremy has not seen her either?"

"I can vouch for the fact that he has not — we have been together all day. Were you unaware that Garia paid a visit to one of her pensioners this morning? Perhaps she rode from there to join the hunt as she intended and got lost. If that is the case — "

"Lost? Garia?" Josepha gave a weak laugh. "She knows this country too well for that. But no, Brutus is even now in his box and has not been ridden today."

Fear began to inch its way down Torin's spine, but he remained outwardly calm as he bid Lady Ivory be seated. "There must be a logical explanation for her absence. She might have wandered off with the younger boys, or — "

"They were with me. We drove to Carrick this morning to visit the shops." Josepha bit her lip and looked down at her saffron-coloured lap. "When we returned, we found the servants in an uproar. How old McCurdie's jaw dropped when I entered the house with the children! At first I paid him no mind — you know how Irish servants always put the worst face on everything, and with the slightest of causes. I fancied Garia might have returned to Dromana without being seen and joined the hunt as planned. But when Erris said that he was never ordered to saddle Brutus, I began to worry. And then McCurdie said Garia had run off with Mr. Ruan, and I knew I must come to you, however much I dread the appearance of talebearing."

Both occupants of the salon were startled when Jeremy, who had been listening from the doorway, flung himself into the room. "What have you done to drive Garia away?" he asked his mother furiously. "I hate you — all of us hate you!"

Torin gripped the angry boy by the shoulders and gave him a strong shake. "Jeremy, control yourself! Your outburst is nothing to the purpose. Lady Ivory, are you quite sure Mr. Ruan was at Dromana today?"

"Yes. McCurdie swears Garia went off with him in his chaise. I can think of only one reason she would have done so," Josepha said gravely, "although I cannot believe it of her."

Jeremy broke free of Torin's slackened hold. "You may try to shift the blame to Mr. Ruan, but if Garia has gone, it's all because of *you*!"

Josepha flinched. "It may be that I did have a hand in her disappearance, but it was all unknowing."

"Tell me all that you do know — and quickly!" was Torin's urgent command.

Josepha took a deep breath. "Well, to begin with, Mr. Ruan summoned me from Paris. I doubt very much Garia is aware of it."

"What do you mean, he *summoned* you?"

"That is the only word for it, because a few weeks ago he wrote to tell me I was entitled to some money. And although I'd never considered returning to Ireland, I was in need of funds, and" — she glanced toward Jeremy — "it was an opportunity to see my sons again. But as soon as I arrived in Waterford, I realised I had come on a fool's errand, for the lawyer then claimed he had been mistaken about the bequest to me. Still, he offered to give me a large sum himself, if only I would agree to help him win his way back into Garia's good graces."

"Go on," Torin said grimly.

"He instructed me to pretend that I'd come here to lay claim to my late husband's estate and threaten Garia with a lawsuit. He seemed to think she would then turn to him for advice."

"What else did he say?"

"He promised to send my sons to a good school if that was my wish." Once more Josepha glanced at Jeremy, who was standing stiffly beside the Earl, and she said sadly, "I haven't been a good mother — well, no mother at all, to be perfectly candid. But I do want the best for my boys. What woman does not? I could never afford to educate them or to help them into careers by myself, but Mr. Ruan, I judged, was well able to do so. So when I reached Dromana, I played the part of grasping woman to the hilt. But the next day I learned of Garia's engagement to you, and I began to suspect Ruan's hopes of wedding her were wholly unfounded."

Torin turned to Jeremy. "Hurry to the stables, my boy, and tell Con O'Patrick to harness my greys to the curricle immediately! And I want Mr. Montrose horsed and ready to ride as soon as possible. Quickly, now, Jeremy! You, too, must prepare for some fast riding — we may have to scour the countryside for news of your sister. Are you up to it?"

"I should say so!" the youth replied staunchly.

"Garia's reputation may well be at stake, so not a word to anyone of our purpose. Understood?"

Jeremy nodded, and with one final accusing glance at his parent, he raced out of the room.

Torin walked over to the window, struggling to contain the emotions that threatened to overwhelm him. After a moment he said coolly, "Now, Josepha — you don't mind if I call you so? What was it you hoped to gain when you told Garia you intended to take your sons away?"

"But I never did that," she told him, startled.

"I distinctly recall her saying that was your intention. She said she must either give up Dromana to you, or lose the boys."

"Mr. Ruan may have told her something to that effect," Josepha said angrily, "but it's not true! I hope I know better than to ask Garia to give up the children, for I am in no doubt of what her reply would be — she'd tell me to go straight to the devil! Nor would I pain her by making such a demand, for I've always honoured her for her love of my sons. So Ruan told lies about me, did he?" The blue eyes glittered dangerously as she said, "Lord Lindal, I hope you find that villain and run him through, and not only for Garia's sake! All along he has been most insulting, treating me like a harlot. Which I never was, whatever else I may have been!"

Torin smiled, but it was a mechanical gesture, and devoid of warmth. He rang for the butler and asked for his driving coat and a pair of pistols, then turned back to Josepha. "You may be sure Ruan will answer for his crimes — all of them. I must ask that you return to Dromana for the present. Do not refuse, for I have no need of you now, and you've already done a great deal to assist our effort to find Garia. But you'll be an even greater help by keeping Bennet and Egan comforted, and in as much ignorance about the true circumstances as possible. And I need hardly add that the same applies for the servants."

"Yes, but what will I say? McCurdie and the rest know that she went off with Mr. Ruan."

"You must strive to keep them quiet about it."

Josepha followed him to the door, saying, "My lord, I hope she hasn't — that is, you don't think she would go with him willingly, do you?"

"I don't know," he admitted.

Josepha's downcast face was transformed by her beautiful, brilliant smile as she said encouragingly, "Well, I can't believe Garia would play you false, and certainly not with such a creature as that, my lord. Sinners that we have been, you and I, and reformed rakes that we now are, both of us know better than to judge her too hastily. I pray you will find her quickly, my lord — and Godspeed!"

Torin gripped her outstretched hand, then ran down the front steps. Before climbing into his waiting curricle, he paused to speak to Jeremy and Thomas, both on horseback. The search party dispersed beyond the Castle gates: Thomas rode toward Carrick-on-Suir and points north, while Jeremy galloped *ventre-à-terre* in the direction of Waterford. Torin was prey to a nagging doubt about the efficiency of this system, but it was the best he could devise. The horses might be fresh but the riders were not, having been in the saddle since early morn, and moreover, Ruan was already many miles and several hours to the advantage.

He and Con O'Patrick set out for Kilkenny on one of the lesser roads. At the Blackthorne Tree, a posting house along the way, they learned that Mr. Ruan's chaise had been seen to pass by earlier in the day. This intelligence was enough to convince Lindal that he had blundered onto the scent; he decided to stick to the country lane, which wove its way toward the River Suir.

"Which town lies across the bridge, Con?" he asked his groom as they bowled along.

" 'Tis Fiddown, your honour."

Along the way Torin considered what he would do when he met up with Ruan. First he must determine whether or not Garia had been constrained to accompany him. But if the lawyer's object had been to force her into marriage, Torin would take great pleasure in calling him out for it. He had faced more than one man from a distance of twenty paces, and with far less provocation. The thought of his gentle love in the clutches of a desperate man was unendurable; if Ruan was so consumed by jealousy that he would abduct Garia, he might be capable of anything.

Torin tried not to believe the worst, that Garia had been a willing party to an elopement with her former suitor. But when he recalled her strange manner of late, it was hard to disregard that possibility. She had always defended the lawyer and called him her friend. And Torin had never been completely convinced that she accepted their betrothal. But if she loved Ruan, she was a more accomplished actress than he'd ever guessed, because she had never given the slightest hint that she held the man in affection.

Torin now regretted his failure to enter the lists against the attorney from the beginning; he should have courted Garia first, thereby granting her the opportunity to make a free choice. That would have been more risky, of course, but at least he would not be eaten up with uncertainties about her feelings. He knew he had acted recklessly in using the betrothal contract to coerce her into an engagement. In the process he may have ruined his chances of ever winning her love, besides making an enemy of his rival. And Torin knew that although he'd been more than half in love with the lady at the time, his had been a ruthless stratagem, which the lawyer had now answered with an act of equal ruthlessness.

These bitter reflexions were interrupted by Con's thoughtful voice. "Ye know, your honour, I was a fisherman once. I've been thinkin' this whileen that if 'twere me, an' I was hopin' not to be followed nor found, what I'd do is lose my carriage and hie to the water."

Torin looked over at him and asked, "Do you mean the sea, Con? But we're nearly twenty miles from the coast."

The groom shook his head. "Nay, your honour, not the sea, but the river! The River Suir flows toward Waterfordtown, where this Ruan lives. And where there's churches and priests, and a port, if he was wishful of hiring a fishing boat or taking a smuggler's vessel out of the country."

Struck by this observation, Torin said consideringly, "You know, Con, I believe you may have something there. And how might we determine whether or not our man has resorted to the waterway?"

"Oh, there's taverns and inns all along the Suir. 'Tis a gamble, but one nivver knows what one will find along a waterfront!"

"Are you acquainted with any of boatmen's haunts?"

"Nay. But even your lordship's honour must have heard tell o' the Rock and Anchor, fast by the bridge."

"I have not, but it is high time I put an end to my ignorance." Torin teased the greys with his whip, a new hope rising in his heart.

When they reached the Rock and Anchor, Torin left the curricle in the hands of an unprepossessing urchin loitering in the yard and pulled a pistol out of his deep coat pocket. He handed it to Con, saying, "Keep this by you, but take care — it's loaded and will go off at a touch. I've another with me. Come along — let's find the proprietor of this seedy establishment with no loss of time."

They found their quarry in the taproom, leaning against the bar. He was a stocky individual with a thatch of unruly hair that had greyed to a faint pinkish colour from its original red. He glared at his potential customers in a far from friendly fashion and said belligerently, "What might ye be wantin'?"

"A word with you, no more," Torin said. "Did a carriage and four stop here earlier today?"

"'Tis bitter weather for travel," was the evasive reply.

Torin reached into his pocket and brought forth a silver coin, which he regarded speculatively. "That is true," he conceded.

"Well," said the publican, shifting from one foot to another as he, too, eyed the shilling, "it *may* be that I remember a carriage stopping here just before noontime."

"And perhaps you might tell me what sort of conveyance your visitors may have hired from you."

"Not me horse, for him I've loaned to Liam Glanbally to pull his cart," the old man declared, grinning at what he deemed his own wit. "And I keep no carts nor carriages." He wheezed sibilantly through the gap in his front teeth.

Torin and his groom exchanged glances. "And what of boats? Did you, by chance, provide one for a lady and gentleman sometime this morning?"

The old fellow smiled, a crafty grimace, and asked, "How much might yer honour be wishful of knowin'? And how much might ye pay for me to spill it?"

Con took umbrage at this. "Watch yourself, gaffer. 'Tis the Earl o' Lindal ye're talkin' to!"

"That's enough, Con. Go wait for me in the curricle. I won't be long."

The publican, unimpressed by titles, spat on the floor. "Aye, ye're an Earl, maybe, and an Englishman, belike. We have no love for such in these parts."

"An unnecessary prejudice — my title is as Irish as the dirt beneath your feet. Are you going to answer my questions, or must I speak with each of your employees in turn?"

"'Tis none but Molly, and she's no gobber." The pinkish brows moved downwards over the hooked nose, and the publican asked petulantly, "Ye're not the one from the castle, are ye?"

There was an arrested expression in Torin's eyes when he queried, "What castle?"

"I'm after forgettin' it meself. But wait." The stocky man turned towards the doorway and bellowed, "Molly!"

Footsteps sounded in the passage and a buxom young tavern maid barged into the taproom, her hands buried in an enormous black muff, an item of gentility that Torin recognised as Garia's property. The girl was obviously displeased by the peremptory summons and asked crossly, "Whyfore are ye bellowin' at me, old man?" But upon seeing Torin she bobbed a sketchy curtsey and added, "Good day to yer honour."

"Molly, what was the name o' that castle? Clonnycan? Cloncallan?"

"'Twas too many letters for me to be rememberin'," she said, shaking her curly head. Then, with another sidewise glance at Torin, she clutched the muff more tightly than ever. "Anyways, that letter has been destroyed entirely — I used it to set the kitchen fire."

Torin had seen and heard enough to convince him that he was on a very fresh scent indeed. Fixing the young woman with his most compelling frown, he demanded further information.

"Well," said the girl, "after the young lady fainted, the gentleman carried her down to the barge. Sure, and the only ones who knows where they be are the bargeman himself and his horse!"

"You say the lady swooned?"

The publican spoke up once more, as if jealous of the flattering attention his subordinate was receiving. "Aye, 'twas ill entirely she looked, poor lass! I ne'er saw anyone fall sick *before* they was on the water!" His chuckle was a ghastly rattle. "She e'en left her fur pillow behind, as ye can see. Molly found it on the floor when she went to tidy up the parlour."

"And I mean to keep it, sure!" the buxom beauty declared, a militant spark in her eye.

"The barge was bound for Wateyford-town," the old man called out as the gentleman exited the taproom, but his first attempt to be helpful was ignored.

Garia could not have gone with Ruan of her own free will, then, Torin told himself jubilantly. Somehow she had managed to pen a plea for help, and perhaps she had feigned some infirmity to slow the attorney down. And even if she really had fallen ill, her safety was assured, for not even Ruan would harm her further — or so he hoped. As Torin climbed into the curricle he realised that he still clutched the silver coin. He flung it impatiently into the mud before picking up the reins. Meeting Con's questioning glance he said grimly, "Waterford — by means of the river, just as you thought. Good God, we are an hour behind them now, possibly more! How fast *can a barge travel downriver?*"

Con sighed and his laconic reply was hardly encouraging. " 'Twould depend what the cargo and how heavy, your honour."

19

Brightness of weapons glints in the air,
Warriors' manifold voices shake
the frame of sky.
— Sedulius Scottus

A sudden, violent impact jolted Garia into consciousness. She opened her eyes and found herself in near-darkness. When she tried to move her head, she discovered that her neck was cramped from lying in one position too long, and she twisted this way and that to ease the stiffness. Her eyes ached and her mouth was painfully dry; she longed for a long drink of cool water. That, she knew, was an effect of the laudanum.

As she gradually grew accustomed to the darkness of her surroundings, she received the impression that she was lying in a low-ceilinged room. Small cracks in the ceiling let in tiny pinpoints of light, and from this she deduced that it was daytime still. Feeling about with her hands, she discovered that her bedding was a pile of damp canvas. Sails? Was she on some sort of ship? The sound of lapping water told her this must be true, yet there was no rocking, wavelike motion.

Her cloak was still wrapped close about her, and she derived some comfort from stroking the woollen cloth; something, at least, was familiar in this strange place. She must have lost her hat somewhere. Or had she been wearing one before? Cobwebs clogged her mind and memory — another lingering effect of the drug. She sank back upon the canvas, closing her eyes, and forced her groggy mind to sort through the events that had led to her present confused state.

She could hear someone pacing the floorboards above, and Charles Ruan's voice growled, "You fool, I did not pay you so handsomely to run me aground!" At the sound of another voice, that of a stranger, she lifted her head again.

"Now how was I to know my tow-horse would break his harness?" the other man asked. "By Peter and all the Saints, I ought nivver to have touched your honour's money. It's mad I was to agree to transport a female downriver, and she so sick, poor lady. 'Twas dead entirely she looked, and I'll not be carryin' no corpses into the port! There's no way I can make the Watey-ford docks in the time you set! 'Tis a heavy burden we carry — a load of quarried stone is no featherweight!"

"Keep your voice down, Sheehy. We must shove off this bank at once."

Even in her half-waking state Garia realised the import of this complaint. They were on the river and not on the high seas — she was not so very far from Dromana after all! Their conveyance must be one of the barges that carried goods from Carrick to Waterford, and she lay in the tiny hold.

She heard the pounding of thick, heavy boots on wooden planks, then the stranger spoke again. "We can do nothing without my poor runaway beast."

"Then *you* can chase after him," Mr. Ruan said sharply. "For if we aren't on our way within the hour, you'll not receive the bonus I promised!"

Garia heard the faint click of his watch snapping shut, and she knew he stood on the other side of the door. She abated her breathing and lay motionless, lest he hear her and enter. One of her legs felt numb and prickly, but she didn't even dare to flex it. If he should enter, she would feign sleep rather than reveal her wakefulness. She would feign death, if need be, and serve him right to think he had killed her. Laudanum! Only let him think she had died of the stuff: then he would be in a quandary.

She wished she knew where on the Suir they

had run aground. The river coursed a scant two miles from Cloncavan at one point on its winding route to Waterford. She tried to remember the names of the other villages that dotted its banks, but the exercise benefitted her not at all, for the vessel could just as easily have come to a halt along one of the broad stretches of waste land, miles from any town.

She could not let Ruan carry her to Waterford, where he probably intended to find some waterfront church and wed her while she was still under the effect of the drug. In the darkness she clenched her fists and thrust out her chin. If he had reckoned upon her bending to his will like a scared and silly schoolgirl, he was mistaken. Somehow she would manage to get away from him, and if she failed, she would refuse all food and drink from his hands. And if he tried to force himself on her in some way, she would fight him with all of her strength.

She heard splashing and thumping, interspersed with curses in Gaelic and English as the two men attempted to dislodge the barge from the bank. The bargeman was adamant in his belief that one of them should seek help at the nearest village — a suggestion that found no favour with the lawyer. Garia smiled to hear Charles Ruan denounce the bargeman as a villain, and she rained silent blessings on the head of the stubborn Sheehy.

Torin and his groom had ridden only a few miles southwards from the Rock and Anchor when they came to another public house by the river. Whether or not it actually possessed a licence permitting the purveyance of spiritous liquors was doubtful, but a half dozen men sat in brokendown chairs outside, and each clutched a mug of ale in his beefy fist.

"Take the reins, Con, and wait for me here," Torin commanded his henchman before climbing down from the curricle. He strode towards the group of men, whose mouths fell agape at the sight of so elegant an equipage and so distinguished a gentleman in their rural midst. At his approach they rose as one, offering various and sundry greetings, largely unintelligible. There was much tugging at caps; one short, wiry fellow, obviously the proprietor of the dubious establishment, asked if he might draw some ale for the gentleman's honour.

Torin declined this handsome offer. "Can you tell me if a barge has lately passed this vantage point?" He addressed the publican but his glance included the entire company.

The wiry gentleman scratched his matted black head. "Peter Sheehy passed by a whileen ago, yer honour. There's nothing to wonder at in that, for he does so twice a week, but 'tis true he was veering mightily off course."

"His pony looked a mite skittish," said another. "Faith, he'll have run aground did he continue that way."

"'Twas my suspicion that poor Peter had drink taken. Though sure, 'tis not like him, he bein' a sober, well-behaved lad."

"Had he any passengers?"

"I couldn't say, yer honour. Sure, and someone could have been down in the hold, but who's to say?" The man lifted one bony shoulder with the question.

"I thought I saw a man standin' on the deck," someone offered helpfully.

The eldest of the group said scathingly, "Don't ye be listenin' to *him*. He's as poor-sighted as Tam O'Leary's blind dog, that one!"

"What cargo does this Sheehy carry?" Torin asked.

"Sometimes limestone or marble from the quarries at Kilkenny, sometimes barley." The short man grinned out one side of his mouth as he said, "Now, I'm not after sayin' there wasn't a mite o' potheen on that barge as well. 'Twould be a miracle an there wasn't! Peter's brother brews the best and charges him with takin' it to their cousin at Watey-ford now and again."

A chorus of "Aye" and " 'Tis true enough"

and several guffaws greeted this sally. Torin bid the men good-day, and left them to speculate about him at great length.

His greys were fast goers, but they were nearly destroyed by the pace he had set thus far. Nevertheless, he did not scruple to whip them into a gallop and told Con to keep a watch for the barge.

"There 'tis!" the groom cried a few minutes later, pointing toward the river. "Sure, and they've run aground, your honour. There's Ruan and the bargeman tryin' to shift it, but I don't see no tow-horse. Nor the lady," he realised.

Torin reined in beside a stand of trees that he hoped would conceal the curricle for the time being. The two men were as yet unaware of his presence, for their heads and backs were bent as they tried to dislodge the craft from the riverbank. That this was a futile effort was obvious. "Let me have my other pistol," he told Con, "and if aught happens to me, see Miss Ivory safely back to Dromana." He sprang down from the carriage and began making his way stealthily toward the stranded vessel.

Garia began to explore her tiny, low-ceilinged prison, knowing that her movements would go undetected so long as Charles Ruan and Sheehy struggled to free the barge. Although her limbs were weak, she managed to pull herself into a kneeling position and crawl slowly through the darkness towards the door, frequently tripping on the mounds of sailcloth in her path. Her progress was further impeded by several heavy objects, and she crouched down to determine what they were. As she swept her hands across each cool, glazed surface, she had to stifle her impulse to laugh out loud. Jugs, a dozen of them at least, and they could contain only one thing: Irish potheen.

She eased one cork up and wrinkled her nose in distaste as the fumes assailed her nostrils. But thirsty as she was, she would not resort to drinking the stuff, for its effect would be as debilitating as the laudanum.

She resumed her laborious way towards the small door, which she discovered to be so warped and cracked that her slightest push was sufficient to open it. The light outside hit Garia's eyes with blinding force, and she shivered as the wind struck her. She didn't see Ruan or the bargeman, but she could hear both of them huffing and heaving. Opening the door a few inches more, she saw that she was only a few feet away from the riverbank. She climbed to her feet and gathered up the long skirt of her habit, but just as she was about to negotiate the two steps to the deck a movement on the higher ground above caught her eye.

It was Torin, and he was making his way slowly and stealthily down the sloping hillside. He held a deadly-looking pistol in his hand, and his dear, dark face was contorted with an anger so intense that Garia scarcely recognised him. On a sharp intake of breath, she hurriedly backed into the hold, for as much as she longed to rush to him, she dared not give him away. But her heart hammered so furiously from her exertions and her joy that she fancied Charles Ruan could hear it.

He couldn't, and it was sheer impulse that prompted him to give up his labours and look in on his prisoner. The lawyer was halfway across the deck when a sudden command stayed him.

"Stop there, Ruan," Torin called, stepping out from behind an oak. "If you take another step, you'll regret it."

In a lightning motion, the lawyer thrust his hand into his coat pocket and brought forth a pistol of his own.

Torin and his adversary faced each other like a pair of angry, stiff-legged dogs, their weapons pointed chest high. "Where is Garia?" he asked.

To his great relief, a faint, disembodied

voice responded from below. "I'm here!"

"Stay out of the way then, until I give the all clear," Torin told her before saying furiously, "By God, Ruan, you will answer for this."

"You'll be in no condition to accept my answer, Lord Lindal," Mr. Ruan replied, sneering. "I'll put a bullet in you and be off without a blink. By sundown Miss Ivory will be my wife, and it will be as though you had never crossed her path!"

"A forced marriage is not a legal one, as you of all men should know," said Torin in a steely voice. "And Garia will be a most reluctant bride, knowing as soon she will the extent of your perfidy. Lady Ivory has explained a great deal, so you may as well accept that your game is at an end."

"I'd expect a rogue like you to believe the lies of a whore!" was the lawyer's reply.

Torin's pistol hand twitched. "You will answer for that insult to her ladyship, as well as for abducting Miss Ivory!"

Mr. Sheehy, a stunned observer of this exchange, suddenly exclaimed, "Sure, and he nivver told me 'twas abduction! I'll have no part in such — and will be takin' meself off after me poor horse, leavin' both your honours to your quarrel." He walked past the tall gentleman in the long driving coat, and to his surprise and delight was given a pistol and commanded to stay.

"Now, Ruan," Torin said triumphantly, "you are outmanned, and overpowered. Turn Garia over to me that I may send her back to Dromana with my groom. Then you and I can settle this between ourselves." But the other gentleman made no reply, and to his dismay, Ruan bounded down the shallow steps leading to the hold. Torin cried hoarsely, "Take care, Garia — stand aside from the door! He's coming your way!"

Frantically Garia felt along the floor for a stick, a board, some weapon with which to arm herself. Her hand connected with one of the jugs, and she struggled to lift it. Her arms were so weak, and she strained with the effort as she prepared to hurl the heavy object as forcefully as possible. But then a better plan occurred to her. She tugged at the cork, and managed to pull it out just as Charles Ruan flung open the door of the hold.

She dashed the contents of the jug into his face, and the clear liquid splashed over him. With an agonised cry he dropped his pistol and fell to his knees. Pressing his knuckles to his burning eyes, he cried out in pain.

Garia paid him no heed, but picked up her skirts and plunged through the door towards the fresh air and the light. She stumbled up the steps, and by the time Torin's strong arms closed around her, her legs had given away, but it didn't matter at all.

20

Our engagement is made now, and love in my heart for you, there's half of my soul that will never part from you.
— Owen Roe O'Sullivan

Charles Ruan, still rubbing his eyes, gasped in agony, "I'm *blinded!* I cannot open my eyes!"

The bargeman, who had been watching as the lordly gentleman embraced the lady, gave a sharp bark of laughter. "Nay, sir, the hurt will go off in a bit, I've no doubt. 'Tis well-served ye are for your evil, abductin' ways." He stepped forwards to say to Garia, "'Twas the cleverest thing I ever saw, Miss, and 'tis glad I am the potheen was to hand! Won't me brother laugh when I tell him how his brew was used this day! I only wish I'd thought o' that trick meself, though to be sure, I did what I could." He bent down to pick up the tow-rope and waved it gleefully.

"You cut the line yourself!" Garia cried as the bargeman grinned at her. "'Tis no wonder your horse ran off."

"Aye, 'twas all I could think to do by way of helpin'. Himself was so fierce, and you so ill."

Torin cocked an eye at Garia. "Shamming it, my love?"

"He put laudanum in my wine," she replied, continuing to lean on his supporting arm. "But Mr. Sheehy, what about your poor horse?"

"Oh, he's a good one, he is, and won't have strayed too far. I could've whistled him back had I wanted to."

"You ran aground very neatly," said Torin, "but don't be shocked when your friends charge you with being inebriated!" He pulled a small leather purse from his breast pocket and handed it to the bargeman with a smile. "Here, you've earned this, but it's hardly sufficient payment, for I'm greatly in your debt. I hope you will do me the favour of conveying your unwelcome passenger to Waterford. He'll not be any trouble to you now, and I've no wish to be bothered with him at present."

Sheehy nodded, his eyes twinkling. " 'Tis sure I am that ye don't. Shall I be givin' him over to the law?"

As Torin considered the question, his eyes never left the lady's worried face. "What do you say?" he asked gently. "I will happily swear a complaint against him, if that's your wish."

But Garia, drained of all rancour and incapable of feeling any emotion but relief, shook her head. "I cannot bear the gossip and outcry we'd provoke if we publicised his disgraceful action. If only I could be sure he will leave us in peace, for truly, that is all I care about."

Torin approached the afflicted gentleman, who still lay sprawled upon the steps. "I strongly advise you never to mention today's business to a living soul, Ruan. And if you continue to make trouble for Miss Ivory, or disturb her in any way, I swear I will ruin you most thoroughly, and take great joy in it. Do you understand me?" A vicious oath erupted from Mr. Ruan's lips, and Torin judged that his point had been well-taken.

He put an arm around Garia's waist and said gently, "Come now, we mustn't linger. It is so cold, and you know your family will want to know you're safe."

She looked up at him and asked, "The boys — they are well, aren't they?"

"Indeed they are, and wait for you at Dromana."

Satisfied, she permitted him to assist her up the hill. They found Con O'Patrick stretched out comfortably in the seat of the curricle, a blade of grass between his teeth. He jumped down, and as Torin helped

Garia into the vehicle, he offered his enthusiastic endorsement of her unorthodox tactics.

"I thought I told you to mind my horses," Torin said, but his smile belied the censorious words. He took up the ribbons and his whip, and asked, "Have you any money about you, Con?"

"Ay, m'lord."

"After you've help Sheehy find his horse, walk on to the nearest village and send some men back here to help him move his barge. Hire a horse for yourself at a posting-house and return home at your leisure. I have no more need of you."

Torin took his eyes away from his horses long enough to inspect Garia's weary countenance. "Ruan laid no finger on you, I trust? By God, if he did, I'll go back to finish the work you began so well!"

She clutched the sleeve of his driving coat as if to restrain him. "Oh, no, he never touched me, or — or hurt me in any way."

"You must banish that crease in your brow forevermore," he chided her gently. "I think I can exert sufficient persuasion upon Charles Ruan to ensure that he will remove himself to Dublin-town. That would make you more comfortable, I know, and I don't want him hanging about here, troubling us with his presence. To say nothing of his lies. For whatever he might have told you to the contrary, Josepha never had any intention of taking the boys from you."

"How do you know?"

"She told me. And after you've spoken with her yourself, I'm sure you, too, will acquit her of any malicious intent. She was also duped by Ruan." He explained to her how the lawyer had tempted Lady Ivory to come to Ireland with his false promises of riches and favours.

"He may have had another reason for enticing Josepha to Ireland," Garia said thoughtfully, when he was done. "He had always heard that she was beautiful and greedy. I think perhaps he regarded my stepmother as bait and believed she was the sort of woman who might lure you away from me."

"That woman does not exist," Torin declared. He tugged on the reins, and when the greys obediently halted, he put his arm around Garia's waist and pulled her closer. Looking down into her eyes he confessed, "For a very long time now, I have hoped for far more than your loyalty or your compliance. I want your love, Garia, and I'll not be satisfied with anything less. When I thought I'd lost you, I wished I'd told you this before — and I hope I haven't waited too long. Please tell me I need not despair of my heart's desire."

"Oh, Torin," she said on a blissful sigh, "it is precisely the same with *me*. And though I managed to persuade myself that my dreams were foolish ones, I never quite surrendered them. I have been too afraid to tell you how I felt, that I didn't want ours to be a marriage of convenience." And any persistent fears were banished forever as Torin pressed his lips to hers in an ardent kiss. Garia twined her arms about him and responded with all the passion she had long been so careful to conceal from him.

Their embrace lasted until one of the horses gave a restive and impatient snort. With a self-conscious laugh, the lovers separated. When Torin drove on, Garia laid her cheek on his broad shoulder, and after a period of silence she said, "Josepha has a legitimate claim to one-third of Papa's estate. I must honour his obligation to her somehow, although I don't know where the money will come from. I don't really care, so long as I need not lose Dromana. You realise it's the only dowry I have."

"Not at all, dearest. The boys are your dowry!" he said merrily. "And you mustn't worry about Josepha, for I'm going to provide her with an ample income. In return, she will no doubt allow me to make your stepbrothers my wards."

Garia lifted her head to gaze at him wonderingly. "You would do that?"

"Of course," he replied, "and willingly. They will live with us at the Castle, and whenever we travel to England, the three of them and their tutor will accompany us. Does that meet with your approval?"

She hastened to assure him that it did. "But I am afraid Jeremy will never be able to overcome his dislike of his mother. If only he could, I should be perfectly happy."

"Josepha's part in today's business is more that of a heroine than an accomplice, and with a little finesse we can convince him of it."

"Do you think so?" she asked doubtfully.

"I'm sure of it. And there is another plan of mine that I hope you will support," Torin told her. "After you gratify me by becoming my Countess, I'm going to settle Dromana upon you. Thus it will once again become the dower property of Cloncavan Castle, as it was in former times. And I propose that we let it to Thomas and his bride — assuming he can convince Miss Frances to accept him." Looking down at his betrothed, he said in surprise, "My poor darling, why in heaven's name are you crying? I hadn't thought it possible to reduce the intrepid Miss Ivory to tears!" Torin reached for his handkerchief, which he offered to the weeping lady. Wisely, he said nothing more, but let her shed the tears that he knew had sprung from her exhaustion as much as from elation.

When they reached Dromana, a host of boys, servants, and a noisy dog tumbled down the front steps. McCurdie and Mrs. Aglish were damp about the eyes, but the young Howards were wildly exuberant.

As Jeremy handed his sister down from the curricle, he told Torin excitedly, "When we came up empty at Carrick and Waterford, Mr. Montrose and I decided that you must have had some success. Such hard riding as we have done this day — there was never anything like it! I vow, I was ready to drop, but now I could dance a jig!"

Bennet flung his arms around his stepsister's waist. His muffled assurances that he was glad to see her were accompanied by Nonny's hysterical barks and capering, which the child interpreted for her. "Nonny has been as worried as Mama and us, and he's awfully happy that you're home." He released Garia and fixed his huge blue eyes on Torin. "Did you challenge Mr. Ruan to a duel this time?" he asked hopefully. "Did you kill him dead?"

"I did not, you bloodthirsty young pup!" was the disappointing reply.

Josepha came forward. "Garia, whatever Mr. Ruan may have told you, I had no part in his scheme. It was purest mischance that brought him to Dromana after the boys and I left for Carrick."

Smiling, Garia extended her hand to her stepmother. "Torin explained everything to me, Josepha, and I have good reason to be grateful to you. If you had not gone to the Castle to warn him, I should not be standing here now." She was pleased to note the effect this brief speech had upon Jeremy, who regarded his mother more benignly. As she and Josepha preceded the others into the house, she murmured, "Will you be so kind as to come upstairs and help me out of my habit? Before it becomes permanently affixed to my skin," she added with a soft laugh.

When the two women were alone, Garia explained the Earl's decision to make the Howards his wards, saying, "It is a thing Papa would have done eventually, although I daresay Mr. Ruan would have advised him against it."

"Your father was a generous man," Josepha said, fingering the items on Garia's dressing table. "I was always conscious of it. You never really understood why he wed me, did you?"

"No," Garia replied. "And though I never asked, I will now, for I should like to know."

Josepha drifted over to the window seat and perched on the edge. Beginning her tale without preamble, she said "At the time I met Sir Andrew, I hoped to be married to one of his closest friends. But unfortunately the gentleman abandoned me as soon as he discovered my ambition. He left me in terrible straits, and I was in grave danger of being arrested for debt when news of my plight reached your father's ears. He very kindly paid off my creditors, which led me to suppose he was himself a very wealthy man. He would visit me regularly, bringing my sons toys and books, and it was natural that I should transfer my hopes to him. But he knew me for what I was, and therefore he could not love me. Nor did I love him." She looked up and added apologetically, "Pray excuse my plain-speaking; I meant no offense."

Garia replied calmly, "Of course you didn't. Anyway, I had rather hear the truth of it."

"When Sir Andrew offered for me, I own I was surprised — but I think it was the boys who won him. And for their sakes, I accepted. But imagine, if you can, how it feels to be wed out of pity." Josepha swallowed, then went on. "I *should* have been content then, for at last I had a protector who could never cast me aside, and my boys had a real home for the first time in their lives. But I was selfish and stupid and spoiled. Though I knew your father was only comfortably well off, I spent his money too freely and ran up more debts. And as you know, during our marriage I had far too many flirts and spent too much time up in Dublin, and then I bolted with the first pretty fellow who promised me the moon. At the time I salved my conscience by telling myself that your father and my sons — and you — would all be better off without me. But it was a horrid thing to do," she said huskily.

Garia walked over to the woman whose confession had answered the questions and slayed so many of the suspicions she'd harboured all these years. "I thank you for your candour, Josepha. It is a relief to know you did not deliberately set out to ruin my father, as I had always supposed."

"Nor did I intend to ruin you either," Josepha hastened to say, "regardless of what Charles Ruan may have told you."

"I know that too." Garia sat down beside her stepmother. "And will you permit Torin to become the boys' guardian? He and I would never try to keep you from seeing them. When we travel to England, they will go with us, and certainly your allowance will make possible regular visits to Ireland. You will always be welcome at Cloncavan Castle."

Lady Ivory smiled her lovely smile. "How *could* I object, when my sons will be the wards of an Earl? But I am very much afraid that after your marriage, Lord Lindal will regard me in the light of a mother-in-law. As we are very near in age, it would be so lowering for me, you understand."

"You needn't worry about that," Garia promised her with a smile. "For certainly I can no longer look upon you as my stepmother." The other woman's face fell, and she hastened to add, "I very much hope you will consent to be my friend." And when she held out her hand, Josepha clasped it warmly.

After changing into a simple muslin gown, Garia hurried downstairs to the drawing room. But her well-wishers had all dispersed, and only Torin remained to bear her company.

He lifted his wineglass in a toast and said merrily, "To the future Lady Lindal, vanquisher of abductors and most admired of women!"

"Foolish Torin! What, pray tell, have you done with all my brothers?"

"I merely exerted my authority, and you see with what admirable results!" he said, setting his glass on the mantel. "Undoubtedly I will be a creditable influence upon them."

"Oh, very!" she agreed with a laugh as she went to meet him. "I shall count myself fortunate if Bennet is not challenging people to duels by the time he is ten, and likely Egan will be seducing chambermaids before he enters his teens! I don't know what plans you have for Jeremy, but — "

He brought her mocking tirade to a swift conclusion by placing his forefinger upon her lips. "I have no interest whatsoever in duels — nor in chambermaids. I beg you to spare my blushes by never again referring to that most reprehensible episode of my past. Yet I cannot regret it entirely, for ten years ago I could never have appreciated you as I do now, my beloved Garia!"

"No, for I was extremely silly, and a child, besides. But let us not speak of the past." And she leaned forwards and lifted her lips for his kiss. But Torin astonished her by backing away. He glared down at her, his arms folded across his chest, and she wondered what she had done to displease him.

"Miss Ivory, not a single kiss will you have until you promise to marry me soon — before Christmas!"

She tested his resolve by stepping towards him, her hands outstretched, imploring. As she expected, his arms encircled her, nearly squeezing the answer from her. "I would happily wed you tomorrow, as brazen as that sounds. Now, if you please, I want my kiss. And when I've had it, we will chase after the imps who are even now peering at us through the keyhole! Your authority extends to meting out spankings, does it not, my lord?"

As he bent his dark head to hers, the sound of three pairs of scampering feet could be heard echoing along the hallway of Dromana House.